TWO MORE SOLITUDES

TWO MORE SOLITUDES

a novel

BY SHELDON CURRIE

KEY PORTER BOOKS

Library and Archives Canada Cataloguing in Publication

Currie, Sheldon
        Two more solitudes : a novel / Sheldon Currie.

ISBN 978-1-55470-303-6

        I. Title.

PS8555.U74T86 2010   C813'.54   C2010-901209-7

ONTARIO ARTS COUNCIL
CONSEIL DES ARTS DE L'ONTARIO

The publisher gratefully acknowledges the support of the Canada Council for the Arts and the Ontario Arts Council for its publishing program. We acknowledge the support of the Government of Ontario through the Ontario Media Development Corporation's Ontario Book Initiative.

We acknowledge the financial support of the Government of Canada through the Book Publishing Industry Development Program (BPIDP) for our publishing activities.

Key Porter Books Limited
Six Adelaide Street East, Tenth Floor
Toronto, Ontario
Canada M5C 1H6

www.keyporter.com

Text design and electronic formatting: Alison Carr

Printed and bound in the United States of America

10 11 12 13 5 4 3 2 1

For Clare, who got me going and kept me going.

Love consists in this,
that two solitudes protect
and touch, and greet each other.

—Rainer Maria Rilke
Quoted by Hugh MacLennan in *Two Solitudes*

PROLOGUE

Mephistopheles:
Why this is hell nor am I out of it.
—Doctor Faustus, *scene III*

THE WINTER QUIT. Along Chemin Ste. Foy, Quatre Bourgeois, St. Louis, Laurier and Champlain, the steep, dirty snow banks crumbled, melted, drained onto the pavement, and transformed into arteries of slush flooding toward the Plains of Abraham, through the streets of Ville de Quebec on their way to the St. Lawrence River and the oblivion of the Atlantic Ocean.

Along Rue St. Jean in Ville de Quebec a bus sloshed through the river of slush and skidded to a stop against the curb at a transparent bus shelter illuminated by a street lamp. The only passenger, a man in his mid-twenties, already wet, got soaked again by the wind-driven rain as he leapt from the bus onto the sidewalk and dashed to the shelter. He shook the rain from his hair, brushed the wet from his eyebrows and watched the bus as it bumped its tires over a low, narrow bridge made of pairs of two-by-six planks supported by firebricks that spanned the torrent rushing to fill the wake behind the departing bus. He looked across the street, his eyes searching. All the buildings were dark save for a crimson light shining through the window of a street door. He peered through the rain, up and down the street, but except for the light above the bus shelter and a blinking amber traffic light at a distant intersection the street was dark.

After spending the previous night at a motel, his baggage still at the airport, he wore scant clothing against the cold rain, a T-shirt under a light windbreaker, jeans and running shoes. Reluctant to leave the shelter in the torrential rain, holding on to the wall, he stretched out the doorway to get a longer look down the street for some sign of life. At that moment the door across the street opened and from it emerged a long woman dressed in the multi-coloured, diamond-patterned suit of a harlequin with bulbous pantaloons and a tunic. On her feet were yellow rubber knee boots decorated with black harlequins. She stopped on the sidewalk and unfolded an enormous multi-coloured umbrella and, with both hands on the shaft, pushed it against the wind. Avoiding the plank bridge, she splashed her way across the street-stream and stood at the door of the shelter. She lifted the umbrella to reveal eyes smiling through a white mask.

"*Allez-vous a L'Enfer?*" she asked. "You go to L'Enfer?"

"Yes, I am," he said. "Where is it?" He backed deeper into the shelter to make room for her to come in but she beckoned him with a tilt of her head to join her under the umbrella. She raised her voice above the noise of the wind and rain. She spoke in English and French, having a little trouble with English. "Good. *Bien. Viens sous le parapluie.* Come with me, *il pleut à verse.* I am called Sharon; I am the clown. Your escort. I guide you over. Your sneaks are soaked."

He stepped from the shelter and under the protection of the umbrella. They huddled for a moment on the sidewalk, her clothing billowing in the wind, pushing against him. Slush rolled around her boots and soaked his sneakers and the bottom of his jeans. Large, hard raindrops, almost hail, clattered on the umbrella and streamed down from its edges in a circle, enclosing them in a crystal curtain, tinged yellow by the dim light hanging from the street lamp over the sidewalk. Sharon pointed to the luminous door across the street and, guiding him with her hand on his elbow, stepped into the street-stream up to her ankles and urged him onto the narrow plank and firebrick bridge spanning the rushing stream.

"Keep on the sticks... How do you call yourself? Are you Ian, maybe?"

"Yes, I am Ian."

"Keep on the sticks, Ian. Your feet are soaked, but keep on the sticks the same. The jeans are getting wet. Must be freezing on the toes."

Ian balanced himself against the wind on the planks and walked with Sharon beside him, protecting him with her umbrella, which she now held with one hand bracing it against her shoulder, guiding him by the elbow with the other, the wind and rain at their backs, soaking his pant legs again. With the help of her guiding hand he managed to balance himself and walk the planks until they reached the sidewalk in front of the luminous door. At the entrance Sharon collapsed the umbrella, opened the door and led him into a vestibule at the top of a narrow winding stair, unlit itself, but bright from the glow that flowed from below along with the sounds of voices and harp music.

"Descend, Ian," Sharon said, pointing down the spiraled steps. "I must return for the next bus. The people will be coming and I have to do them the umbrella. Wait for Mr. Griet at the doorway and tell him the name, who you are. He expects an Ian and he is going to take you to your seat."

Ian stepped into the stairwell and, holding on to the metal rail, walked down the spiral into the glow, the music and the low buzz of voices. In a semicircle over an archway at the bottom of the stair the name of the bar, L'Enfer Sous Terre, gleamed in red neon. Once inside, he stopped and scanned the room. To the right of the door at one end of the room a bar and bar-stools stretched across the full width of the space. Two waiters wearing white shirts, maroon vests and black pants sat on stools, their backs to the bar, scanning the space before them for customers looking for service. At the opposite end a small stage, about half the width of the space, thrusting in an arc, formed a semicircle into the room.

The space between the barstools and the stage contained about eighteen small, round, ebony tables, each with a tiny red candelabrum holding three tiny, purple candles in its centre. Four chairs surrounded each table. In the space in the centre of each circle of tables a platform on a pedestal held a cast-iron fondue cook-stove heating a small copper cauldron of boiling oil. Beside the cook-stove a gold-coloured, cylindrical container held a fag-got of silver-forked skewers meant for spearing and dipping cubes of meat—beef, pork, lamb, veal, chicken—in the boiling oil. The room contained chairs enough for about six dozen souls. Early patrons, scattered about, occupied about half the chairs.

A spectacular display of scarlet, neon, dancing flames formed the wall at the back of the stage. At centre stage a human-sized capital letter B shot silent flames from its edges and through its two internal holes. At intervals along the side walls of the room, between a half-dozen *fausses-fenêtres* filled with stained glass, triangular sconces displayed cylindrical torches of scarlet neon. The room was aglow.

A young man—Peter Greit, according to his nametag—dressed in the same costume as the waiters but with an in-charge look on his face, approached him and when Ian identified himself the man beckoned him to follow and led him to a table with just two chairs close to the stage and apart from the circular arrangements.

"Vergile's table," Mr. Greit said, putting one hand on the table and the other hand on a chair. "Have a seat. She thought you might show up. When she finishes her act she'll come and sit here." He placed his hand on the other chair. "Would you like something to drink while you wait? A beer, or…"

"A beer would be fine."

"I'll send a waiter."

Stepping on stage in front of the flaming B, a musician, the word *Vergile* emblazoned in black letters across her breasts, began to warm up by playing arpeggios on a harp. Beside her a three-pronged fork stood upright in a sleeve-like stand. After a flourish of arpeggios she played twice through twelve bars of blues in the key of E major and, accompanied by recorded music from speakers playing the same tune, she faded on the final twelfth bar in B major, stood up from her stool, pulled the three-pronged fork from its scabbard and walked to the apex of the semi-circular stage. She spotted Ian, flicked him a little finger wave of recognition and smiled down at him as he sipped beer from his glass. He raised an eyebrow and offered a wry smile.

He watched in astonishment as she began to hum a tune to the chords that were still playing on the sound system. Good God, he thought, could this be the same woman he met earlier that day on the ferry who followed him back to the house in her black walking shoes, ankle-length grey skirt, white buttoned-up blouse and a kerchief tied under her chin covering most of her mousy blond hair? She was very helpful then and promised to be more helpful, but now only the angelic smile and the blue laughing eyes revealed her identity.

A scarlet suit of Stanfield's combination underwear covered her body from her neck to below the tops of her ankle-high goatskin boots decorated with artificial goat hooves. A helmet of shiny black hair covered her head like a steel dome. She plucked a microphone from the middle prong of the fork, and with fork in one hand, microphone in the other, she waltzed the stage while her recorded harp sounds continued playing through the speakers from the flaming wall behind her. In a throaty, torch-song voice she sang "The Dispossession Blues," while latecomers entering the bar quietly, politely waited and watched her performance from near the door.

I once had everything, but that's all gone
It was all mine and mine alone
I dropped the ball, don't really understand
Got the dispossession blues and I feel down low.

Oh, they used to call me Beelzebub
And I hung around in a better pub
I was an angel, I was Lucifer

But now I am banned forevermore, I
Got the dispossession blues and I feel so bad

So please don't pin your hopes on worldly things
On houses, clothes, cars and on diamond rings
You don't want to end up a wretch like me
And live a life of misery, I
Got the dispossession blues and I feel so sad.

The song done, the audience at the tables offered enthusiastic applause and the late arrivals under Mr. Greit's guidance
arranged themselves in seats, filling up all the tables and chairs.
Vergile continued to reprise the tune, humming to the recorded
sound. She put the fork back in its scabbard and carried the
microphone down the steps at the side of the stage and across
the floor. She stood by Ian's table and sang to him.

So don't pin your hopes on worldly things
You got the dispossession blues and I feel so sad.

More applause. She sat across from Ian, switched off the
microphone and placed it on the table between them.

He smiled at the microphone, gave it a mock-suspicious
look. "Are you going to interview me?"

"Don't worry," she laughed, "it's off. But come to think of
it, interviews might make an interesting variation in the enter-
tainment. Everybody has a sad and woeful tale."

"I doubt it would be interesting."

"Oh, I don't know, lost souls are always interesting, especially in this ambience. I might suggest it to the management; every night an interview with a volunteer from the audience. Try it anyway, you never know what might happen. My act is pretty predictable, a little serendipity to spice up the evening couldn't hurt. What do you think?"

"You might attract crazies, desperate for attention."

"Crazies can be interesting, in the short run. I recognized you, you know, the minute I saw you."

"What, you think I'm crazy?"

"No, no, not that. I knew the minute I laid eyes on you, in the funicular. It wasn't the descent that scared you, although it's scary enough descending in that glass cage. It wasn't the going down. It was the going at all."

"What? What do you mean you knew? You knew what?"

"You're lost. A chronic case."

"So what is that big flaming B for?" Ian asked, quickly changing the subject.

She smiled. "What do you think?"

"Beelzebub?"

"That's what everybody thinks."

"So it's a trick?"

"No, not a trick. Stands for my name. My initial."

"B for Vergile?"

"No. Although B and V are very close, linguistically."

A waiter interrupted. He wore the maroon vest jacket Ian saw on the other waiters, with a coral, wing-shaped epaulette on each shoulder. He placed a crystal chalice of red wine on the table.

"There you go, sister. The usual for you." He turned to Ian. "Welcome sir to L'Enfer. We love to greet new customers. I'm the head waiter. If there is anything you need don't hesitate.

Nasty evening out there, but it's comfy in here and the heat will dry your clothes. How about I bring you a hot rum and honey toddy, on the house, to warm your heart. We're getting busy but I'll be back soon as I can."

"Thanks, Bub," Vergile said. "This is Ian."

"Nice to meet you, Ian. Enjoy your evening."

The waiter threaded his way through the circles of the animated crowd toward the bar at the other end of the room. Ian and Vergile sipped their drinks.

"Where were we, Ian? Oh yeah, no, no trick, Ian, B is my real initial."

"A code is it?"

She laughed. "No."

"Okay. A new alphabet. An acrostic alphabet. The fourth last letter of the standard alphabet, in the new alphabet stands for the second letter of the standard alphabet and so on. Pretty hard to learn that one."

"No, no, it's nothing clever. The B is for *papillon*."

"B for *papillon*. How does that work? Does it make sense? Or is it clever after all?"

"It makes sense, believe it or not. When I was born my face looked like a scarlet prune. My father said I was ugly as sin. But the next week I became beautiful, or so they tell me. When the priest baptized me he poured the water and said, 'What is the child's name?'

"My father blurted out, '*Papillon*.' In my imagination I can see my mother's chin drop to her breast. Years later when she told me about it she said, 'I couldn't get my mouth closed or my tongue to work.' She wanted to call me Beatrice after my grandmother so she took to calling me B for butterfly and everybody called me Bea and thought my name was Beatrice. So sometimes I'm B and sometimes I'm V depending on who, when, where, and sometimes why. And now, my boy, it's time for me to get back to work."

Ian wondered which of the two women attracted him more, the plain, angelic creature who followed him from the funicular to the ferry, from the ferry to the house, or this scarlet harping demon in Nova Scotia underwear. But he was eager to investigate further while he seemed to have her complete attention.

"Would you like to go out later, have a drink, listen to my sad and woeful tale?"

"Yeah…" She hesitated. "But I should warn you…"

"Uh oh, something scary?"

She laughed. "No, no, nothing scary. It's just, we won't be 'going out,' in the usual sense, like on a date."

"Oh. Why not?"

"For now, anyway, I can only see you on a professional basis."

"You're kidding?"

She smiled. "No, Ian, I'm not kidding."

"You want me to hire you to sing?"

She laughed, enjoying his confusion. "No. You're hiring me to sing right now, if you paid for your beer. By the way, your hot rum and honey toddy hasn't come yet. Where is Bub? No, Ian, I don't want you to hire me to sing. Singing is not my profession."

"You're not a prostitute?"

"No, no, no. I don't want you to hire me at all. I work for free. Remember that old song, 'Bewitched, Bothered and Bewildered'? That's what you look like now. "

Ian sipped the last of his beer, gazed across his empty glass and studied Vergile's laughing eyes. The list of professionals who work for free must be a pretty meager list, he thought. "If it's a guessing game," he said finally, "I give up. What is your profession?"

"I'm a nun." She watched Ian's search for an expression that might adequately respond to this surprising revelation.

His face settled for a bland stare, his mouth and tongue searched for words to adequately express his astonishment. Finally, he lowered his glass and said simply, "A nun."

Vergile lowered her chalice to the table and repeated, "Yes, a nun."

He stared across at her. "Why would I hire a nun? And you don't look like a nun, certainly not now, although I guess on the ferry you did."

"I'm not for hire, Ian. Are you paying attention? I work for free, which is why I took this job, singing for my supper, to support my day job. Something like an actor, eh, wait on tables by day, but the real work is strutting the boards by night. But for me it's the opposite, I take the stage by night, I work by day."

"And what would you be doing for me?"

Vergile smiled. "What you just suggested. Listen to your sad and woeful tale. Your problems."

"What problems?"

Bub finally arrived, picked up Ian's beer glass, put it on his tray full of drinks and replaced it with a steaming mug while he reminded Vergile that the audience was getting expectant and she was about due on stage. He moved on, serving drinks to the people sitting in the circles of tables, which were now all occupied. The murmur of voices raised to a buzz, the heat making patrons hang their jackets on the back of chairs. Vergile picked up the microphone from the table, stood for a moment with her free hand on Ian's forearm.

"Well, dear," she said, "if you don't have problems you don't need me. Let me entertain you. But you sure looked lost on the ferry yesterday. That's why I spoke. We try to help the lost and dispossessed. Hang around for a while. I have to ply my avocation now. After I sing I'll come back if you are still here."

She mounted the stage, inserted the microphone into the three-pronged fork and accompanied by the pre-recorded harp music emanating from the wall of fire, sang a couple of French folk songs. Ending the set, she looked straight at Ian and sang:

On a boat to nowhere, in the dead of night
On a boat to nowhere, not a star in sight
Every time we get there, and we think we're home
We find we're where we started, once again we roam

I like to be a sailor, but I need a star
Like to leave the harbour, like to travel far
But when a sailor's weary, on a darkened sea
Sailor needs a foothold, sailor needs a tree

When the task is over, when the battle's won
When it's time for sinking with the evening sun
When it's time for drowning in the dark, dark, dark
Sailor needs a foothold from a shattered bark

After her song, Vergile walked through rousing applause down the steps at the side of the stage, resumed her place at

Ian's table and once again placed her hand on his forearm. The crowd applauded for an encore, some of them standing up, but she waved them off with a promise to return the following night.

He looked around to see the people who were standing, applauding. The applause diminished and the patrons reluctantly sat down. "They want you to sing again."

"Yes."

"So…"

"Always leave them happy, but never leave them satisfied. When they're hungry they come back. That's how I earn my money. Now, as for you, there are three kinds of lost and dispossessed. Those who don't realize they are lost and dispossessed—they are the worst off. Those who know, realize they are lost and dispossessed—that's better. And those lucky few who know it's normal—that's the best way to be."

"That's normal, lost and dispossessed?"

"We're pilgrims. Wayfarers. Sailors on the sea of time. We're looking for a star to navigate by. You—" she pointed her finger "—you need a star."

"Do you have a star?" he asked.

"I do." She smiled.

"What is it?"

"You can't have my star. Everybody needs a personal star. And anyway its bad karma to talk about your star."

"How do I know you're not a nut?"

"Well, there you go. Maybe I am. I'm off work now. I'll go change and come back as a patron. You tell me your sad and woeful tale. If I am a nut and you're crazy maybe we'll end up in the sack after all."

The waiter came back with a new mug of hot toddy. Ian stood and took off his jacket and hung it on the back of his chair. "Well, my clothes are dry now and my heart is getting warm, so why not," he said as he took a sip from the hot mug and wrapped his fingers around it. "Now tell me, is that why you get a chalice and I get a beer glass and a coffee mug, because you're a nun?"

"No," she laughed. "It's part of the decor. We don't expect patrons to participate in the decor. When I come back Bub will give me an ordinary glass."

"It wouldn't be the first time I participated in a decor. This waiter is not my first Beelzebub, and you're not my first nun, you might want to know. I went to Halifax to enter the seminary, but instead I entered Marie."

"There you go, Ian," Vergile laughed. "Sounds like the beginning of a sad and woeful tale. We can talk here. People are beginning to leave so it won't be so noisy, just a little buzz and my harp music coming from the flames."

PART ONE

PART ONE

ONE

If you don't know where you're going
you'll probably end up somewhere else.
—*Yogi Berra*

FROM THE PITCHER'S MOUND Ian stares at the left-handed batter. He takes off his hat and wipes the sweat from his brow with the sleeve of his jersey, a blue-and-white shirt with the word *Saints* written across the chest and across the back *The University of Glace Bay*. The scoreboard shows the Saints are ahead two to one in the ninth inning. There's one out, runners on second and third. The runner on third base is a couple of feet off the bag waiting for the pitcher's windup. The third baseman stays close, holding the runner until the pitcher releases the ball. Ian looks in at Mark, the catcher, sees the sign, then looks at the dugout, nods at the manager, calls time out and steps off the mound. Mark and Father Angus rush out and the three of them discuss the situation.

Father Angus says, "I think they're going to try the suicide squeeze."

"Okay," Ian says, "that's easy, I'll burn his nose, make him jump out of the way."

Father Angus looks at his catcher. "What do you think, Mark?"

"Ian's right. Make him duck his head. Take a slow windup. If it looks like the runner is staying at third, throw a strike. If he breaks, throw it at the batter's head. He'll duck—he's not that stupid—and we'll nail the runner."

"What about brushing him back?" Father Angus says.

"I might hit him. He might take a hit on the hip to get a walk, but he's not gonna take a hit on the head. The next guy up is a good clutch hitter. This guy is nervous. If we get the runner then get the batter its over, we win. If we put him on and the next guy hits fair the game is over, we lose."

"Okay," Father Angus says, "this is it, the championship is on the line. He might take the first pitch hoping for a walk, so if it's a strike they'll have to try the bunt on the second pitch or risk bunting on two strikes." He pauses. "Keep talking until the umpire comes out. The longer the batter stands there the more nervous he'll get."

"So what do we talk about?" Ian says.

Mark gives Father Angus a sly smile. "Let's talk about Ian's future."

"What future?" Father Angus says.

"Play ball," the umpire yells from behind the catcher.

"He wants to be a priest."

"Are you crazy?" Father Angus says.

"Play ball!"

"Yes, I'm crazy, didn't you know that?"

"Here he comes," Mark says. "Better scatter."

"Warn him, Mark," Father Angus says. "And you two come see me in my office after you shower."

Mark walks to his position and as he passes the batter, he whispers, "Watch your noggin, buddy."

Ian gets back on the rubber, stares at the batter, takes a long windup, the runner fakes a break and stops, Ian throws.

"Strike one."

Ian catches the ball from Mark, stares at the batter until he calls time and steps out of the batter's box, looks at the third base coach for guidance. When he steps back in Ian pitches immediately with no windup, the batter sets to bunt, the runner breaks, the batter ducks under the ball, sits on the ground and scrambles out of the way. Mark catches the ball and stands astraddle the plate while the runner tries to knock him over but Mark has lots of time to plant himself and is immovable. He tags the runner out. The batter picks himself off the ground, insulted, humiliated.

Mark smirks. "Awful hard to bunt those high buggers, eh?"

The batter turns crimson. He streaks for the mound with Mark on his heels. Father Angus rushes in from the dugout. Ian drops his glove, waits until the last minute and, with the batter nearly on top of him, jumps at him with two fists flying and knees him in the groin. The batter drops to the ground curled in pain. The players from both teams circle around them. After a lot of pushing and shoving the umpires and the coaches restore order.

Once the batter straightens out his body he walks back to the plate and resumes his place well back in the batter's box and strikes out with two weak swings at two fastballs down the outside edge of the plate. He waits until Mark takes off his catcher's mask and swings the bat again. Mark grabs the big end of the bat with his catcher's mitt two inches from his nose.

"You're not supposed to do that," Mark says to him, eye to eye over the bat. "Why don't you go home and get your girl-friend to give you a nice massage, then you can go to confession tomorrow and 'fess up all your sins." He yanks the bat out of the batter's hand, drops it on the plate and walks off the field. The batter bends to pick up the bat again but the umpire's foot is cementing it to the ground.

After the game Ian and Mark shower and change into street clothes, jeans and T-shirts with *University of Glace Bay* printed across the front along with its emblem, a steel rail embedded in a lump of coal embossed on the Cape Breton tartan. They walk across the outfield of the ball diamond inside the wire fence along the cliff. The waves of the North Atlantic slap at the giant boulders that over the years have fallen from the eroding cliff to the gravel beach. Seagulls using the boulders as take-off and landing pads lift off, climb and swoop, catching updrafts and downdrafts, ride the wind, circle, and dive and plunge into the waves, fishing for food.

"Think they enjoy it, Ian?"

"Who? Enjoy what?"

"The gulls. Are they having fun d'ya think, or is it just food? They're competing for food, yeah, but is it like working for a living, or is it like playing ball—you know, something you'd do even if you didn't get paid?"

"Who cares?"

"I guess. But wouldn't it be a shame if they don't enjoy themselves? All that effort just for a bite to eat. Just think if we could do that, whooshing around in the air having a great time, grabbing a fish every now and again, like trout fishing, only fly-ing too. Riding on the wind." Mark pauses, then adds, "You were in the air force. What was it like, flying?"

"We didn't do much fishing."

"Isn't it the same thing? You fly around, you kill something, you make a living but you have fun doing it?"

"I didn't kill anything. I nearly killed myself."

"What's wrong with you today?"

"I'm not in the mood to worry about a flock of birds and their fun and games. I'm thinking about what Father Angus wants. 'Come see me in my office after the game' does not sound promising. I think he's pissed off."

"Well, you nearly took the guy's head off. You didn't have to try to take his balls off too. That makes Father A nervous."

They enter the main building of the university and walk the halls past offices and classrooms until they find Father Angus seated behind his desk. They sit in the two chairs positioned in front of the desk.

Father Angus' baseball cap is still on his head, pulled down tight over his forehead so that he has to cant his head back to look up at them. With his chin stuck out and his eyes squinting against the sun flooding the room, he gives the two a quizzical look. His baseball uniform rests in a heap on a pile of towels on the floor in the corner of the office. Patches of the floor not covered with newspapers, periodicals and books are littered with baseball bats, buckets of baseballs and an assortment of new and abused baseball gear. He wears a university T-shirt identical to Ian's and Mark's with the emblem covered by a black dickey. His roman collar hangs open on his chest.

The walls are covered with bookcases, collections of poetry, novels, baseball and hockey instructional manuals, but mostly books of psychology, theology, anthropology and philosophy.

A map of the Middle East hangs from two bookcases and covers half a section of books.

"I've got the collar on," Father Angus says, taking off his ballcap and throwing it on the heap of uniforms on the floor, "because now I'm not the coach, I'm the counsellor, one of my many jobs I'm not too good at. I don't want to talk about the game except to say I hope you noticed that violence breeds violence, it's a boomerang, comes right back at you."

"We learned it from you," Mark replies.

"Yes. I know. To my shame. But, forget that, I want to talk about your future."

"Okay," Mark says. "What am I doing here? I'm not even graduating."

"You're a witness. He'll listen better if someone else is listening. If you paid more attention in psychology class you'd learn things like that. And since, like Ian here—though I guess he's changed his mind—you're planning to become a failed professional ball player, that's the kind of thing you need to know."

"How do you know what I'm gonna do?" Mark says.

"Because I paid attention in psychology class, and because I know you are not quite a good enough athlete. And that means you are a very good athlete and good enough to think you can play major league baseball. And that means you'll try and you'll fail. So my advice to you is to fail early so you won't spend your good years in hopeless hope in the minor leagues until even you know the truth and settle for a job selling cars. Go ahead and prove me wrong but do it quick."

"Hey, I thought this was all about him."

"Hey, I'll get to him, but you're here now and I like to shoot

30

ducks when they fly into sight. But now that I've finished with you, listen while I finish with him."

"I know the drill anyway," Ian mumbles. "I heard it all before."

"Yeah, you heard it all before, but did you listen? Now you'll hear it again and if you don't listen again we got a witness and later on he can tell you what I really said, and not what you think you remember I said. So, you wanted to be a ball player?" Father Angus says, and pauses, closes his fist and hits it into his left palm. He nods at Ian, and raises his right palm as if to say, don't talk, I'm not finished, and points his left forefinger at Mark as if to say, pay attention. "And you want to be a Gaelic scholar, and you want to be a theologian, and now you want to be a priest and you want to be the best. That right?"

"That's right. What's wrong with that?"

Father Angus laughs. "For one thing, you can't be a professional ball player and a priest except in your crazy imagination. For another thing, you have got a hot hopping fastball and a devastating change up, but you know as well as I do you couldn't hit the broad side of your grandfather's barn with your curveball. That's not good enough."

"I'm getting better."

"Yes, you are. And you can get a lot better. You can get so good that you can join your buddy Mark here on a ten-year tour of second-rate ball teams. Then you can come back to Glace Bay and sell vacuum cleaners."

"That's a little harsh."

"Yes, it is. And that's just for two things. Another thing: you want to be everything but a coal miner, which is just as well since they don't make coal mines anymore."

"Why not?"

"Be everything? Why not be everything? Because for one thing you need ability, determination, luck, and I mean good luck and lots of it."

"He's got all that," Mark says.

"He's got determination. If he had to knock the head off that dumb batter to get the out he would've."

"He hasn't killed anybody yet."

"Ability," Father Angus says, and looks at Mark. "Were you listening? We just talked about that. He's got lots of ability, just like you, but not enough."

"I heard you, but just because you say it doesn't make it right."

"That's right. I could be wrong. And if you go for it I hope I am wrong. But like I said, when I see a duck on the fly I shoot before it's out of sight. But we haven't talked about luck. Is he lucky? Yes. He's lucky to have determination and ability, but luck is opportunity too, and that kind of luck comes and goes."

"We make our own luck," Mark says, "like we made that batter duck."

"Sure, we make our own luck but it only works until we're arrested."

They sit in silence for a long moment.

"I could still be an athlete. You're a priest," Ian says, slowly, as if he were playing the five of trump on a jack, "you're an athlete, you're a scholar. What d'you think, nobody can do it but you?"

"Yeah, that's me, jack of many trades, ace of none. But never mind that for now. Listen, you studied Gaelic because your

32

grandmother taught you a few words and a few songs and you loved her bitter black currents. You studied Celtic history and convinced yourself that you're a victim of a British plot to destroy Highland Scots' culture and you became a patriot, an ethnic with an axe to grind."

"Well, isn't it true?"

"It's somewhat true and somewhat false. That's the problem. Because now you consider yourself to be a scholar as well as everything else."

"I'm over all that. Now I just want to be a scholar. What's wrong with that?"

"I hope you are over all that, because a patriot trying to play the scholar is playing a dangerous game."

"Dangerous?"

"A patriot thrives on half-truths, a scholar's loyalty is to the whole truth. A ball game is not the Battle of Culloden where there is no next year and everybody is dead. And a theologian's allegiance is to the truth, not to the bishop, and bishops have a hard time understanding that and if you want to be a priest/scholar you better be ready for that. I know that's complicated but you think about it. In the meantime, since you want to do everything and you think you can multiply your loyalties to a variety of vocations as if they were different sports on different playing fields, well, I guess it's obvious you'll need to start with one of them."

"That's right."

"So?"

"So what?"

"So don't be an arsehole, what are you going to do first?"

"First, I'm heading for Halifax. I'll check out the seminary, perhaps get to be a priest, just like you did, but I'll be tougher, less pussyfooty," he says and smiles to show he is joking. "I'll play senior ball on summer vacations and see what happens. If it has to be one or the other, well, so be it. Keep the options open."

"Yes, I know you are fond of options, but options are only useful if you opt, a fact of life you seem to have trouble with. So you're going to try the seminary?"

"That's it."

"Did you talk to the bishop?"

"Not yet. I think I'll look it over first."

"Oh, good idea," Father Angus says, and he gets up from behind his desk and goes to the window to study the clouds drifting across the sky. When he turns back he takes a long look at Ian and an impish smile crawls across the priest's face. Ian and Mark exchange glances. They know that smile and they know it means something they won't find out about until later, an hour maybe, a week, a year, but when the time comes, the revelation will arrive like an explosive dawn after a long, comfortable sleep.

"Do me a favour, would you," Father Angus says. "I have a friend in Halifax. Your friend too, your old girlfriend, Marie. I met her when she came to summer school last year. Would you look her up and say hello? She knows where the seminary is. She can show you where it is. And oh yes, before I forget, congratulations on the win, the team played real baseball today, especially you two. I'm proud of you, and thank you, you made me look good too. I'm afraid I can't join you for the victory party but I imagine you can manage without me."

Ian and Mark get up, move to the door and step out into the hall. Father Angus follows them out, they shake hands and

34

he thanks them again. Ian and Mark look at each other and grin, then stand side by side at attention and with mocking little boy voices they intone in unison, "Thank you, Father Angus," and they turn like two boy soldiers and walk down the hall. After a few steps Ian turns and smiles. "I think I can find the seminary."

Father Angus smiles, enjoying himself. "Don't be too cocksure. Things can happen when you turn your back. And remember, if you can't get what you want, you might have to want what you get."

"I never turn my back," Ian says, turns and catching up to Mark walks to the end of the hall and out the exit.

"Don't get lost, Ian," Father Angus yells as the glass door shuts behind them. He stands watching through the door as the two continue down the long corridor and vanish around the next turn.

two

Is it not delightful to have friends coming from distant quarters?
—*Confucius*

WHILE HER FRIEND, co-worker and patient Jocelyn Au Coin sucks from a machine in brief gasps the last cubic litre of oxygen her lungs would ever enjoy, Marie walks down the hospital hallway, breathing easily in spite of a two-flight stair climb. She continues her usual exercise routine, passing by the elevator on each floor, walking the hall and climbing the stairs at the other end. Her healthy 85 pulse will drop to 65 soon after she reaches her destination. She watches herself put one foot in front of the other in a straight line. "Here I am exercising when my best friend may soon be dead. Absolutely incredible!" she mumbles to herself. "As Jocelyn would say, if Jocelyn could put one foot in front of the other."

I am not bored, she thinks, as she watches the toes of her black shoes disappear and reappear under her downward gaze. Things are lousy but not boring, stupid but interesting, trivial but overwhelming, especially overwhelming Jocelyn. And here I am walking down the corridor of the hospital, a nurse on her day off, in my crumpled trench coat, hoping for Jocelyn. Hoping. Jocelyn, Ms. Energy, Ms. Immune System, Ms. Never Had the Flu, Ms. Never Heard Herself Cough, now this.

Marie climbs the stairs to the seventh floor, pushes open the door of room 1755 and closes it softly behind her. Jocelyn lies on her back, her black hair in braids folded over the front of her shoulders, her face white and wasted, her lower lip, once full and red, now a thin pink line clinging to her teeth, her eyes, staring at a picture of a boat on the wall opposite her bed, wide open, stark, blank, dead.

Marie pauses, closes her eyes for a moment, then moves toward the bed. Jocelyn's hands, folded over her belly, hold a white, sealed envelope with Marie's name scrawled on its front. Marie lifts it from Jocelyn's hands and sits in the chair at the foot of the bed, tears it open and reads:

Dear Marie,

Welcome to the expulsion of the Acadian. How in hell are you, as we always said to each other when we plied our trades in our chosen infernos. But this is for the last time. By the time you get this letter you might truthfully wonder how in hell I am. Think of all the fun we had together, Marie, always think of all the fun.

Can you tell how calm I am? I didn't think I would be calm. It's because I still have the feeling of control. But I know it won't last. That's the trouble being nurses. We know too much. I'll soon have to die whether I agree to it or not. But I am ready to go. I don't want to go, but I am ready. I'm writing this letter in advance because I know that soon I won't be able to, maybe even not really soon but soon enough. I'll tell you about this letter but I don't want you to read it until I'm gone. As you know I always have to have the last word.

I'm looking at the picture of my grandfather in his boat. I have a feeling he is waiting for me. It's a great comfort. It's the picture that looks most like him so I got it enlarged and framed. I want you to have it so make sure you get it. Take it now. I imagine myself slipping out of bed and into the boat and off we go. We'll be together forever. When your time comes, just get into the boat. In the meantime, keep us with you. Leave the picture to the one you love the most.

Too bad we won't get a chance to visit Grande Rivière again together, visiting our roots. We had such a good time there. We should have gone more often when we did have the chance. We thought we'd have lots of time for that. Too busy trying to convert the world. Remember that, Marie. Whatever it is, don't wait, do it.

Au revoir,
Jocelyn

P.S. Give something from me to Lynn, whatever you think. Keep anything that fits you if you like it and give the rest away. S.A.G.

The enlarged and framed photograph hangs on the wall across from Jocelyn's blank gaze. When she and Marie made their vacation trip to Grande Rivière Jocelyn found the picture wrapped in wax paper in a steamer trunk in the attic of her old home. She scoured the beach for two hours picking up and choosing pieces of driftwood. She boiled two pots of dye, a red made from beets, rosehips and Kool-Aid, a yellow made from onion skins, burdock and King Cole tea. She framed the photograph with pieces of the grey wood, spliced together and reinforced with lengths of dyed, braided, red and yellow strands of rope that she found in her grandfather's old tackle box in the attic trunk.

Marie lifts the picture from the wall and puts it on the pillow beside Jocelyn. She stands back beside the bed and looks at the two faces. She had looked at the picture many times when it hung in their apartment and on her daily visits to the hospital room. But now she is struck by Jocelyn's resemblance to her grandfather: the same eyes, shiny, brown, wide, shaded by thick eyebrows, long lashes over high cheekbones, the same little bump halfway down the nose, ample, bright, eloquent lips, in life curved in a smile, now flattened, darkened, like her eyes, to incomprehension.

Marie leans over, closes Jocelyn's eyes, takes the photograph of the grandfather and sets it on the foot of the bed then sits in a chair beside the bed and reads the letter again until Ian appears in the open doorway.

"Here you are, Ian, come on in. I'm just ready to go. Saying goodbye to Jocelyn."

Ian stands at the foot of the bed and picks up the photograph of the old man standing in his boat, his sou'wester pushed to the back of his head, one hand winding or unwinding a rope that ties the dory to a wharf, the other hand bent in a beckoning wave, an avuncular, benign smile shining from his eyes.

"That's Jocelyn's grandfather. You won't be meeting him for a while. And this is Jocelyn and you'll have to wait to meet her too. So you're stuck with me, you poor thing. Good to see you again, how are you?"

"I'm okay," he whispers.

"No need to whisper, Ian. This is not a library, not a church."

"I don't want to wake her up."

"Not to worry, she's dead to the world. She won't wake up.

Anyway, I'm ready to go. You grab that picture for me if you don't mind. I'm taking it with me."

Ian carries the picture of Jocelyn's grandfather, the hanging wire on his fingers, his thumb curved over the top, and Marie carries her huge purse on a shoulder strap. She leads him out of the hospital, across the parking lot and they walk up South Park to Spring Garden and turn right at the Lord Nelson Hotel. The day is still occasionally bright with the sun shining intermittently through breaks in the clouds, but the dark is thickening on the eastern horizon.

Marie stops on the sidewalk across from Nova Scotia Tech between the french fry truck and the library with its statue of Winston Churchill decorated with pigeons waiting to swoop down for any french fries that people dropped on the sidewalk. She stops to talk to Dr. Deedy who sits on the stone wall with a large paper cup of fries and a styrofoam cup of coffee.

"Good God, Ira," she laughs. "Is this your idea of a coffee break? Is that what you tell your cardiac patients to eat?"

"Can't walk by the french fry truck, just like everybody else. Never before in the history of Halifax have so many french fries been consumed by so many. Maybe I'll go on a diet of kale and carrots for the rest of the week. Here, have a couple, they are delicious."

"Thank you, Ira." She takes a handful of fries, pops two into her mouth and hands the rest to Ian.

"Who's your friend, Marie?"

"This is Ian. Ian, this is Ira Deedy, a cardiologist extraordinaire who should marry a dietician or soon he'll be ending his days with a nurse."

"Hello, Ian. Welcome to the land of what'll they say next.

41

Are you a mere friend, or did she finally fish out a boyfriend?"

"He used to be a boyfriend," Marie says, "but he was a trout, and you know how hard they are to keep once you take the hook out. They wiggle and pop from your hand to the water and in a flash away they go up the river. Looks like rain, don't you think? Look at that sky. Grumble rumble pretty soon I'd say."

"Well, that's what you get for fly fishing, Marie," Deedy says. "The flies catch them on the lips. You should fish with worms. A trout will swallow the worm and the hook along with it. Not much wiggle left in them after that. Did you meet here in Halifax?"

Marie considers the question as if it were worth a lot of consideration. The coffee-break crowd begins to fill the side-walk, engineering students and professors from Nova Scotia Tech, clerks from up the street and the librarians. The pigeons flee the sidewalk and fly over the stone wall to the library lawn under the majestic Winston Churchill where they wait on the generosity of the french fry truck patrons. Ian listens to the conversation while he breaks his fries into pieces and flings them over the wall to the scrambling birds.

Marie puts her hand on Ian's shoulder. "Meet here? God, no. Well today we did. No, we were childhood neighbours. Well, he wasn't really my neighbour. His grandparents lived in the same duplex as my family. And when he was six," she laughs, "his family couldn't tolerate him anymore, put the run on him and he lived a lot with his grandmother, so we were childhood neighbours, then childhood friends, and then we got into the grocery business together and we became an item. He was the delivery trucker for the Co-op and I was the clerk, filling boxes with orders that came over the phone. Between his delivery trips we'd take a break in the back shop after he loaded the new orders of groceries onto his half-ton. I'd make two cups of coffee and we'd sit on a bag of oats and share a banana."

Ira Deedy cracks a smile and nearly chokes on a french fry.

"Don't you dare laugh. It was just a banana," Marie laughs. "Sometimes, you know, a banana is just a banana. Anyway, as they say, we became thick. Can I have another fry?" she says and takes two and gives one to Ian. "We better get going."

"Oh," Deedy says. "How's Jocelyn doing today; did you drop in yet?"

"Yeah," Marie says, as she turns to walk away. "Yeah, she's resting peacefully."

"Keep ahead of the storm. It'll be wet and windy. Nice to meet you, Ian." He waves them off.

"So, what's the story on Dr. Deedy?"

"He's a doctor."

"No kidding. He likes you. His eyes lit up when you suggested he'd end up with a nurse."

"He likes me now."

"And you? You like him now?"

"He's not my type."

"And what is your type?"

"Oh, I don't know, somebody better than you used to be."

"And who would that be?"

"Good question. What about you? Are you better than you used to be?"

She leads him down toward Barrington Street and as they pass St. Mary's Basilica she blesses herself. Ian gives her a look and she laughs.

"I can't help it. I don't go to church much anymore, but it got to be such a habit and I never bothered to give it up. It's like a superstition. Every time I pass a Catholic church I do it, even in the city where nobody else does it. I often get a look like you just laid on me."

"I do it myself sometimes, but only at churches I used to go to a lot."

"Funny, isn't it, Ian? Even Jocelyn quit going to Mass a few years ago. She always said people started quitting after Kennedy was assassinated. I don't know why that would be, but maybe she was right."

"Just a coincidence maybe," Ian says. "Or maybe the shock made people stop and think."

They cross Barrington and she leads him down the steep slope and across Lower Water Street to the edge of the harbour and into her favourite coffee shop. They sit on stools at a tall, round table for two at the window overlooking a wide expanse of wharf. A variety of vessels moored against the jetties bob slightly with the waves produced by an oil tanker moving up the harbour. They sit and watch as a tugboat finishes nudging a navy destroyer against its mooring before it turns and disappears down the harbour. Marie takes her wallet from her purse and slips it into a pocket of her trench coat.

"Look after my purse and the picture," she says, "and I'll go get the coffee. I know the good stuff. Want a muffin?"

"No, thanks."

He watches her walk to the counter. He remembers her walk. She always seemed to know where she was going, always seemed to want to get there. The counter clerk sees her coming and starts to serve her before she arrives at the counter. As Ian watches the two of them talk he sees each of them in turn touch her head and run fingers down a few strands of hair. Marie's hair is cut short now, very different from the hair he remembers. She glances over her shoulder at him and catches him looking before she turns to walk back to their table.

When she returns with the steaming mugs they sip coffee and watch through the glass wall as crew members of an American submarine assemble on deck. Marie and Ian are close enough to see their expectant smiles. As the sailors chat and gesture to each other they seem unimpressed by the sinister growl of thunder in the distance, or by the bulbous phalanx of angry clouds advancing over the water from the Dartmouth side of the harbour. The swirling wind is beginning to produce tiny cyclones of dust and gum wrappers along the wharf.

They sip coffee and share a ham and cheese croissant at the little round island of a table surrounded on three sides by the buzz of the crowded restaurant. They watch through the window as outside on the quay between the restaurant and the submarine a pair of buskers, a juggler and a fiddler, entertain the submariners, the strollers and joggers passing by. The door out to the quay is shut tight against the damp and the coming storm but the occasional strain of the fiddle penetrates the glass wall of the café. When she hears the music Marie taps her fingers against her coffee cup.

"The coffee here is pretty good," Ian says, "but it doesn't taste as good as the Nescafé you used to make, do you think?"

"It must be pretty bad then. I know you pretended to like the coffee but I could read your face, every time you swallowed you winced, and you never drank the whole cup. It was the bananas you liked."

"It was you I liked. The coffee was a small price to pay."

"You liked me. Listen here. I had your number, mister man,

when you tried to seduce me right there in the back shop of the Co-op."

Somebody opens the door to the quay and they can hear the fiddler playing "Farewell to Nova Scotia." Although they can't hear his voice the juggler seems to be singing the song, which is amusing the submariners who have just arrived and are obviously preparing to spend some time in the city.

"They're playing your song, Ian."

"Come on, Marie. I liked you is all."

"You liked me all right. You had a hard problem to solve and I was handy."

"I liked you though."

"Oh, yes. I knew that. Liked me! You loved me! I could tell because you didn't dress up in nice clothes and come at me with flowers and chocolates, and wine me and dine me like some smooth guy might try to pull off. No, you just tried to bang me on a bag of oats in your overalls."

"Well, I was only young."

"You were old enough. We were both young and old enough. What I felt bad about was that poor priest, our old demented pastor, standing there, bawling his eyes out. I'll never get over that."

"I doubt he even saw us."

"Then why was he crying?"

"He had Alzheimer's. The nuns were looking after him in the convent. They let him wander. He was always showing up somewhere, lost and crying. He wouldn't know where he was or how he got there or who we were."

"He knew us all through school. He seemed to have a great influence on your life, him and his library. He might remember. God knows how long he was standing there behind the bananas.

I'll never forget that day. Remember his face, like a mask of melting wax. Mind you, I was crying myself, looking at him through tears; I had to go to the washroom to fix my face before I went back to work. You can imagine what fun those two meat-cutters would have with me if they got one look at my face like that."

Marie looks out the window past the buskers and the submarine with its deck full of sailors and watches the ferry carry its load of passengers toward Dartmouth. In the opposite direction a new set of angry clouds, denser and darker and closer to the water, follows the returning ferry across the harbour toward Halifax. The smell of coffee and food obliterated the dank smell of the air when they entered the restaurant. Now the diminishing light brings back the feeling of heaviness. Marie looks at the drooping sky and picks up her purse.

"Oh well, he was an old-fashioned priest. We better go, Ian, before the downpour starts. Maybe he sensed we were already becoming new-fashioned."

They linger a while watching the submariners debark and walk quickly across the quay as if already looking for shelter, some of them slowing down long enough to throw change into the busker's open fiddle case.

"You were telling me about Deedy."

"Oh, you know already, he's a cardiologist, a tight-assed nose-in-the-air. When Jocelyn and I landed at the hospital the fur flew for a while but we straightened him out—I should say, loosened him up—and he's a happier man now."

After the last sailor disappears past the restaurant the fiddler scoops the money from the case and pours it into her purse, zips it up and puts away the fiddle; the juggler stuffs his balls into a drawstring sack, and swinging their instruments, the two walk toward the restaurant.

Ian and Marie leave the coffee shop through the sidewalk door and walk up the steep streets and cross Barrington Street to Spring Garden Road. Despite the threatening weather crowds of pedestrians fill the sidewalks. They walk past St. Mary's Basilica, past the library and Winston Churchill and his pigeons, past the stores along the bustling shopping district of Spring Garden, and turn right onto South Park at the Lord Nelson Hotel. At the end of South Park Marie points and explains in her tour guide imitation voice: "And here to your right, folks, is the famous and storied Citadel Hill, seen from the south side."

"I remember it. If we keep going we'll come to Quinpool Road, right?"

"How could you remember that? You told me you only ever came to Halifax the one time, to begin your oh-so-important career in the air force, and you never moved off Barrington Street."

"I remember it from Hugh McLennan's novel, *Barometer Rising*, about the Halifax explosion."

"When was that, I forget?"

"More than fifty years ago now. Two boats, the Imo and the Mont Blanc, crashed and blew the whole downtown to bits, the biggest explosion ever heard of until Hiroshima and Nagasaki. A lot of people killed. A lot wounded."

"Was it a love story?"

"Neil, the main character, came back from the war and walked up here like we're doing now. Came to see his girl. What else do you know about Citadel Hill?"

"Nothing. Well next to nothing. It's a nice place for a picnic on a nice day, hint, hint. Oh yeah, and it has a sister citadel in

Quebec. You know what, Ian? Wouldn't it be nice to get a jug of wine and a couple of buns and a hunk of cheese?"

"That's a good idea, but where will we go in the rain?"

"Let's get the wine and cheese and we'll see. We can always take it back to my place."

They walk along the base of Citadel Hill, pause for a while and watch the Bengal Lancers, young girls who are guiding their horses through various manoeuvres, riding down lanes and leaping over pole fences. The rain holds off but the air is so damp they can see that the cooling wind is condensing water on the poles of the fences. Ian and Marie hold their breaths for a moment as one young teenager gallops her horse toward the rail fence. She makes the jump but knocks over the top rail. When the horse hits the ground its knees buckle, the horse tumbles, the girl flies off, rolls away, then picks herself up, picks up her peaked cap, laughing, holding up her thumb and forefinger to show she missed the jump by just a fraction of an inch. She walks over to the recovered horse, standing, patiently waiting, gives it a pat on the head and a hug, climbs back into the saddle, and then horse and rider return to the start line.

"Atta girl, give it another go," Marie whispers and raises her fist as horse and girl race toward the hurdle.

Further along near the end of the Commons they stop to watch an inning of softball. According to their T-shirts the Crocodiles are pitched against the Alligators, and by the sound of their battle cries, they feel themselves in mortal combat. But the ferocity of most of these two sets of middle-aged, reptilian men and women seem sadly mitigated by the girth of their middles and the lethargy of their legs.

"Do you still play ball, Ian?"

"Oh yeah. Just finished playing for the university in Glace Bay. We won the championship. I graduated just before I came to Halifax."

"So you did go back home, and you went to the university."

"I did."

"Well, good for you."

A well-rounded batter hits what should have been an in-the-park home run and Ian and Marie watch as he chugs around the bases and almost overruns the two base runners in front of him. He stops halfway down the third base line and hurries back to third as the ball comes in to the catcher just a second too late to catch the first two runners.

"Now tell me, Bucko," Marie says, "how did you know to find me? How did you get my phone number? It's not in the book."

"When I left Glace Bay Father Angus suggested I call you."

"Did he now? Well, how sweet."

"He said you could give me the tour. He said make sure she takes you up Quinpool. Tell her to show you the seminary."

"Did he now? How very sweet. He must be getting nostalgic, missing the old torture chamber. Good, then let's go, the liquor store is on the way, and I'll bring you up to the seminary."

The inning ends with a strike out and they leave the ball game behind them, cross the Robie Street intersection at the Willow Tree and walk along Quinpool past St. Pat's High School.

"So, the hero," Marie says, "in *Barometer Rising*, Neil, did he get killed in Halifax after surviving the war? Did he hit a home run? Did he and his girl crash together and go boom, blow up like the two boats and the city? Or did he just leave her and join the air force?"

She smiles and turns to search his face for a reaction, but he ignores the jab in her last remark. "No," he says, "I don't remember exactly, but probably like a lot of people they survived by being here behind Citadel Hill. It deflected the blast. Saved a lot of people. They got married, lived with their daughter and all that."

"Kinda boring."

"Not for them."

"I guess not," Marie says. "Come to think of it, isn't that the way it should be? Life in books should be exciting, but in real life it's probably more fun if it's boring. Watch your daughter play softball, watch her jump her horse over wooden fences, hold your breath when she takes a fall, be proud of her when she jumps up laughing, praise her for giving it another go, take her for a walk along the waterfront and count the boats, treat her to an ice cream or french fries, sit on the edge of the wharf to eat and watch the buskers juggle balls and play their fiddles, drive her to school on rainy days, take her to church, help with her homework, dress her up like a witch on Halloween and go trick or treating, hold her two-wheel bike by the seat until she gets the knack of balance, her excitement is your excitement, make sure she doesn't get killed or raped, hope she doesn't fall in love with some jerk, like you, who runs off to join the air force instead of getting married to a nice girl like me. Yes, a nice boring life, doing corny stuff, living happily ever after."

"The woman in the book was a lot like you."

"How do you mean?"

"Oh, tough, smart, bitchy." He puts his arm across her shoulders and gives her a squeeze.

"God, Ian, don't do that."

"What?"

"You're turning my crank. If you'd've used your mouth

instead of your hand in the back shop you might've turned out like your friend Neil in the book with a wife and a daughter to buy a horse for and a nice corny life living happily ever after."

He gives her a sly look and takes her hand.

"Thank God," she says, "I'm old enough to know better now."

"What?"

"Your tongue is no more dependable than your hand."

"How can you be sure?"

"Don't make me laugh. Why did you come to Halifax? Don't try to tell me you came to see me."

"I had a good reason to come, but when I heard you were here, I came anyway."

"Don't make me laugh. The back hand of flattery. Thanks though, anyway. Let's pretend we're all happy just in case we are."

They walk slowly and stop now and again to punctuate the rhythm of their conversation. The clouds that followed them from the harbour overtake them now. Not raining yet but getting darker and the invisible mist saturates the air with damp. "We'd better get a move on," she says, "if we don't want to get drenched."

"C'mon then," he says. "Let's get up Quinpool and see if we can find what we're looking for."

"Oh, we will. Indeed we will. You know for someone who never ventured off Barrington you seem to know your way around."

"It's all in the book."

"I don't think it's all in the book."

"How do you mean?"

"I don't know what I mean but I know I'm right."

They stop along Quinpool first at a bakery where Ian buys some rolls and cheese, then the liquor store and Marie buys a bottle of red wine in a brown bag. They continue along the sidewalk. Ian pulls the bottle from the bag, reads the label and puts it back. "Châteauneuf-du-Pape, the Pope's New Castle," Ian says. "I never heard of it."

She puts the bag and wine along with the bread and cheese in her purse. "Me and Jocelyn, we wouldn't drink anything else. And how appropriate now."

"Appropriate? How?"

"You'll see, buddy boy."

The clouds are letting go their burden of rain now and the wind changes direction from south to west and blows a drizzle into their faces. Ian puts Jocelyn's grandfather's picture inside his suit coat to protect it from the rain. Marie leads him across the street and they take shelter in the recessed doorway of a book-store and sit on bundles of *Playboy* magazines, delivered but not yet un-roped and taken inside for distribution to the laity. The right hand dog-ear on the front page of a particularly lurid tabloid reveals the angelic smile of Hugh Hefner, neo-priest, shining like a gibbous moon.

Marie fishes some tissue from her purse, they wipe the rain from their glasses and contemplate the building across the street. The iron fence along the sidewalk is broken at the centre, the iron bars of its double gate flattened onto the lawn by the large crane poised in front of the two-storey building. A huge ball hangs from the arm of the crane at the level of the second-floor windows. A man in coveralls opens the door of the crane, climbs down the ladder and disappears through the black hole that replaces the stoved-in door.

"Well, Ian, there you are. You have arrived. Behold the structure you seek. There she stands, at least some of it, but apparently not for long."

"The seminary?"

"That's her."

"So that's why Father Angus had a big grin on when he told me you'd lead me to it." Ian pulls the top of the paper bag down over the neck of the bottle, unwraps the top covering, digs the cork out of the bottle with the blade of his pocket knife and passes the bag to Marie to begin their little ceremony. After a few drinks from the bottle and a few wafers of bread, sliced off the roll with his jackknife, Ian stands and delivers a brief homily.

"*Vere dignum et justum est.* It is fitting indeed and just, no doubt, and a tad ironic—" he glances at the magazines and surveys the sex paraphernalia in the store window "—to be sucking on a bottle of Châteauneuf-du-Pape from a bag, like a wino with nowhere to go but drunk, surrounded by artificial faces, plastic teeth a-smiling, and airbrushed tits and renovated arses, imported from New York and California to assuage my loneliness as I watch the deconstruction of the Pope's old Château."

Marie looks up at him laughing, but not surprised. She knew soon after they met he was what she called a fabulator. When they worked at the Co-op he told her a new story every time he came in for a new load of groceries, always a story based on some crazy encounter with a customer or someone he met on the road. At first she believed him but soon realized he must be making at least half of it up; nobody could have that many interesting events in a week much less in a day. But he assured her that these things happen to everybody. People just don't notice. They're not paying attention. But today, since they left the hospital, he seemed subdued, until now, for some reason, excited by the destruction of the seminary, nourished by the wine and the bread, he is on fire. "My God, Ian, could you be that drunk on a few slugs of wine? Pardon me for laughing. Are you delirious?"

"I am drunk with disappointment. Contemplating disappointment. Delirious too. Why not? It looks like a day of reckoning so let's reckon."

"Holy Mary Mother of God, maybe you are drunk. I must say it suits you better than sober."

"What d'you mean, girl?" Ian raises the bottle in the wet, wrinkled bag in a sort of salute.

Marie snatches it from his hand and takes a swallow. "Winos don't get drunk sipping Châteauneuf-du-Pape from bottles in bags and they don't talk in Latin as a rule, and what the hell are you talking about? I think that's what I mean. I always think it's better if I know what's going on."

The windows are gone from the holes in the wall of the brick building across the street, the roof and half the second storey gone. Shards of plaster from the gutted building litter the lawn. Drizzle turns to rain. Tires rolling up and down Quinpool Road begin to hiss and splash puddles up on the sidewalks. From their storefront porch Ian and Marie watch the crane operator come out from the door hole in the wall, search his pockets, climb up the ladder to the cab of his machine, get in, pull a lever, lower the huge ball to the ground, then raise it again a foot or so and climb down the ladder to the ground.

The operator approaches the ball and with a stick starts poking at the debris under the hanging ball. He carries the stick back into the building.

Ian takes a swig of wine and gives Marie a smile. "Saved for the moment," he says.

Marie looks at him, her face twisted in a puzzle. "So it's the seminary. What's it got to do with you?"

"I came to Halifax to go there."

"To be a priest? You must be joking."

"That's what Father Angus said. But if you are serious, he said, look up Marie, get her to show you where it is. I guess he meant where it isn't. Now I know the reason for that fat smile on his face. Why does everybody think I'm joking?"

"Why do you think they're demolishing the building?" she says.

Ian doesn't answer for a moment but then says, "I'll give it some thought."

"Well, my thought is they probably don't need it anymore. And you? Is that what you want? Are you sure?"

"No, but I don't think they should tear it apart until I am." He laughs.

"Well, for Christ's sake let's put a stop to it." She jumps up and rushes into the store. Ian takes a swig of wine, watching her go. She comes back out carrying a clipboard with several pages of blank paper. On the top half of the first page she writes a variety of illegible scrawls and the name and address of the seminary. She pins a plastic card on the lapel of her trench coat and writes on it in large letters: Halifax Historical Society. "C'mon, dummy, I'll show you how to do this."

With his head tilted down toward the big steel ball, from behind his eyebrows the crane operator watches their approach through the gate and over the lawn full of wallboard and shingles, led by Marie in aggressive stride, her trench coat trailing in the breeze. As they close in on him he looks up for a moment then bends his head again and kicks a shingle. He puts his hands in his pockets.

"On the other hand," she says to Ian, loud enough for the crane operator to hear, "perhaps you better stay with me 'til we settle this one."

"What about MacKenzie?" Ian asks, following Marie's instructions.

"Never mind that son of a whore, he knows if he touches a brick, he'll be in court in the morning." She leans into the crane operator and says, "Are you in charge here?"

"Jes' drive the crane."

"What's your name?"

"Danny MacIntyre."

"Well, Mr. MacIntyre, you've got quite a mess going here."

"I jes' got here."

"And what do you propose to do here?"

"Sent me down to knock her over."

She waves the clipboard at him. "Do you realize we have a court injunction prohibiting any interference with this property? This is one of the oldest buildings in the city."

"Suits me," Danny says. "I got the flu anyhow. Jes' as soon be home in bed. Lost my watch in this junk. Let me lift this here ball a little higher. Would you mind taking a look, jes' take a minute, eh. Look under see if it's there. I looked a bit but I didn't look good; I didn't see it."

He climbs the ladder to the cab. When he lifts the ball Ian kicks at the shards of glass and wet plaster, spots the watch and picks it up it by the strap. The crystal and the hands are gone. He holds it up for Marie to see.

"It's none o'clock," she says, and touches him on the shoulder. "I guess we're starting from zero."

Danny takes the watch from Ian and looks at it as if it were a favourite dog that had to be put down for pity's sake. "Pretty well shot, ain't she? Good strap though. She was getting pretty rickety anyways. Always showed the wrong time on her. Never knew was she fast or slow." He threads out the leather strap and throws the watch into the shards of glass and plaster; he coughs, spits and trudges to an ancient Monarch parked outside the failed fence. The car grumbles to a start, backfires and Danny hisses off down the wet street.

"Quite the performance, Marie. For a nurse you're a pretty good actor."

"You think that was fun, than jes' you wait, my lad, jes' you wait 'til I take you to supper. You won't know are you coming or going. Let's go get another bottle of pape juice and amble on downtown. I can't wait to see your eyes pop."

"Where to?"

"We're going back the way we came. And I just thought of something. We walked past the house Hugh MacLennan lived in for a while. I never read his books but somebody once told me where he lived, right next to the CBC radio station. Told me he hated the house and always slept on the porch. I don't know why but when I pass by I always think of him sleeping on the porch even though he's long gone now. But today I forgot about it. Anyway we'll go by it on our way to a place, my one-time, would-be lover, a place fitting and just, and jes' a tad ironic, and we will eat and we will mourn."

"And what does that mean?"

"You'll see." She smiles.

THREE

And, after all, what is a lie?
'Tis but a truth in Masquerade.
—*Byron*

THEY REACH THE DOWNTOWN RESTAURANT, The Loaves and Fishes, on Water Street, living on the edge of their second bottle of Châteauneuf-du-Pape, hand in hand, pleased with themselves, each other, a delicate, fragile pleasure, and self-conscious of how they must look, her in a crinkled trench coat, himself in a rumpled suit, a comfortable couple, looking like Ingrid Bergman and Humphrey Bogart without the hats in dim and misty Casablanca without the aircraft waiting on the tarmac. They put the empty bottle of Châteauneuf-du-Pape in its wrinkled paper bag on the sidewalk, open the heavy mahogany door and walk inside.

So touching they appear, as they stand in the vestibule and look down the aisle of the restaurant, that the host, astonished, rushes to them, his soutane flapping swooshing noises around his legs.

"Oh my God," he says, leaning back to take them in, "Bergman and Bogart look-alikes. Would you mind terribly? Would you just wait here? I'm a big fan. I'd love to get a photo. Would you wait just for a moment? I'll get my camera and I'll be right back."

"Sure," Ian says. His eyes focus on the soutane, his eyebrows knitting, his lips sucked into an amused smile.

"Don't move," the host says, holding up the palm of his right hand. He turns and rushes down the aisle past a silverware caddy and through a curtain of black lace. He reappears with a camera and snaps several shots from various angles and distances. "Thank you," he says. "I'm a bird watcher by avocation but I like to shoot people too."

They stand in the pleasure and mystery of a silent moment until Ian asks, "Could we get something to eat?"

"Of course, *bien sûr*," the host says, and, still infected by their charm and his own, he steps between them when they let go of each others' hands and puts his arms around their shoulders. "My name is Frankie; I'll be your host. May I ask yours?"

"Rick," Ian says.

"Ilsa," Marie says.

"Goodness, we'd better sit you down, you'll miss your plane if you don't hurry. Or I guess that would be a boat in this part of town. You look familiar, Ilsa, you've been here before."

"No, first time, but I've got a twin sister. I think she comes here a lot with her girlfriend."

"Oh yes, those two, I remember them, laughing all the time and drinking the Château," Frankie says. He drops his arms from their shoulders, steps ahead of them and with a flourish of his arm leads them on a short but labyrinthine trek, down an aisle between two sections of altar rail, turns left at the end of the aisle into the eating area, passes by a bandstand behind another section of altar rail, turns left again and sits them opposite the bandstand at a low rectangular table, next to a large window overlooking Halifax Harbour. They hang their coats on the back of their chairs to dry. Marie puts her voluminous purse on the floor beside her chair, takes the picture of Jocelyn's grandfather from Ian and leans it against the purse.

"We don't want to forget that," she says. They settle in with their elbows on the table and look out on the harbour. The restaurant is higher up the hill than the café where they drank their coffee earlier. Now they are overlooking the buildings on the lower side of Water Street and the obscured view of the wharves and the navy ships docked at them. As they watch, a three-masted schooner full of sails appears from behind a warehouse built on one of the wharves.

"That must be the *Bluenose*, Ian. Doesn't it make you feel like the nineteenth century, or would it be the eighteenth?"

"Hard to know what century it looks like from here," Ian says, then, realizing that Frankie is still hovering, looks over at him and says, "What d'you think, Frankie?"

"I'm not into centuries, but it is the *Bluenose*. I heard on the radio that it tried to sail to Quebec but a storm in the Gulf chased it back home."

The restaurant is large and quiet, with a handful of customers scattered here and there. The faint sound of Gregorian chant flows in a barely audible whisper from speakers disguised as statues of Mary and Joseph on either side of the bandstand. A couple of waiters sit at a table looking at menus and chatting and blowing smoke in each other's faces. Another man sits alone eating soup. Marie looks around. She says to Frankie, "Where is everybody? Are we too early?"

"Don't worry. No problem. We're not busy yet, so you have my undivided attention. It is a little early but you are welcome. A little early for choir night. We don't get a lot of guy-girl couples here, not that we don't want to, we are ecumenical and you are completely welcome. On choir night people tend to come in later to enjoy the music while they eat. Look, there're a few couples coming in now. I'll be right back to set you up."

Frankie greets two pairs of young women and one couple of young men and escorts them to seats. Ian watches and turns to Marie.

"What's it mean?"

"What, you mean guy-girl, girl-girl, guy-guy? I guess it means in the reformed church various freedoms of choice are the new dispensation. Now where did that Frankie go? He said he'd be back to set us up."

"I feel like I've been set up already," Ian says. "What is this, Marie? Gregorian chant, altar railings. Any why is Frankie decked out in that rig, a soutane for God's sake?"

"Don't mind Frankie. He loves to talk. He should have been a professor. He's a camera fanatic and a movie fan. But to answer your question, I thought you might find that this place is indeed fitting and a tad ironic, *vere dignum et justum est*, you might say. Can't you guess?"

"Well," Ian says, and takes a deep breath through his nose. "It's awful churchy. Some nut dressed up like a priest. And the music coming from the statues. And those things, cut-off pieces of altar rail, what do they mean? Are they fences?"

"Look behind the bandstand, Sherlock. See if you can find another clue."

Stained glass windows from floor to ceiling decorate the

wall at the back of the bandstand. Neon lights across the top, bottom and sides illuminate the words and figures painted on the glass. Ian studies the stained-glass panels and realizes they must have been arranged originally with a representational logic and perhaps were disassembled for moving and cleaning and put together in their new location by someone who didn't know, or didn't care, or perhaps simply preferred a non-representational presentation.

Consequently it came to pass that when St. John the Baptist was beheaded, St. Catherine's head rolled on the grass. St. John's head turned up on St. Clare, with St. Francis of Assisi behind her giving it a haircut, so that she could take the veil. Later, down the wall a bit, she got her own head back in time to pray against the Saracens. The various historical and biographical revisions are comical and probably sacrilegious, but the chief value of the confusion lay in the fact that canny spectators could design their own arrangement and bend history or biography to suit their wills or whims.

"It's the seminary," Ian says, holding up the palms of his hands. "This is all salvage."

Marie tilts her head and offers a weak smile of congratulation. "Do you like my hair like this, Ian?"

He looks at her hair. He remembers when it fell like a frame of woven waves around her face and fanned across her neck and shoulders. He remembers the feel of it on his face. He remembers whispering through it and the feel of it on his lips. The last time he thought about her hair he was reading a poem in English class at the university. He could only remember a snatch of the poem, "those great honey coloured ramparts at her ear." Marie's ramparts then were not honey coloured but brown, like the brown fur of a fawn. And now they are gone. He reaches across the table and feels the air beneath her ear. "Your hair is lovely." He smiles. "But most of it has gone somewhere."

"Yes. It went to the past. Like so many other things we used to enjoy. Disappeared into the wild blue yonder, something like yourself. Me and Joss, we chopped it short so when we put our nurse hats in our pockets and hung stethoscopes around our necks, we looked like doctors. It's amazing the difference it makes. We tried to get the doctors to wear our hats but they wouldn't do it. Got snippy about it too. Our friend Deedy was one of the worst."

Ian takes another look around the restaurant. Another couple comes in and waits to be seated. "Where is he?"

"Yes, where's that Frankie? We need some wine." Frankie comes out through the lace curtain and leads the couple to a table. "Oh, oh there he is, speak of the devil. Now doesn't that old chestnut take on new meaning in a joint like this? The Châteauneuf-du-Pape is the house wine. Joss and I came here if we ran out at home. Here he comes. Be patient, Ian, he's a non-stop talker and you're a fresh ear. Just keep interrupting him until it gets busy and he won't have a lot of time for us."

Frankie arrives with a fat smile on his face and a surplice worn over his soutane like a vest, cut short, bleached white, with short, wide sleeves trimmed with starched lace at the ends and on the bottom. He carries two narrow, four-foot lengths of black cloth draped over his outstretched hands and two menus trapped under his upper left arm.

"Would you like to wear these? You don't have to of course, but some people enjoy getting into the spirit of the place."

"Is that a stole?" Ian asks.

"Yes. Well, am I ever impressed. So you're conversant with the liturgy."

"Why not?" Marie says. "Let's."

"Sure. Why in hell not?"

"Good then." Frankie drapes the long pieces of linen around their necks and folds the ends on their laps.

"Where'd you get these things?" Ian asks.

"We got our seamstress to make them. The ancient Romans used them like we use napkins to keep food from soiling their togas. We printed an explanation on the placemats, which we call altar stones," he says and as they glance down at the placemats, Frankie abruptly departs, the menus still under his arm.

"Where in hell did he go?" Marie says. "I didn't get a chance to order the wine."

Ian reads a few lines from the placemat to Marie. "'The church copied the garments of the Roman nobility, turning them into rituals, the stole an imitation of the bib; priests wear them to hear confessions.' Why? Maybe to keep the sinners from spilling sins on the priest's lap, ha, ha. ...'"

"That's enough of that, Ian, I read it all before."

Ian stops reading it out loud but skips a paragraph and reads a little bit more to himself. "The church abandoned the seminary and developers bought it as a tear-down so they could build a shopping centre and we rented a truck and hauled away the contents. Their junk became our treasure. . ."

Marie is drumming her fingernails on the table when Ian finally stops reading. Frankie suddenly reappears with the menus still tucked under his arm. He lights the candle on the table with a taper, and begins to talk.

"You should have seen our old place, the Catacombs.

Nothing but a name and an old Halifax basement with a fire-brick foundation. Talk about creepy. It had a secret underground passage to the harbour and we made up stories to give it historical significance but you couldn't walk it without meeting a dozen rats so we couldn't give a tour. Now in this location Governor Cornwallis used to get drunk every night and that's true historical significance. So we bought it and created our decor. It has a spooky basement too but no rats. It's our wine cellar. We call it the Catacombs and this—" Frankie waves his hand to include the room "—is the Upper Room. And we're right downtown. In Halifax you have to have location and interesting decor, and of course a full menu. The days of fish and chips, salt and vinegar are long gone."

He asks, "How about a cocktail before you order? We have all the regular drinks but our Mortal Sin is a favourite, and of course we have our popular non-alcoholic beverage, the Venial Sin, for children and teetotalers but you don't look like the venial-sin type. Me either. Just the other day I was saying to Luke, my partner, I don't want to go to purgatory. For me it's heaven or hell, though I might need a deathbed confession to get into heaven. Are you with me on that, Ilsa?" he says to Marie who is drumming a finger on the table and nodding her head and smiling the patient smile of a person who is waiting for somebody to shut up.

"No," Marie says. "I'm with him."

"The Mortal Sin sounds interesting," Ian says, "but I think we'll stick with wine. A bottle of Châteauneuf-du-Pape, please."

"Okay then, that's fine. Perhaps you'll feel like a Mortal Sin later in the evening. People often do after a bottle of wine."

"I thought they did away with mortal sins," Ian says.

"Not at all," Frankie says. "They changed the name is all. For the names of things you can't beat the old-time religion. Now they call sin antisocial behaviour, which I guess could still land you in some kind of hell, but Antisocial Behaviour wouldn't be a suitable name for a cocktail. No, no. I don't think so. Here are your menus."

The cover page of the menu is decorated with five varieties of bread and five species of fish, a half dozen crustaceans and, written in script, the words:

LOAVES AND FISHES
The menu according to Mark

Frankie puts his finger on the name Mark on Ian's menu. "Mark is our chef," he explains. "If you want anything not on the menu he can make it. It's amazing what he can do with a fish and a loaf of bread..." He pauses for effect, raises his eyebrows and smiles a knowing smile. "Miraculous, almost."

"Where's the crucifix?" Ian asks.

"Pardon?"

"They must have had a crucifix in the chapel in the seminary. Did they keep it?"

"Oh yes, there was a crucifix. We had to take it. They said we could take everything as long as it wasn't nailed or bolted to the building. We put the crucifix with some other useless stuff downstairs in the Catacombs."

"Why don't you put it over there on that empty wall?" Ian says.

"Matter of fact, Matthew suggested that very thing; he's

67

one of our partners. We had a big meeting here after hours one night. We lugged it up from the Catacombs and nailed it to the wall to see how it would look, tried to imagine what effect it would have on our patrons. But in the end we thought, no. There was nothing nice about it at all. If it was one of those Renaissance ones with a positive image, you know, Christ triumphant, well, maybe. But no, no, blood all over the legs, hair matted with blood from a halo of thorns sticking into his scalp, one god-awful grimace on his bloody face, ugly slash across his belly, and those big Jesus railroad-tie spikes sticking out of his hands and feet, and except for a blood-soaked diaper, not a stitch on him. No, all in all, not an awfully appetizing decor for a gourmet restaurant. And then too, we didn't want to go too far. Even these days there is such a thing as blasphemy. We put it in the Catacombs." And with a self-satisfied look, he dashes off.

"Well, Ian," Marie says, her chin in her hand, her lips pursed in a half smile.

"Well what?"

"Well, you got quite the look on your face. A little bewildered are you? What's the matter? Don't you think it's fitting and just and a tad ironic?"

"Let's just call it interesting."

"If you don't stop asking Frankie questions, we're going to sober up, if we don't starve to death first or fall asleep listening to him drone on and on. Like my father used to say, he's got a tongue on him like a loose board on a bane wagon."

Frankie comes back leading two pimply teenagers, each in surplice and soutane, one carrying a carafe of red wine and the other two silver chalices. "Christian Brothers Burgundy," Frankie explains as he pours, "because we ran out of Châteauneuf-du-Pape. These altar boys will take your orders. This is Peter and this is Daniel. If you order fish I recommend the Baked Sole à la Beelzebub, we call it 'The Bub.'"

"Any lobster?" Ian asks.

"Pardon?"

"Lobster. You have a picture of a lobster on the menu."

"You have to read the footnote," Frankie says.

Ian looks, and there actually is a footnote on the menu. An asterisk above the left eye of the lobster leading to a twin asterisk at the bottom of the menu and an explanation:

Customers are advised that lobster will not be available until Quinquagesima Sunday and will continue to be served all through Lent. Otherwise it will be available on Ember Days and during Advent, the four weeks before Christmas.

Ian reads the footnote to himself while Frankie and the altar boys shift their weight from foot to foot and Marie drums her fingers on the table. Then, oblivious, he reads it out loud to Marie, and tapping his finger on the footnote explanation he asks Frankie, "What's the point?"

"There's no point," Frankie says. "It's just a rule we made up."

"Just like the real church," Marie laughs, "and just like it used to be."

"Okay, I'll have the baked sole."

"And for Ilsa?"

"Me too," Marie says.

"It comes with baked potato and fiddleheads, but we can substitute if you prefer something else."

Marie and Ian nod approval and the teenagers scribble on their order pads and retreat. Frankie stays until they sip the wine. "How do you like it?"

"It's a very nice wine," Ian says. "Meek but with a hint of inner strength."

"There you go. You are into the spirit of the place. Yes, it's an excellent wine. We copied the recipe from The Christian Brothers. It's their burgundy. We like to have liturgical sounding wines and what could be better. We used to just buy it when the monks made it themselves but then we couldn't get it. They must have stopped making it; we don't know why."

"Maybe they ran out of monks," Marie says.

Ian answers Frankie's statement as if it were a question. "If you want a liturgical wine, why not Blue Nun?" he suggests. "You could hire an altar girl to serve it."

"What a marvelous idea. We do have the wine, but yes, we should rent or maybe we could buy a nun costume, dye it blue and hire one of our sisters to pour. Or one of our slight, slender boys. One of them looks a little girly anyway. Yes indeed, marvelous. I'll bring you a complimentary half-litre for that idea. And by the way, this is your lucky night, did I mention? You just happened to come on choir night. I asked them to come out a tad early so you won't miss their performance and that you might have a request or two. I told them you were celebrating a special night. I have a sixth sense you know, I can spot an occasion a mile away. This is an occasion, is it not?"

"Oh yes," Marie says. "This is indeed an occasion, a fitting occasion, and just, and a tad ironic."

Frankie smiles the smile of a person who misses the point of a joke but doesn't want to admit it. "I see our customers are starting to come in," he says to cover his confusion. "We always get a big crowd on choir night, but most people come late." He looks around to admire the growing crowd. "Enjoy your meal. If you need anything give the altar bell a tinkle," he says, and places a little golden bell on the table between them.

The altar boys return with a basket of bread and utensils wrapped in napkins and set the table in silence.

"So," Marie says, with the bread and wine finally between them on the table, "alone at last together, and imitation Christian Brothers Burgundy coursing through our veins chasing the Châteauneuf-du-Pape. Are we happy, or should we give Frankie a tinkle?"

"Perhaps we could ask him to consecrate the bread and wine."

"Frankie might think that would be going too far. Blasphemy, my dear, might trump decor if it goes too far. And to tell the truth I'd appreciate it if you don't give Frankie any tinkles 'til absolutely necessary. He might talk the legs off the table and we'd have to hold it up with our knees. Are you serious about going into the seminary?"

Ian doesn't answer her question right away. He looks as if he might not answer at all. He butters a slice of bread, his head down, while Marie sips wine, smiles and waits. When he finishes chewing he looks around at the broken pieces of altar rail and the confused, neon-lit stained-glass wall behind the bandstand. Frankie leads a couple of young women to a table and as they pass in front of the bandstand they turn to each other and dance along the altar rail to the Gregorian chant emanating from the statues mounted beside the stained-glass wall. Ian turns back to the table and hums a mirthless laugh.

The altar boys return with plates of food and set them down. Ian focuses on his plate, takes a bite of sole, digs his fork into the split baked potato and takes a small bite and then a fiddlehead and chews his food slowly. "I don't know," he says. "I guess this is the seminary, and I guess I'm in it. Father Angus will get a good laugh. Maybe I'll go to Quebec. They must have one there, though I wonder if it makes sense anymore. It was a strong idea in my head I had to follow up."

"Wine tends to dilute strong ideas."

"Oh well, let's not bother with it now, this is not the time nor place."

"I kind of like this place, Ian. You know why? I'll tell you." She slides down her chair stretching her legs under the table until her knees bump into his. "It's the only restaurant in town where two people can touch knees without disappearing under the table."

"Oh, you're a bad one, Marie."

"It's not me, Ian, it's the Christian Brothers made me say it, the little devils. They're not as innocent as you might think."

"I propose a toast, Marie, to our knees and the Christian Brothers who encourage them."

"Our knees," they say in unison.

"Our knees," toasts Marie, "long may they rub."

"Our knees," toasts Ian, "rub a dub, Bub."

"You know, Ian, while I'm in a burgundy kind of mood, I'd like to say I don't think you are all that priesty."

"It's not a question of being priesty. It's a question of doing something worth doing. What d'you mean priesty?"

"You don't seem to me all that holy. I've been holy myself, and you don't seem holy to me."

"How do I seem to you?"

"There is an h-word for it, something like holy, but the Christian Brothers won't let me say it until the Châteauneuf-du-Pape escapes my blood stream. They don't like the competition."

"Say it anyway."

"I don't want to sound corny, but I doubt the 'h' word goes with my decor."

"Does it go with your heart?"

"Oh yes. And my decor is subject to change." She nudges him under the table with her knee and gives him a wide-eyed innocent look. "And here is another toast for our occasion. Here's to our success. To celebrate our success." She raises her wine glass with both hands. He follows her lead and they clink their glasses.

"What success?"

Marie picks at the food on her plate. "God, Ian, you have a poor memory. Don't you recall, try hard now, a couple of hours ago we confronted man and machine trying to tear down the past and put a grocery store in its place. And we won. We did it."

"Oh yes, the capitalist dog and his timeless watch. He put his tail between his legs and slunk off. Don't forget, Marie, tomorrow will see more dogs in the yard and nobody with a clipboard and a pencil to muzzle them."

Marie takes a sip of wine. "True. But we fought the good fight. *Something worth doing*," she says slowly. "There are still lots of things worth doing. We all lose in the long run, nurses know that, but I hate to lose in the short run."

"Okay, let's clink to the short run." *Clink* go the chalices.

"Here comes the band," Marie says. "But not the choir;

didn't he say choir night? Do choirs sing with bands? I can't imagine this won't be interesting."

A drummer sits on his stool behind the altar rail and begins a soft rhythm with his brushes. He wears the brown habit of a monk with the hood bunched back at the neck. Another musician in the same garb sits at the organ, and another with a clarinet sits on the altar rail and they begin to trade riffs to the rhythms of the drummer. The room is nearly half full now and a comfortable murmur rolls around the room under the music.

"That's a nice sound, Ian."

"Yeah and here comes the choir."

The four singers file in from the kitchen wearing the same costumes as the other musicians but with white hoods covering their heads and full beards and mustaches disguising their faces. As they fit themselves in front of the band behind the altar rail, several tables full of people begin to clap. Light streaks through the stained-glass windows behind the bandstand, throwing shadows over the white hoods of the singers so that even their eyes are obscured and in the psychedelic haze they look like ghosts wrapped in brown sheets.

The clarinet player rests his instrument on the floor, picks up a microphone and greets the audience. "Good evening, ladies and gentlemen. Tonight is choir night and we have with us the ever-popular Castrati. Look on the back of your altar stones for information about our first tune, our signature tune. The music itself is authentic."

Ian twists in his chair to see the clarinet player make his speech, then turns back and as the band plays an introduction and the four singers in the choir ready themselves, he reads on the placemat:

Authentic music and lyrics were all taken from the Paroissien Romain, contenant la messe et l'office pour les dimanches et les fêtes, chant Grégorien extrait de l'édition Vaticane et signes rhythmiques des Bénédictins de solesmes. *Members of the choir did the translations.*

The note is followed by several verses of the *Dies Irae* and then a translation of the first few lines:

Wrathful day, dreaded day
The day Sibyl and David said
Would be the day beyond the dead.

As they listen to the music Ian reads, "The choir took its name from the infamous 'castrati.' The church forbade women to sing in the choir so they employed castrati to sing the high parts of the Mass music ..."

"Oh, shut up, Ian," Marie says. "We know all that."

"Don't you think it's interesting?"

"No."

"Okay."

"They're not real, you know," she says, pointing to the choir.

"Who?"

"Those so-called castrati. They're not men. They're women wearing false beards and mustaches masquerading as men."

"Get out."

"Are you stunned or what?"

"It's all a fake?"

"So what? It's just decor."

After the mock castrati finish singing several authentic verses in Latin and English, Ian looks at Marie and sees her eyes shining, beads of tears falling from her cheeks into her chalice of wine.

"Marie, what? Is it the music?"

"Yes. The music. So beautiful. And Jocelyn. Dead."

"Jocelyn? She's dead? We just left her a while ago. How do you know?"

"She's dead. She's dead. She was dead when we left her at the hospital. Nobody with her when she died. I was late. I was late. She left me a note. I couldn't bear to tell anybody until I got used to it."

"Are you used to it now? Would you rather talk about it, or not talk about it?" Ian asks.

"We can talk about it for a bit to see. I'm holding it at arm's length. But the music got to me for a minute. I'm okay now, I think. The *Dies Irae* was our favourite tune. Sometimes we'd go to the funerals of strangers just to hear the choir sing it."

"What an odd favourite tune for two nurses."

"Oh, we weren't nurses to start with. We were nuns. We met in the novitiate."

Ian stops eating, watching Marie continue to push the food around her plate. "You were a nun?"

She takes a tiny bite of fish. "It wasn't the plan. The plan was, after I got my sister and brother through school, I thought, okay, when that's done, I'll quit my job at the Co-op, get married to you, and we'd have babies and they'd grow up and we'd put them all through school. Isn't that what people did in those days? They got themselves to nunneries, or they got themselves to seminaries. Those days are over, mister man."

"Well, you didn't tell me your plan."

"You're not supposed to have to tell people stuff like that. You are supposed to twig to stuff like that, Mister Oblivious. You go out on a date, then you go steady, he takes you to the prom, he buys you a Christmas present way too expensive and you pretend you can't accept it and you know the rest, a cedar chest the next Christmas, then the ring. It was all written down in our brains."

"How was I supposed to know what you wanted if you didn't tell me?"

"I told you, I didn't think I had to tell you. But stupid me I guess what I didn't realize is that all those customs and arrangements were withering away like apples clinging to a tree long after the leaves on the ground are buried under the snow."

"I guess boys don't think about that stuff."

"No, I guess not. I guess we know what boys think about," she says and reaches across and touches his arm to show him she is only pretending to be cross. He is staring at her as she keeps talking faster and faster, spilling out words in paragraphs, inhaling gasps of air in between.

"I was shy. By the time I was brazen enough to speak out, you were long gone upstream and there wasn't much of a pool to fish in. The men left over, any with fewer than two heads and enough arms and legs were long gone too, along with my brother and sister.

"Or if they did hang around Cape Breton they were two kids into a marriage already, so I hemmed and hawed and finally entered the convent. Like you, behind the times, not realizing that convents and seminaries, nuns and priests were going out of fashion."

She takes a deep breath and continues. "'See you in a week,' my mother said and laughed her head off. She would have been right too except the first person I met in the convent was Jocelyn. On our own we would have caught on we picked the wrong place at the wrong time, but together we enjoyed it and stuck it out quite a while."

After that breakneck speech her tears disappear and she starts to laugh and he starts to laugh and when they stop laughing he says, "Well, talk about Frankie's tongue, you can say a mouthful yourself once you get going. So what happened?"

"We dug right in at the beginning. We wanted to be nurses but they said they had enough nurses. We were thinking Florence Nightingale. They needed teachers. We tried. We studied, theology, philosophy, Latin, and all that university stuff, English, history, biology, everything, and presto, we were kindergarten teachers, and we spent our days peeling ski pants and overshoes and scarves and mittens off the cute kids, and the most fun of all, playing nits and boogies on the cute kids' heads.

"So after all that, even getting a kick out of it for a while, one day Jocelyn said, 'Marie, this is kinda comical, but do we want to spend our whole lives as clowns?' They wouldn't let us retrain as nurses so we turned in our hoods, gave Mother Superior a big hug and off we tripped hi-ho to the hospital."

"She didn't mind?"

"I don't think so. When we left she said, 'Probably just as well, you two are too *you-two* for life in a convent. Our loyalty is to the church not to each other. Sooner or later we'd have to send you off in different directions and then you'd probably quit. You might as well quit now.' And she was right."

"Well, what if you got married? That would've separated the two of you."

"Sister Superior said that too. We told her we were looking for a set of Siamese twins to marry. That would keep us together. She didn't laugh. I think she thought we were serious."

Their laughter soars over the now crowded restaurant. The buzz of conversation diminishes and Marie and Ian can feel heads turn and eyes focus. They slip into silence and when the waiters clear the table of dishes they slide their elbows onto the table and with their heads almost touching they form a tent and begin to whisper as the buzz returns to the sea of people around them.

"So you became nurses and lived happily ever after?"

"No, dammit, no. And without Jocelyn, I don't know if I can hack it any longer. We liked nursing. But we didn't get a chance to do a lot of real nursing. Same nonsense all over again. How much physiology do you need to help somebody piss in a pan? And doctors expecting us to be servants and gophers. Jocelyn said, 'You know, Marie, this is kinda comical, and some of these doctors are cute, but do we want to spend the rest of our lives as flunkies? Let's do something else. Let's save the world.'"

"But then she got sick. And now she's dead. We had a lot of fun. We loved that tune and the Mass for the Dead that it's in, and now she's dead, and nobody to put her into the grave but me, and there's very few outside this room who could sing her song. Maybe I can hire this castrati bunch and maybe you and I could join in."

"What should we do then, go back to the hospital?"

"I've been thinking about what Jocelyn would want."

"And…"

"Jocelyn would say, don't sit there like a goddamn fool, get thee a bottle of wine, get thee to our apartment and celebrate the reunion of me and my grandfather. Bring Ian with you, we'll have a double reunion."

"She knew about me?"

"She knew everything that I knew."

"Have you got wine at your place? Aren't the liquor stores closed?"

The tears are gone but Marie is sniffling now. Her nose is running. "I can get the wine. If I can shut down the demolition of the seminary, I'll not be daunted by the lack of a bottle of wine. You leave that to me."

"We could always switch to Mortal Sins."

"Indeed. I have the makings for those too," she laughs. "God, Ian, between sniffling and sobbing I don't know if I'm laughing or crying, but I know Jocelyn would be laughing her head off. Do me a favour will you, go see if they can do the *Pange Lingua*."

Ian approaches the altar rail and asks the clarinet player if they can play the *Pange Lingua*. The musician looks to the choir leader who answers with bright enthusiasm, "Oh yes, indeed we do, and how delightful to be asked. We'll sing it for you. I see you are quite conversant with the liturgy."

"There's not much left of it though is there?"

"That's so true, but we try to keep it going. As long as we're doing it, somebody's doing it."

Ian returns to the table and sits with Marie and listens to the choir.

When they finish the hymn, Ian makes a sign that perhaps they should leave but Marie says that she sent Frankie with another request to the choir and that he is coming back with the cheque. As she speaks the clarinet player announces, "We have a request for Psalm 129, dedicated to Jocelyn who could not be here tonight in the flesh but is here in spirit." The band plays an introduction and then the choir chants a capella:

De profundis clamo ad te Domine
Audi vocem meum

Marie takes Ian's two hands and they hold each other across the table. He looks into her moist eyes. "Do you know what the song says?" she asks in a whisper.

"Yes, I remember. 'Out of the depths I cry to you, Lord. Hear my voice.' But I guess we'll all soon forget."

"I just remembered," Marie whispers, "what Jocelyn used to say when we came here. She'd say 'Isn't it kinda comical, just when the church is giving things up, Frankie and his crowd are keeping them going?'"

When the choir finishes the tune, Marie suggests that Ian pay the bill and she look after the tip and the wine to bring with them.

"You can't buy wine in a restaurant," he says.

Marie puts her finger to her lips and gives him a straight look. She takes a fistful of bills from her bag and writes a note and stuffs it with the bills in an envelope. When Frankie arrives she explains that the tip is inside the fat envelope along with instructions on how to divide it among the waiters, himself and the choir. He holds out his hand but she picks up the cheque and the money Ian left on the table to pay it and adds it to the envelope, which she holds behind her back.

"We'd like to see the crucifix," she says.

"Pardon?"

"We'd like to see the crucifix."

Frankie, after a long moment, with his eyes averted, trying to process Marie's brazen request, says, "The crucifix is in the wine cellar."

"That's okay," Marie says, flashing the envelope thick with money, "we'd like to see the crucifix in the wine cellar." She drops the envelope into her handbag and picks it up along with the picture of Jocelyn's grandfather, grabs her trench coat from the back of her chair where she insisted on keeping it when she came in. "Let's go down and have a look."

For a while they can't find the Christ. The cellar is a maze of randomly placed wine shelves and piles of ecclesiastical paraphernalia. They search, poking and pulling at the heaps and piles and finally find the crucifix under a heap of candelabra, a station of the cross with the inscription, *Mary Magdalene Wipes the Face of Jesus*, a rusty holy-water font, the door of a confessional with its hinges and handle hanging loose, a wooden altar corroded from damp and dirt and collapsed on itself like an old, wet cardboard box, its tabernacle door gaping open and empty. The cross is upside down, the top stick broken off, the crown of thorns embedded in the dirt cellar floor. Frankie grabs the bottom stick but he can't pull it out.

"I can't budge the Jesus thing," Frankie says. "Give me a hand, Rick."

Ian takes hold of the nail sticking out of Jesus' feet and together he and Frankie jerk the thing from the rubble and lay it out on the floor, look it over and reattach the parts. "There you go," Frankie says. "It should hold together for now. Wouldn't take much to firm it up, crazy glue maybe, and a splint on the back of it out of sight."

While Frankie and Ian struggle with the crucifix Marie

quietly helps herself to a bottle of imitation Christian Brothers Burgundy and stuffs it into her handbag.

"Do you think it's an antique? Do you want to buy it?"

"Why in the name of God would we want it?" Marie says.

"You said you wanted it."

"I didn't say we wanted it. Rick, did I say we wanted it? I said we wanted to see it. He just asked you if you kept it. He didn't say he wanted it. I don't believe he wants it."

"I hope to God after all that pulling and dragging and lugging it out of that mess, you're gonna take it."

"What do you think, Ilsa?" Ian says.

"If you want to carry it, Rick, feel free. We could take it as an act of charity, for Frankie's sake."

"All right," Ian says, and picks it up where the beams cross and holds it up under his arm in the crook of his elbow. "Let's take it. Let's go back upstairs and get out of here." He heads for the stairs. The crucifix is taller than Ian and he has to let the back end drag a furrow across the dirt floor toward the stair.

"No, no, no," Frankie says. "Not that way. Good Christ, you can't haul that thing through the restaurant. I'll let you out the basement door into the alley."

Frankie opens the ancient door to a ladder of broken steps leading to the dark night full of rain. "You two go on up," Frankie says, "and I'll push it up to you. Be careful, the top step is rotten and one of the steps in the middle is missing altogether."

He takes the cross from Ian and when they get over the top step Frankie pushes the cross up and Marie and Ian each take an arm of the crossbeam and back up with it as Frankie walks it up holding the bottom. Once in the alley Frankie helps Ian shoulder the cross and Ian and Marie walk toward the street leaving Frankie standing at the open basement door holding the envelope full of money for tips and Marie's estimated cost of the wine.

"Thank you," Frankie hollers after them.

They walk up the alley and turn down the steep street with the gentle wind from Halifax Harbour flowing around them, caressing their faces, the rain soaking their hair. Marie carries the picture of Jocelyn's grandfather and her handbag full of wine. Ian holds the crucifix on his left shoulder, his free hand swinging Marie's hand in time to the tune of *Dies Irae*, as they sing and hum their way down the sidewalk. They are drunk on wine and adventure, their eyes glow with the suspicion that some wonderful gift is on the way to visit their good mood. They can't remember all the words so they repeat the first two lines of the song over and over. *Dies Irae, dies illa solvet saeclum in favilla.* At an intersection they pass two prostitutes and a pimp huddled in a storefront doorway who watch in astonishment as the two pilgrims fade into the dark.

"Did you see that?"

"Jesus Christ, I think I did. What did you see?"

"Holy Virgin Mary, as my mother used to say, I'm not sure, but if you saw it, whatever it was, I guess I saw it too. What did you see, Joe?"

"I don't think it could have been Mary, she's too young to be his mother. It must have been Mary Magdalene. What was that song they were singing?"

"I don't know. I remember it from somewhere though. Cute tune."

"We couldn't all be going crazy at the same time, could we?"

fOUR

Love is anterior to Life
Posterior to Death
—*Emily Dickenson*

IAN AND MARIE walk along Water Street parallel to the harbour. In the dark and drizzle the ships moored at the docks appear as huge shadows. In spite of their high spirits and good moods, as they approach the apartment she shared with Jocelyn, memories of her exploits with her friend keep returning. She doesn't say if they are making her sad or happy. Some she relates to Ian: "Jocelyn used to…" or, "One time we…" trying not to darken their mood.

Jocelyn. Marie tells Ian about Jocelyn, how she always described herself as "a natural born daughter of disaster." "But being happy in the rain is the only way to live." At thirteen she survived the death of her father, Pierre Le Blanc, because he refused to take her out fishing that Saturday for fear of a possible storm.

"Jocelyn described that day for me. She told me that in the shelter of the fish plant, with her mother's arm around her shoulder, she watched as the few boats not yet safe in the harbour fought to breast the sea swells against the south-east gale blowing over the mountain across the village and out to sea. One by one the boats struggled through the rain and wind and sailed past the lighthouse through the north opening of the harbour and tied up in port between Grande Rivière Island and the village. Her father's boat was not among them. One by one the women and children quit peering at the empty Gulf of St. Lawrence and trudged up the road, bent into the wind and pelting rain to the quiet of their houses or to L'Église St. Joseph D'Étang to say a prayer of thanksgiving.

"Jocelyn and Magdeleine waited, their skirts and shirts soaked against their skin, their wet, black hair flat against their heads and necks and shoulders, waited until long after the air was too dense with rain and twilight to see beyond the breakers crashing on the shore.

"They waited until the parish priest came. 'You might as well wait at home,' he told them. 'Perhaps they went ashore in New Brunswick or Isles de la Madeleine and if they did they'll send a message.'

"So they walked home, silent, two arms behind them around each other's waist, two arms in front of them, the fingers of their two hands knitted together under their breasts. No message ever came from New Brunswick or anywhere else."

Marie pauses in her narrative, glances at Ian then continues. "At fourteen Jocelyn held her silent mother's hand as she died of cancer. Before she lost the ability to speak, to think, to focus, Magdeleine said to her daughter, 'Don't let it get you down, dear. Live while you can, learn and live, conquer the world,' and she laughed while she could still laugh.

"Jocelyn didn't have any brothers or sisters, so she moved in with her grandmother, a former teacher of French and English, and her grandfather, a fisherman who was home with the flu on the day of the storm. She dedicated herself to learning. In school she studied in French and in English, after school she studied music and painting with *Les Filles de Jesus*, Sister Noella and Sister Térèse, and outside school she learned fishing, basketball, photography. The nuns loved her.

"'She could be one of us,' they frequently said to each other.

"She was so energetic. In her spare time, she volunteered at the hospital as a nurse's aide and became a favourite of the nuns who ran the hospital and provided most of the nurses. She left Grande Rivière and moved to Halifax to enter the convent, and when she met me we soon figured out that we were distant cousins.

"My grandfather, François Au Coin, left Grande Rivière in the thirties to work in the coal mines in Glace Bay, and my grandmother, the petite Félicité Etang Le Blanc, finished grade nine in Petite Rivière and travelled to Reserve Mines to live with her sister and work as a housekeeper for the manager of the coal mine. At a dance sponsored by La Société L'Assumption in Reserve Mines, François walked across the floor, offered his hand and invited her to dance. She put her hand in his and they danced until "God Save the King."

"My grandmother told me that their hands never separated until after he walked her to her employer's home. While they walked she asked him what he most wanted in life and he spoke in English and said with a smile so she would know it was a joke, 'I want to be a big fish in a small pond.'

"She didn't understand English then, so she said, '*Qu'est-ce*

87

que ça veut dire?' and laughed because she knew it was a joke. He smiled and he said, 'You'll see,' but because he said it in English she didn't understand his joke until after they were married and she mastered English and then she figured out that she was the small pond and he was the big fish. The day she caught on she gave him one of her token backhanders across his bearded cheek." Marie lets go of Ian's hand and demonstrates her grandmother's gesture on Ian's cheek.

They continue to walk in the thickening fog along the invisible harbour until the drizzle of rain suddenly turns into a downpour and they take shelter in the darkened doorway of a furniture store. Once standing still and as the effect of the wine and food wear off they begin to realize how odd they must look, two lost pilgrims, soaking wet, trudging along the sidewalk carrying a cross. They watch the rain in silence for a moment, looking across the sidewalk into the street. A couple walk by under an umbrella and give them a puzzled look when they see the end of the cross sticking out from the doorway. Ian and Marie wait another moment in silence feeling even more self-conscious, until Ian asks: "Does it help or hurt to talk about Jocelyn?"

"I'm not sure, Ian. I know I feel better when I'm talking so I'd rather talk, and I feel better when I'm walking, and I've only got two things on my mind at the moment—you and Jocelyn. So let's walk, and I'll talk and I'll tell you about Jocelyn and me. Let me tell you about our winter vacation. It's a story with an ending that might be very interesting to you and your half-hearted ambitions."

fIVE

The world, uncertain, comes and goes,
The lover, rooted, stays.
—*Ralph Waldo Emerson, in "Friendship"*

WHEN IT WAS JOCELYN'S TURN to decide where they would go for their vacation she announced, "This year we are going to take a week in February."

"February?" Marie said, wrinkled her brow and laughed. "The middle of winter. Are we going south then?"

"No, Marie, we are not. We are going north."

"Let me guess, the sunny Northwest Territories."

"No, afraid not. We are going to the windy Grande Rivière, Cape Breton Island, Isle Magnifique. Home of our ancestors. We'll dig up our roots."

"Dig up our roots. In the middle of February. Won't the ground be frozen?"

"The roots of people grow above the ground, like kohlrabies, and the frost can't penetrate their thick skins. It's my year to pick where we go and I think it's time you visited your roots."

"But I can't speak French."

"Not yet. But you won't need to. Everybody in Grande Rivière speaks English. And anyway, you won't need to speak at all because you're going to be a mummy, a dummy mummy. Speaking is optional."

"I give up, what's this all about?"

"It will be *mi-carême* in Grande Rivière and also in Petite Rivière and in all the *rivières* and all the *étangs*."

"What's *mi-carême*? And for that matter what's an *étang*?"

"An *étang* is a pond. And *mi-carême* is mid-Lent. It's the middle of Lent. Everybody takes the week off from fasting, those who still fast for Lent, or give up smoking or drinking or whatever they think they do too much of, and we have a big party all week. Like Mardi Gras but Acadians do it in the middle of Lent instead of the week before. Everybody dresses in disguise to visit each other's homes and people try to guess who they are. Everybody knows everybody so you have to have really good disguises."

In the weeks leading up to the trip Jocelyn fashioned two jolly face masks of papier-maché. She took two extra-large suits of Stanfield long johns, dyed them red, stuffed them with two pillows and transformed herself and Marie into Santa and Mrs. Claus. She dyed a bed sheet red and sewed it up to make a bag and they filled the bag full of cheap toys and trinkets.

They rented a car. Marie drove from Halifax to the end of mainland Nova Scotia and across the causeway over the Strait of Canso to Cape Breton Island. Jocelyn took the wheel then and became the tour guide as they turned north and fled along the coast of the Northumberland Strait and the Gulf of St. Lawrence, the frigid waters of the North Atlantic Ocean.

Marie didn't recognize the scenery of the rural Cape Breton

she had seen hanging on the walls of their Halifax apartment—squares and rectangles of colourful, idyllic displays of seascape and landscape painted with Jocelyn's nostalgic brush: little foamy waves lapping against white boats, riding high in the water, ready to leave the harbour and roll over the gentle swells of the friendly ocean. On the rising land leading up to the mountains the roads and paths wrapped around the shoulders of the hills like the arms of loving uncles. The sun drenched everything, warming the land and the sea, nourishing the flowers standing straight on the slopes or bowing like girls in pretty dresses in the gentle breeze. People walked in and out of houses and churches or ambled along the summer roads. Fields full of sheep, gated behind barbed wire or electric fencing, herded by a black-and-white border collie and guarded by a watchful donkey were the only signs of menace.

As they sped along the cliffs, skirting the seashore, Marie could see no sign of Jocelyn's bucolic scenes. The boats were gone from the harbours, but not gone to play on the ocean. The few she did see cringed in yards by the leeward side of houses or crouched under makeshift canopies beside barns or in copses of trees. Sheep, dogs and donkeys were nowhere to be seen. The back roads, covered in snow, seemed to be waiting for a plow, perhaps to free waiting prisoners from their homes. The recent snowstorm was over and the main road was clear but the northeast wind continued to roar down the hills between the clouds covering the tops of the mountains and the white fields descending to the sea. The flowers of summer were dead and buried. Along the beaches rows of ice chunks, pushed ashore by the ferocious waves, munched on the crusts of snow at the high-water mark. Smoke from the chimneys of the buttoned-up houses, whisked away by the wind, was the only sign of warmth between the mountains and the sea. Every once in a while the wind would blow a cloud of snow across the road before them, blurring visibility to almost zero.

They drove to Petite Rivière and stayed with Jocelyn's friend Angélique, a former *Fille de Jesus* who operated a religious articles shop out of her home along the road between Petite Rivière and Grande Rivière. They swore Angélique to secrecy so nobody in either village would know they were there.

"We have a new priest," Angélique said. "We don't know what he's like yet so don't tell him you're not going to Mass these days."

They spent the week, sometimes just the two of them, sometimes joining other "*mi-carêmes*" going from house to house, handing out toys and taunting people to guess who was hiding behind their disguises. Jocelyn ho, ho, hoed and answered questions in French or in English, sometimes telling the truth and sometimes telling it slant and Marie hee, hee, heed but otherwise kept mum. They began at the beginning with "*Laissons entrer les mi-carêmes.*" On the second evening out they landed at the home of the Chiasson sisters, Françoise and Marguerite, two old ladies famed for their ability to guess the faces behind the masks. The large living room was full of people and Jocelyn and Marie handed out toys and trinkets while another couple dressed as doctor and nurse mock-measured the guests' blood pressures and pulses and offered advice: "Don't walk barefoot in the snow. Always get up in the morning before you go to work." They wrote prescriptions for hot rum-cinnamon-honey toddies, moonshine martinis and homemade wine.

"Take off your gloves," Françoise said to Santa Claus.

"Hold out your hands," Marguerite said.

"Ah ha. This one is a nurse; look at the ring. We know all the nurses, Marguerite. Don't we?"

"We do. Okay, Santa, answer me this, *qui amarre tes souliers?*"

"*Moi-mêmes.*"

"*Peut-tu faire chiard ou tchaude?*"

"*Oui.*"

"So you are from here, the two of you?"

"No."

"Ah, so you are lying or a come-back-home, or one of you is."

"Are you Céleste, or Sophie, or Nicole?"

"No."

"That's everybody about their age from Sydney. Must be Halifax or Montreal."

"Are you Marie?"

"Not me," said Santa.

"Ah ha. A Marie, and another nurse. Are you Marie? Take off your gloves."

Marie took off her gloves with a laugh and displayed her fingers with her ring. Marguerite examined her ring, noting her graduation date. She turned to Santa and asked her, "Are you Geneviève, Suzanne, Ysabelle?"

"No."

"Then you must be Jocelyn."

Jocelyn and Marie removed their masks and Françoise and Marguerite embraced them and led them to the table full of food and drink.

All night and all week they grazed on the bountiful tables of Grande Rivière and Petite Rivière: *fricot, chiard, tchaude, pâté à la viande, morue en cabane, crêpes au repage, croquettes au poisson, sauce au boudin, poutine aux raisins.* While they feasted and danced and listened to the fiddles and the guitars they met their distant cousins, their aunts, their uncles, their great aunts.

On the last night everyone gathered for the grand dance at the parish hall, everyone in costume, all but one of them already guessed at. One *mi-carême* imposter, disguised in the mask of the parish priest, had defied recognition all week. He arrived late and Marguerite and Françoise made another try at exposing his identity.

"He must be a man because of the hands and feet."

"Are you from away?" asked Marguerite.

"Sometimes."

"Do you live here?" Françoise asked.

"Yes, sometimes."

"These are not the same answers as before," said Marguerite.

"If it's true there is only one possibility," said Françoise. "We have eliminated everybody but one."

"So we know who it must be," said Marguerite, "don't we, Françoise?"

"Yes, we do," said Françoise, triumphant.

They were on their knees for the examination, in the middle of the dance floor. The band stopped playing and the dancers encircled the two women and the mystery man. The hall hushed. "Who is it?" somebody whispered. "Who is it?" everybody whispered.

Marguerite looked around at the expectant crowd. The sisters rose to their feet. "The parish priest did not show up at *mi-carême* all week."

"The parish priest did not come to the dance tonight," Françoise said.

"The imposter priest is the parish priest," Marguerite said, and sure enough, the mystery man lifted his parish priest mask and revealed the parish priest posing as the parish priest.

Jocelyn and Marie returned to Halifax happy, overwhelmed and exhausted. "Isn't it kinda comical," Jocelyn said to Marie, "the priest masquerading as a priest. It's a sign of the times."

That was then.

SIX

Because they had no roots, they withered away.
—Matthew 13:6

IAN AND MARIE CLIMB to her apartment at the top of a wooden staircase at the back of an old building renovated into apartments. It is more of a fire escape than an entrance. It is not a real apartment, rather one big room, an attic with a high ceiling peaking in the centre and coming halfway down the walls on two sides. A kitchen and dining area share one end of the room. The other end holds a sofa bed between end tables and bed lamps. A door across from the bed opens to a bathroom. Another door on the opposite wall opens to a large walk-in clothes closet and storage space.

It is a dingy building on a dingy street but the simple room is awash in colour and beauty. Every wall displays a gallery of photographs and paintings. Jocelyn's paintings of rural Cape Breton cover one wall. At the top of another wall a green, blue and rust harlequin macaw looks down on a collection of paintings. Directly under the bird hangs a painting containing multi-coloured apples in various stages of decay clinging to a tree denuded of leaves and Jocelyn's signature imprinted at the bottom left corner. Under the apple tree painting runs a series of paintings in a row: first, a print of Picasso's *Harlequin With a Glass* and next to it, as if in response, Miró's *Carnival of Harlequin*, a festival of fractured chaos, followed by two black-and-white photographs, first of the Sistine Chapel and next of the seminary they visited earlier on Quinpool Road, its exterior still intact but obviously gutted and most of its windows broken by a couple of teenagers caught in the act of throwing apples fallen from a tree inside the gates. Beside the seminary photo hangs a print of Picasso's *Guernica* that might make a person think Picasso learned a thing or two from Miró.

"As you can see," Marie says as she juggles the picture of Jocelyn's grandfather while she pulls off her wet coat, "the room is all Jocelyn. This is where we lived. I'd be tempted to move to a regular apartment but it would be like leaving her behind even though I'd take everything with me. It wouldn't be the same. Anyway it's bigger than the room I lived in at the convent. Look at the photos on the wall behind you."

He is standing in the middle of the room, the crucifix still on his shoulder.

"Put the cross down, Ian, you're not going to Calvary tonight."

Ian stands the cross in the corner of the room by the door and goes to the wall between the two windows to look at the photographs, a variety of shots showing Jocelyn and Marie in various locations. "The one on top is me in my habit standing by my bed in my little cell." She throws her coat on the chair beside the Hide-A-Bed.

"Joss snapped that one the day we made our vows. And that one is the two of us in our nurse uniforms standing by a bed at the hospital. God knows what bed I'll be standing by the next time I get my picture taken."

Marie takes her trench coat off the chair and goes to the cross in the corner. She leans the picture of Jocelyn's grandfather in his boat against the bottom of it and takes her trench coat and Ian's blazer and covers the body of Christ. She pulls a pair of pajama bottoms out of a dresser drawer and throws them at him. "Here. They're way too big for me so they should fit you. You better get out of those wet clothes."

While he changes in the bathroom she hurries into her own pajamas, pulls a wooden clothes rack from the closet, spreads it open and hangs her wet clothes. She puts a 45 vinyl record on her turntable and on comes a jazzy version of *Dies Irae* on a saxophone. When Ian comes out she hangs his pants, shirt, underwear and socks on the wooden clothes rack. She kicks off her slippers. "C'mon, wet-head," she says, "let's dance in our naked feet."

When the *Dies Irae* ends Marie searches through her collection and puts on another record and they dance to Louis Armstrong's cornet and gravelly voice.

Oh when we're dancing and you're dangerously near me
I get ideas, I get ideas
I want to hold you so much closer than I dare to
I want to scold you 'cause I care more than I care to
And when you touch me and there's fire in every finger
I kind of think you get ideas too.

"You know what I like about Louis, Ian?"

"What?"

"He always sounds like he's talking right at you. And you know what else?"

"What?"

"We're dancing."

"Yeah."

"We haven't danced since the prom."

"Yeah."

"This is where we left off."

"Yeah."

"It's zero o'clock. Jocelyn predicted this would happen."

"Smart woman."

"Very sage. If she is ever beatified and becomes a saint, we'll look on this as her first miracle."

"Don't forget what Frankie said, there is still such a thing as blasphemy."

"Don't forget what Saint Augustine said, only love and do what you will."

"Wasn't that Saint Paul?"

"Does it matter who said it? We are here, we are dancing, and you are dangerously, dangerously near me, mister wet-head."

"Yeah."

"You know what?"

"What?"

"Your hair is almost dry."

"Yeah. It's pretty warm in here. How about you, Marie, is your hair dry?"

"My hair is dry but I'm still wet."

"Yeah. It's pretty warm in here."

"Your pajama collar got wet from your hair. You better take it off to dry."

When Louis Armstrong finishes "Dancing" he begins a cornet solo of "That Old Black Magic," and Marie leads Ian to the kitchen end of the room and opens a cupboard where she keeps her wine and liquor. "Why don't you make us a drink, Ian?"

"Châteauneuf-du-Pape or Christian Brothers Burgundy?"

"No. Let's make us a cocktail. I think it's time for a Mortal Sin."

Early next morning the rising, yellow sun pours light through the windows, flooding the sofa bed and its rumpled couple. The sofa cushions are stacked between the clothes rack and the crucifix. When Marie peels her eyes open she can see Jocelyn's grandfather smiling at her from the bottom of the cross. She smiles in return, sits up, reaches down and picks her slip off the floor and pulls it over her naked body, gets out of bed and pads barefoot to the kitchen counter and sets some coffee to brew while she goes to the bathroom.

Ian lifts the sheet off his apprehensive face, looks around the empty room, hears the perking coffee, hears the toilet flush, ducks down and covers his face with the sheet.

Humming the *Dies Irae*, Marie dances a two-step across the room to the kitchen counter and pours coffee into two cups decorated with yellow smiling sun faces, adds a dollop of cream and a spoonful of honey. She puts the cups down on the end table beside Ian's covered face and sits on the bed in the curve of his body.

"There's no point pretending you're asleep, my man. I'm a

nurse. I know when people are asleep. I know when they are dead. I know when they are alive. I know when they are awake. You are alive and you are awake." She reaches under the sheet and takes his hand and pulls it onto her lap.

Ian is still. Stiff. Marie turns and spreads a long look over his motionless form under the sheet and nudges him with her elbow until he relents, uncovers his head, pulls his hand from her lap, turns on his back, stacks two pillows behind his head and sits up against the back of the sofa bed. He clasps his two hands behind his head and stares gloomily at the sun pouring through the window. She gives him a puzzled look and turns back to drink her coffee.

"Ian?"

"Mmm."

"You know what?"

"What."

"Mornings are not as good as nights."

"Mmm."

"Mornings are nice. Full of promise. Nights are fulfilling. In the morning you never know what's going to happen. But at night you know. Much more satisfying."

When Ian makes no response, she continues. "What'll we do today? I have to go to the hospital, make arrangements for Jocelyn. But then we're free. What would you like to do?" She turns to face him and her smile fades. "What's wrong, Ian?"

"Nothing."

Marie, alarmed, stares at Ian's eyes but his eyes stare steadfast at the yellow light in the window.

"What's wrong?"

"Nothing."

"Don't you lie to me. Answer me. Are you leaving? Answer me!"

"Yes."

"You're leaving."

"Yes."

"Where are you going?"

"Quebec."

"Quebec?"

"Yes."

"You're going to Quebec? What the hell for?"

"To find a seminary."

Marie leaps from the bed, grabs the sheet and yanks it from Ian's clenched fists leaving him folded, naked, his hands gripping his knees. She pulls his shirt, pants, socks, underwear from the wooden rack and carries them to the door.

"Get up."

Ian rolls to his feet and stands looking for his clothes until he realizes they are tucked under Marie's arm.

"Could I have my clothes, if you don't mind?"

"Why should I mind? They're your clothes. I have to admit you look like you'd make an outstanding priest. It's too bad you're not an Anglican. With balls like that you'd make a formidable canon. Here put these on." She balls up his boxer shorts and throws them at him. He catches them and scrambles into the legs. "Tell me one thing, Ian, before you steam off like the *Bluenose* for Quebec. Tell me. Why?"

"I feel like I need to finish what I started. I can't be distracted."

"Distracted. That would be me? A distraction. Well, let me tell you this, you arsehole, you're going to find your distractions are the best part of your life. And when did it matter to you if you ever finished what you started? You started on me and left, you started on the air force and you left, you started on me again and you are leaving and now I guess you are going to try and start something in French. And what makes you think you are going to finish that?" She takes a deep breath in the silence and starts again.

"Find out! You go. You find out. Go to Quebec. Find out. If you find out you like it, stay. If you find out you don't like it, stay anyway. Goodbye. Good riddance." She throws him his socks, shirt and pants. While he puts them on she gets his coat from the foot of the crucifix and throws it on the bed and while he puts it on she hits him in the belly with one shoe and when he bends to pick it up she hits him on the head with the other. Then she goes to the door and holds it open. He picks up his shoes and takes them out to the platform at the top of the stairs and sits on the top step and puts them on. Marie slams the door. By the time he reaches the bottom she has opened the door again.

"Wait there," she yells down at him. "You wait there one minute." Leaving the door open she crosses the room, grabs hold of the crucifix and hauls it out to the platform. Part falls off and clatters down the stairs and lands at Ian's feet. She tips the crucifix on its crown of thorns, flips it head over heels, sending it crashing down the wooden steps to the bottom. The arms of the cross break off and the three pieces of wood land at Ian's feet, the head comes off and rolls down the lane to the sidewalk.

"Take your junk with you. You wouldn't want to land in Quebec without your cross to bear."

He picks up the pieces and walks with them down the street toward the shadowy *Bluenose* into the vague sunlight trying to burn the cloud of fog off the harbour.

PART TWO

SEVEN

Accidents count for much in
Companionship as in Marriage
—*Henry Brooks Adams*

EVEN EARLY IN THE MORNING tourists fill the Old Quebec streets. But in the stone basilica there are only two, a man and a woman in T-shirts, sneakers, shorts and cameras. Her shirt says, *J'y suis, J'y reste.* His shirt says, *Le Français, on le parle par coeur.*

The cathedral contains three aisles, a wide aisle in the middle between the main entrance and the altar, flanked by two wide rows of pews. Beginning at the side entrances and running up to the two smaller altars, two narrow aisles on either side divide the middle pews and those along the wall. The Stations of the Cross hang on the walls, seven on each side, between the stained-glass windows.

The man roams the back of the church opening doors, poking his nose into confessional boxes, the woman marches up the centre aisle, snaps a picture of the main altar, strolls to the auxiliary altar, gawks at the statues and altar paraphernalia, walks down the side aisle snapping her camera at the Stations of the Cross in backwards order starting with the fourteenth, "Jesus is placed in the tomb."

She finishes her photo shoot on the other side of the church at the first station, "Jesus is condemned to death." She takes this photo from a distance because Jesus and his accusers are contained inside a small section in front of the alternate auxiliary altar, about a dozen pews cordoned off by yellow tape. A sign hanging from the tape advises tourists: This Section Reserved For Worshippers.

An old lady in a black kerchief kneels near the altar and mumbles as she counts her prayers on a rosary. The woman takes a shot of the old lady who, startled by the flash, turns to her, and the woman snaps again at the astonished face.

"Thanks," the woman says and scoots across to the centre aisle to complete her tour where her husband is standing with his camera at the ready.

"For Christ sake, Charlie," she says to him, "let's get out of here. We haven't got all day; I want to get out to the shrine and shoot Sainte-Anne-de-Beaupré."

Charlie says, "A minute, Christine dear, I see my Christmas card coming. I gotta get this photo. Talk about quaint."

"I'll meet you outside."

Graceful, Yvette walks up the side aisle. Petite and slim, she moves with restrained strength like a straw in a rough broom, a low note from a flute. A paisley dress, elastic at the waist, hangs loose to her knees. She glides past the pews that are almost as tall as herself, shaped at the top like little church roofs. Christine Dear now watches impatiently from the rear of the centre aisle. She can see only Yvette's black hair cascading over her shoulders.

When Yvette reaches the end of the aisle she kneels at the altar rail below a low tray of votive candles in maroon cups. A flashbulb obliterates the somber gloom of the basilica and Yvette hears the photographer whisper as he walks toward the back of the church, "Perfect profile in the candlelight."

She closes her eyes and mumbles her prayer: "Thank you for the peaceful death of my father."

Father Légère, his black soutane flapping around his old knees, comes out from the sacristy and walks over to where Yvette is kneeling. "Are you talking to yourself, Yvette?"

"Yes." She smiles. "I am so relieved my father is at peace. I have to say it out loud so I can hear myself say it. Isn't that funny?"

"Oh, I think it's normal. It's hard to think you feel happy or relieved if your father is gone. I guess saying it out loud is a relief, like letting go after holding your breath for thirty seconds. I felt it when my mother died. She was so sick her life had become a torment." Father Légère bends down, picks a finger off the floor and reattaches it to the Virgin Mary's hand. "The poor woman is falling apart," he laughs. "You got your picture taken."

She laughs. "Yes, I don't like it, but what can I do? I heard him tell his wife he's going to put me on his Christmas card." She pauses. "Why don't you buy her a new hand or get a whole new Virgin?"

"We hope to when we get the money. Virgins are hard to find these days so even a second-hand Virgin would cost a lot. But if enough tourists spend money in the gift shop in the vestibule… Oh, I have an idea, perhaps we should make them pay for taking pictures. We don't have many sources of revenue. Not many coming to Mass with their envelopes these days." He laughs. "It's hard enough to get them to come to bingo. We'll all be like you pretty soon, talking to ourselves."

Yvette rises to her feet as Father Légère's voice trails into silence. "Goodbye," she says and flees the church.

☆ ☆ ☆

Yvette's mother died first. When she was trying to die without too much fuss, she called her daughter to her room.

"Yvette."

"Yes, mama?"

"I'm dying."

"Yes, mama."

"God looks after the dead, Yvette. But the living must get by on their own hook."

"Yes, mama."

"Your father is old. Older even than me. But I am going to die first anyway."

Yvette took her mother's hand. "Don't be in such a big hurry, mama."

"I'm not going to get better, you know. Once you know that you have to go… The cow will give you milk; the chickens will give you eggs; the garden will give you vegetables; the pigs will give you meat. You need money. Look after the cow and the pigs and the chickens and the garden and your father can do his work and bring home the money."

"Yes, mama."

"The work and the walk will keep you healthy, Yvette."

Yvette's father Alphonse worked on the ferry collecting tickets from people who want to cross the St. Lawrence River from Lévis to Quebec City and back to Lévis. Because he was old they gave him the day shift, which ended before the heavy, after-work traffic. Yvette could finish her chores by four o'clock and in half an hour or so run the three miles and arrive before the ferry docked after his last trip and catch her breath before he stepped off.

It was uphill most of the way back. Wolfe's men, on the other side, had trouble getting up on the Plains of Abraham side of the St. Lawrence even once; no surprise they grumbled and complained. Yvette and Alphonse climbed the hill on the Lévis side every day so they wasted no breath on complaints.

She took his lunch can from him and gave him a drink of water from her thermos jug in silence, and if the weather was warm, took his sweater and wrapped it around her waist, and in silence they walked and climbed, up the ramp, past the railroad station, up the almost vertical wooden stairs. She knew if he had his heart attack on the stairs she could never hold him back from flying to the pavement. He knew it too and made her do the climb in front of him. After the stairs, up the steep path, through the gardens, lanes and driveways of their neighbours, across the road, through their own field, past the barn and home.

By the time they reached the edge of their farm and walked up and down the stile at the pole fence that separated their property from the field of their nearest neighbour they would both be puffing a bit from the strain of their climb. They sat on the bottom step of the stile for a rest and waited while their dog loped across the field to greet them.

Even standing on the top step of the stile they could see, over the trees surrounding their island of house, barn, shed, garden and hayfield, only the silos or the peaks of the tallest barns of their neighbours. But down the slope, even from their perch on the low step of the stile, they could see the Château Frontenac on the high ground of Quebec City at the edge of the Plains of Abraham. And they could see half the width of the St. Lawrence River that separated them from the city. And they could see the ferry arriving or leaving on the Quebec side. Upriver about four miles or so they could see the top of the superstructure of the bridge connecting the south side of the St. Lawrence to St. Foy on the north.

Sometimes when they began their trek they talked as she took his lunch box and sweater. It was either:

"Why not take a taxi, papa?"

"No, the walk keeps me alive."

Or:

"How did it go today, papa?"

"The same. It's a funny thing. You spend your whole life going over and coming back every day. You never get off on the other side. You always come back. It's like life, I guess. You go to sleep. You wake up. You always come back."

After their rest they ambled across their field to home. Father, daughter and dog enjoying the spring sunshine, the smell of manure from the barn, the moon-eyed stare of the cow and the oblivious, foraging chickens under the watchful eye of the rooster. A bliss it seemed that could go on forever.

But one day he did not come back. When the ferry docked he was not there ready to step off. Instead, her friend and cousin, Gaston, who organized traffic on the ferry, approached her and she knew by the look on Gaston's face that something was wrong.

"He's on the other side, Yvette. He fell unconscious just

before we left while he was taking tickets. Maybe just a dizzy spell. They put him on the wharf, sent for an ambulance. Get on the ferry and we'll rush you back right away, never mind the schedule.

She found him on his back, his eyes open, but staring blank. His fingers gripped the end of the pavement as if it were the edge of a cliff. A line of people filed by heading toward the ferry. A tourist took a picture. Yvette got into the ambulance and sat beside the paramedic and held her father's curled fingers. She looked carefully at the paramedic's professional face. "What's the matter with him?"

"Hard to say. Could be a stroke. Aneurysm. Maybe a concussion if his head hit something when he fell. We'll find out at the hospital."

"Is he going to die?"

"Not today. Don't worry, too early for worry. He's breathing okay. Got a decent pulse."

Yvette learned to be a nurse's aid simply by volunteering to be there, looking after her father, following the staff's instructions. She stayed at the hospital for three months, going home to her chores every evening, coming back in the morning after she milked the cow and fed all the animals. She trained him to move his arms and told him jokes to make him smile. She told him regular jokes she heard on the radio but she peopled them with friends or relatives and she could tell by his smile that he understood. She helped him to drink and to eat. When he was ready to be moved she took him home and reversed the schedule, returning to the hospital in the evenings to work the night shift while he slept through the night. She was by then officially a part-time nurse's aid with a job that paid her a salary. She slept through the day in spurts between farm chores and house-work.

The doctor told her the damage from the stroke was probably permanent and probably progressive. But at the beginning he seemed to understand speech although he could not talk. She read to him. He would have no interest in any of the books she kept on the bookshelf in her bedroom, so every day on the way to work she browsed the bookstores and every payday she bought a cheap paperback if she thought it would interest him. She seldom read the actual words of the story but used them to recreate her own version. Most of the stories she found too boring so she altered them by substituting the characters to describe people they knew and changing the locations to places in Quebec he was familiar with.

But then she discovered Butler's *Lives of the Saints.* Since she couldn't afford to buy it she hid it on a shelf behind the dictionary section. She would read individual entries in the store and re-tailor them for her father if she thought they would amuse him. His favourite was St. Jude.

She propped him up against the bed's headboard with a pillow behind him for comfort. She put his meals on a borrowed hospital tray that slid across the top of the bed. When the meal was over and they sipped their mugs of tea she sat cross-legged at the foot of the bed and read to him from the book she bought that week or she recounted the life of a saint.

"Jude, papa, is the saint of hopeless cases, because one day he met a beggar on the street asking for alms and Jude said, 'Why aren't you working, they're looking for cashiers down at the liquor store.' The man stuck out his tongue and put his finger on the tip of it and made a sound like *ghoolgh*. So Jude took a strip of palm from his pocket, broke two strips off it and formed them into a cross and placed it on the man's tongue. The man swallowed the spit formed on his tongue and spoke.

"'Hey,' he said, 'I can speak.' Alphonse's face broke into a smile.

Yvette took a piece of palm from the waistband of her jeans, broke it into two one-inch pieces, spliced them into a cross and put it on her father's lips. Alphonse stuck out his tongue and licked it.

Yvette continued with her story. "The man kept on talking. 'I used to be a tour guide showing people the sights of the city but I lost my voice so I lost my job. But thanks to you I can work again, and thanks for the tip, I think I'll check out the liquor store.'"

Alphonse made a series of noises like abbreviated hiccups to show he was laughing.

"Too bad, papa, I'm not St. Jude, but anyway we'll pray that you be delivered."

She would try to take him for a walk on her arm after the meal. He could barely slide his feet along the floor and he would only go as far as the bathroom. They lived happily enough for a year. One day she came home and he was there but his lights were out. He would slide to the bathroom on a walker she borrowed from the hospital, he would suck on popsicles she made from a concoction of fruit and berries, but he did not laugh at her stories anymore and his eyes were zeros. She read to him anyway, just in case, and on her way to the bookstore she paid a visit to the Virgin Mary in the cathedral and prayed that he would die. Soon enough he did.

Yvette returns to the basilica. She takes a taper and lights the end of it from a candle and starts a candle of her own and thanks Mary for her father's peaceful death. But she feels the need for another favour.

"*Mon père est mort, je vous remercie. Mais, Vierge, maintenant, il m'en faut an autre.*"

"*Un autre père?*" Mary shakes with laughter and the loose plaster of Paris little finger dangling from her right hand falls to the floor. Yvette spits on it to make it stick when she fits it back into Mary's knuckle. "Thank you, dear," the Virgin Mary says. "But another father, I don't think so." She laughs.

"No, no, no," Yvette protests, "that's foolish. I'm finished with fathers, that's not what I want, I need a chum."

"Oh dear. Have you tried St. Jude?"

"Well. I wasn't thinking I'm a hopeless case," Yvette laughs. "Is that what you think?"

"No, dear, no, no, I'll ask Jesus. It's just you know, I'm a virgin. I don't know a lot about men. We should be able to come up with something."

"Someone who speaks French, maybe. I don't think I'd want a tourist."

"Don't push it, dear."

She leaves the cathedral laughing at herself, relieved that Father Légère didn't come out again and overhear her conversation. He is a nice man and beloved of her parents and she doesn't want to tell him her church-going days are over. She crosses the street to the bookstore. She has no one to read to now but she keeps her schedule. In her reading nook behind the dictionaries she is looking through the window over the top of *The Lives of Alternative Saints* when she sees him jogging past on the street beside the sidewalk. She leans as far as she can into the window but he is out of sight in seconds so she goes to the door and leans out over the sidewalk, her finger keeping her page in the book. He is gone. He must have turned up the alley. She runs to the corner of Rue du Trésor. It is empty except for artists and musicians setting up their easels and music stands for a day's work in the tourist business. She goes back to her nook in the bookstore and continues to read.

St. John of the road, a minor legendary figure. As a youth he became bored with sins of the flesh and retired to a hovel to become a solitary, reading the few books he brought in his knapsack and working as a dishwasher in greasy spoons for food and minimum wage. When the veins of his calves became swollen and purple and sore from standing all day, he used his savings to buy expensive running shoes and began running the streets of the city to improve his musculature. When he got tired he'd stop on a street corner and preach to pedestrians who happened along, undeterred by the consistently apathetic and sometimes hostile responses, about the virtues of strengthening musculature.

Yvette thinks of her father, wishing she could read this one to him and make him laugh. She wouldn't even have to change the words; it is funny enough by itself.

Again the runner flashes across the top of her reading. Yvette rushes for the door but a large store clerk stands in front of it, her arms akimbo, blocking the way. She gives Yvette a stone-faced stare.

"May I help you?"

"I'm just browsing."

"You can't take books to the street unless you pay for them."

Yvette looks at the book in her hand as if seeing it for the first time. She hands it over to the clerk who nevertheless will not budge.

"What are you looking for?"

"My chum," Yvette says, trying to deke the clerk who keeps moving from side to side, blocking her exit.

"Well. This is a bookstore. Not a chum store," she says, and moving sideways around Yvette, strides down the aisle and slots the book into its proper place on the shelf.

Yvette waits on the sidewalk for a while but the runner does not come around again. On her way to work she walks through the Rue du Trésor and talks to one of the artists who is amusing herself by drawing quick, charcoal sketches of the runner. One of the sketches shows a headband flying backwards from the runner's head. She smiles at Yvette and tells her, "Yes, this guy ran through quite a while ago and then again maybe ten minutes ago or so. Maybe he'll come back after a while, he seems to be running in a pretty wide circuit. Maybe tomorrow he'll do it again. Friend of yours?"

"Not yet."

"You want to buy the sketch?"

"Maybe tomorrow."

"Okay. I'll put in some detail. If I see him coming tomorrow, I'll try to stop him and make a really good portrait."

Yvette walks on a few yards and picks up the headband, pulls it over her head and wears it under her hair around her neck. She resigns herself to wait until tomorrow and, realizing she is late for work, hurries off to the hospital. But when she reaches Place D'Youville up past the city wall there he is in the middle of the street on the pavement in front of a taxi, unconscious, his T-shirt torn up to his shoulders, his bloody back scratched, scraped into curls of skin turned white, his head nosed into the pavement, his arms flung out to the right and left like petrified wings, his fingernails dug into the dust and debris of the street. The taxi driver, animated, gesticulating, his arms flying, pleads his innocence to a stoic policeman staring at the body collapsed on the pavement. In the distance an approaching ambulance screams.

"I didn't see him. He popped right out of nowhere."

"Nowhere," the policeman says with a smirk. "Where's nowhere? On the sidewalk? There's nothing here but wind and sunshine. See these white lines? That is a crosswalk. Up there, that's a flashing red light. It means stop. And you are supposed to stop. Even if someone was hiding behind nowhere and planning to run in front of a taxi. You were driving too fast, if those skid marks on the road behind your car mean anything. You better hope he's not dead."

"Could he be dead?"

"Who knows. I don't think so. Lots of damage but it all looks superficial. Knocked out though. You never know."

As the ambulance screams into view, suddenly the runner pulls his hands under his chest, pushes himself to his knees, jumps up and runs off up the street. Yvette chases after him but his long legs soon take him out of sight and she has no idea which direction he took. She appeals to Mary.

"You're not trying hard enough, Virgin," she laughs. "Have a talk with St. Jude, if that's what it takes. I got to get to work before I get fired." Even though she is late she takes her time walking the rest of the way to the hospital hoping he might come her way.

She bypasses a semicircle of pickets with their "on strike" placards surrounding the front steps of the hospital and walks through the emergency ambulance doors at the back of the building. "*J'arrive, j'arrive*," she says, pulling on her uniform, pushing through the doors of the emergency room. A nurse leans over a patient stretched out on a gurney. "*Ô, mon Dieu*," Yvette says when she sees who it is. A doctor, examining one of the patient's running shoes and showing it to a paramedic, looks up when he hears Yvette.

"You know him, Yvette?"

"No, but I just saw him a while ago at Place D'Youville, on the street. He was hit by a taxi. He looked like he was dead, but then he got up and ran away."

"Nothing in the pocket, nothing in the sneaker but the size 12, big feet, that's all we can figure out so far. He's a long bugger too. Where'd you get him, Jacques? What happened to him?"

"Don't know. Some kids found him on the Plains, unconscious. He woke up when we got him in the ambulance, but he wouldn't talk."

"Well, he didn't just faint. Look at his back. *Tabernacle*. He took a hit on the head too. Look at the nice walnut on his forehead. Maybe somebody whacked him for his wallet." He looks into the patient's eyes. "*Comment t'appelles-tu?*" The runner blinks but says nothing.

"Ask him in English."

"What's your name?"

No answer.

"I think he's okay. Nosebleed, nothing serious. Amnesia maybe. His skin's in shreds, must be sore. Here, let's turn him over." The paramedic and the nurse gently roll him over on his back. "Looks like he was plowing with his nose." The doctor pulls up his T-shirt. "Look at that, bruises everywhere, *sacrament*." He pulls the T-shirt back down and reads the slogan spread across the front, *J'y Suis. J'y Reste.*

A nurse takes scissors to the T-shirt and slices it up both sides, pulls it away and holds it up to read for himself. "I'm here, I'm staying," he translates freely.

The doctor smiles. "*Je ne pense pas*," he says, "not for long anyway, and me neither, if I can help it, but in the meantime I don't know where in hell we're going to put him. The union picked a grand time to go on strike. Did you see all those pickets out there? Perhaps if some of them get the flu they'll change their minds if they find themselves in the waiting room at the end of an eight-hour lineup, or worse, in a hospital bed without a nurse."

"Yvette, you're late, but at least you're here. *Sainte Vierge*, I'm supposed to be on vacation since Tuesday and by God after today I'm gone no matter what. Find some place to put him, Yvette. Clean out his ears with hydrogen peroxide—they're full of dirt, maybe he can't hear anything—and get Dr. Marier to check him out tomorrow if she's not on strike too, or late. I think this guy will be okay but we better keep him 'til we know for sure. If I have to forfeit my plane ticket I'll put somebody in the hospital myself. Maybe they'll put me in jail where I'll get some peace and quiet. This place is going crazier every day. I'm going crazy myself, I can tell because I can't stop talking. Come to think of it I could be a medic in prison and get paid while I serve my time. Where is Marier? *Calvaire*, if they're not on strike, they're late, if they're not late, they're sick. Get me out of here."

Yvette wheels the gurney down the hall to the storeroom

where she can check on him whenever she goes there for bandages and equipment needed in emergency. After attending to his wounds, she pares down his fingernails and washes out the dirt with a toothbrush, cuts his toenails, washes his hair, shaves his face. While she cleans out his ears with Q-tips and hydrogen peroxide he stares at her with his lips parted, puckered as if he were trying to form a question, but no sound comes out and he closes his lips and sighs. When she finishes she flicks the two ears with her forefinger to see if he would crack a smile across his worried face. No response.

"*Tu es malade?*"

She pulls his headband from around her neck and offers it to him. He takes it and holds it in his hand but says nothing. His wary eyes watch. She wonders how she could get him home. Would he walk? Would he even sit up? In shorts and T-shirt somebody might notice him leaving. She borrows a pair of hospital pants, a grey hospital shirt and a pair of socks from the paramedics' closet. The runner does not respond to verbal commands but he cooperates with physical persuasion. "*Lève-toi,*" she says, but he doesn't move. With her one hand behind his shoulder and the other behind his neck he sits up and she pulls the shirt's sleeves over his arms. She starts to button it up but he pushes her hands away and finishes it himself. She smiles. "Good for you," she says.

She grabs his knees and pulls his legs around and over the side of the gurney and he steps into the pant legs and pulls them over his shorts. She dresses him in an open lab coat and hangs a stethoscope around his neck and walks him down the back stairs and out the basement door into an alley. She takes off the stethoscope and lab coat, stuffs them into a plastic bag and away they go, to the bus, off the bus at the Château Frontenac, down the funicular, through Place St. Charles, onto the ferry. When she sees people on the ferry that might recognize her she manages to appear to be alone. Once across they follow the route she and her father took so many times, up the steep hill, up the gardens, driveways, fields and home. She puts him in her father's bed and gives him a sleeping pill with a glass of water.

When he falls asleep she takes off his sneakers, the pants and shirt from the hospital, his running shorts and his underwear. The hospital clothes she puts in a plastic bag with the lab coat and stethoscope to bring back to the hospital. With a string she measures his waist and the length of his legs. She puts his clothes in a laundry bag, takes them out to the barn and throws them on the floor of the loft, pitch-forks a pile of hay over them and sticks the pitchfork into the mound of hay.

Back at the house in the bedroom she walks her tiny fingers lightly all over his body, stopping here and there to savour the texture. "His hairs are beautiful," she whispers, "but will he like me?" Then she turns him over on his belly and changes the dressing on his back. Scar tissue has already started to crust over the wounds. She stands and looks him over. "What a cute bum," she whispers, and gives each cheek a little slap and watches it shiver. "He will like me, probably." She covers him with a sheet.

After she finishes her chores she checks on him. He is still asleep. She goes to her bedroom and dozes on top of the blankets until she hears him. By the time she gets to his room he is wrapped in the sheet, looking in the empty closet. "*Viens,*" she says, beckoning, and leads him to the hall and points to the bathroom. She shuts the door behind him, purses her lips, raises her eyes, goes to the kitchen, mixes four aspirin in a glass of water, takes it to the bedroom and puts it on the table beside the bed. She sits on the bed and waits.

He takes a long time in the bathroom and when he comes back he stands in the doorway and won't step into the room until she gets off the bed and backs up to the window. He backs onto the bed, still wrapped in the sheet, leans against the backboard with his knees up, his hands outside the sheet gripping it around his ankles. She hands him the aspirin water. He gulps it down, scrunching up his face from the taste, drops the cup on the bedside table and resumes his position, this time with his hands and arms under the sheet. She inches her way back to the bedside, sits on the edge slowly, the way you might try to get close to a rabbit.

She looks at him and smiles. "*Comment t'appelles-tu?*" she says. He looks at her and tries to smile but squints instead like someone surprised by a mouthful of warm water. "*Comment t'appelles-tu?*" she says again. He looks at the door. "Did you forget your name? Or did you forget how to talk altogether? You will have to learn all over again. I will teach you. We'll start tomorrow. Tonight relax." She grabs his heels through the sheet and tries to pull his legs out straight but he won't let them go. She stretches her hands under the sheet and tries to pry his fingers from around his ankles but his strong hands will not yield. She looks up at him and laughs. "Let go," she says, but he looks worried and won't let go.

She climbs onto the bed, pushes his head and shoulders forward, squeezes in behind him and massages his neck and shoulders until he gives in and stretches out on his side. She urges him over onto his belly and soothes him with her fingers until he falls asleep. She slaps his bum through the sheets.

"Au revoir, mes jumelles, je te verai."

In the morning she awakes ahead of him, wakes him up and gives him a vitamin and a few sleeping pills crushed in a glass of milk. When she is certain he is sound asleep she puts a glass of orange juice on the bedside table, takes the shopping bag with the borrowed stethoscope and hospital clothing and leaves for work. She hopes he will stay asleep until she gets back and finishes her chores.

Sailing the ferry to work that morning Yvette stands with her hands on the railing and watches the sun rise over the edge of the Atlantic Ocean carpeting the St. Lawrence River with its yellow reflection. With no one in sight she feels herself alone on the ferry. She sings the song she composed to put herself to sleep the previous night.

> My lover is a man I want to meet
> I want to know his name
> My lover is a man who's here
> My lover is a man who stays
> My lover is a man who's near
> A man of silent ways
> My lover is the answer to my prayers
> And when I call his name…

The sound of a step behind her startles her. She turns. "Oh, hi, Doctor Rench," she says.

"Hello, Yvette. You're happy today."

"It's such a beautiful day."

"What a beautiful voice. I'm sorry about your father. I haven't seen you since he died. I've been away for a while. Just got back yesterday. A small toothless holiday," he laughs. "You must miss him."

"Yes, but it was a peaceful death. And he missed my mother."

"It must be hard living in that house all by yourself, running the farm too, and now you have to work in town as well. It must be hard."

"I'm used to the farm. And I like my job and the money, I'm getting used to the money. Makes life easier."

"You've got two jobs then. If I can help on the farm, let me know. Any time. I wasn't always an orthodontist, you know. I grew up on a farm. Cows, pigs and all that. Chickens. Work, work, work, dig, plant, weed, spray, collect, gather, store, sell, buy, hammer, saw, chop, never done, never done. Said goodbye to all that though. But I'm all by myself now too."

Yvette looks up at him, as the boat gently bumps into the dock. She could think of nothing to say.

EIGHT

It is a paradox of French-Canadian life:
the more bilingual we become, the less
need there is to be bilingual.
—*Marcel Chaput*

IAN WAKES UP, sits up, bewildered. He throws off the sheet and looks down at his naked body in the bed, with no idea where he is or how he arrived. He scans the room. Nothing much to see. To his right a bulbous red lamp with a mauve shade sits on a bedside table and next to it a glass of orange juice. He runs his tongue over his dry lips, picks up the glass and drains it. On the other side of the bed a hospital table designed to fit across the top of a bed holds nothing but a checkered tablecloth folded in two and then folded under itself at the ends to fit the narrow tabletop. A family photograph—man, woman and child—decorates a maroon-painted wall on one side of the room and on the other side a framed print of the Sacred Heart of Jesus. A crucifix hangs above the open doorway at the end of the room opposite the bed and beside the door a vanity with six drawers and a large dressing mirror attached to its back stands against the wall. Beside the dresser two brown drapes hang from rings, covering the opening to a closet. The picture of the Sacred Heart and the crucifix tug at his memory but he can't place them.

He leans over the side of the bed and looks on the floor for his shoes and socks. Nothing. He puts his bare feet on the floor, wraps the sheet around his naked body, goes to the window beside the table lamp and looks out the rectangular panes: a barn with grey shingles, a bright red door and a mansard roof. A lean-to extends from the barn on the right side and through the open doors he can see the nose and small front wheels of an ancient tractor. Beside the lean-to a rooster and a dozen or so chickens walk freely in and out the open door of a chicken-wire coop. Next to the chicken coop, long horizontal poles form a four-sided corral. Through the spaces between the poles he can see two pigs sheltering from the sun in the shade of a hovel at one end of the corral. An English sheep dog sits near the chicken coop keeping an eye on the chickens as they wander, pecking at the ground.

On the other side of the barn he can see a mound of manure, a small apple orchard next to it. Beside the orchard on a slight grade a six-foot-high fence of chicken wire surrounds a long rectangle of tilled ground. A wooden button keeps closed the garden door made of crisscrossed laths. In the field beyond the garden a jersey cow stands, bending her head down to munch grass and raising it up to chew her cud.

Ian walks to the closet and opens the drapes. Nothing much in there, two black socks pushed into two men's black leather shoes on the floor and a collection of wire hangers hooked over a pole stretching across the top of the closet under a shelf holding a box of Christmas decorations and a sewing basket. A twelve-gauge shotgun and two rifles stand together in the corner of the closet, a bolt-action 303 Lee Enfield army rifle and beside it a bolt-action 22 caliber. He takes each rifle, opens the bolt and checks the chambers for a round of ammunition. He closes and opens the bolt of the 303 to make sure there are no rounds of ammunition in the magazine and puts the two weapons back in the corner. He breaks open the shotgun and checks the barrel for ammunition and puts it back with the rifles. He recognizes the rifles; he knows how to handle them but can't recall how he learned about them or what he used them for.

Nothing in the closet he can wear. The shoes are too narrow, too short for his feet. He squeezes into the socks. They also are too short in the foot but long enough so that with the heels under the curvature of his soles they cover his feet up to his heel.

A crocheted scarf covers the dresser and on it stands a grotto containing a phosphorescent Virgin Mary with a votive candle on either side. He wonders where he has seen such a thing before. Ian pulls open each drawer but finds little: a jackknife, a hunting knife in a leather scabbard, some candles, Christmas wrapping paper, a rosary of black wooden beads and a lot of this and that but nothing to wear except for a necktie covered in *fleur-de-lis*. It is already tied in a Windsor knot and as the sheet falls from his body he puts the noose of the necktie over his head and around his neck, thinking, if I'm going to look ridiculous I might as well go all the way. After a quick look in the mirror he shakes his head and smiles. He picks up the sheet, folds it in two and wraps it around his waist like a skirt. He feels a hint of vertigo and sees himself tilt slightly in the mirror.

"That's probably ridiculous enough," he says to his double.

He takes the glass from the bedside table and, wearing the sheet, the tie and a silly grin, steps into the hallway and walks to the bathroom at the far end.

After a pee and a long drink of water he leaves the bathroom and looks into the room beside the bedroom where he woke up. It too is a bedroom but, with only a cot without bedclothes, it seems to be used mostly for storage. He rummages through a steamer trunk and a couple of suitcases but finds only blankets, quilts, winter coats, gloves, mitts, scarves and toques. A few open cupboards of shelves contain rolls of toilet paper, containers of pills, a variety of medicines and a few towels but none of them large enough to wrap around his slim waist. He goes back down the hall, stands at the top of the stairs and listens but hears no sound from below.

He returns to the bedroom, takes the sheet from his waist, pulls it up over his shoulders and ties it in a knot around his neck. He wraps it around his entire body and clutches it at the front with his right hand. He meets a cat in the hallway and it follows him as he carefully creeps down the stairs, a couple of small towels dangling from his left hand, doubling his front-end protection. At the bottom of the stairs he finds himself in an old-fashioned kitchen with cupboards that look homemade but well constructed of pine darkened with age, a rectangular, varnished, wooden table made with tiger maple and four matching chairs. An electric stove.

At the sink he pours himself another glass of water, walks down the hall until he comes to a closed door decorated with a print of *La Masia* by Joan Miró. He studies it for a moment. A couple of buildings, a large old one and a new one under construction, some farm animals, a tree, a woman, the sun in a blue sky, some tilled ground, a watering can, a ladder, a bucket, and a myriad of hard-to-identify things. An eye hides among the leaves of the tree. An ear protrudes from its trunk. He smiles, the disjointed images of the painting seem like a mirror of the confusion in his mind from waking up groggy in a strange, unintelligible world. He purses his lips, shrugs his shoulders, taps a tentative knock on the door, turns the handle and pushes it open a crack.

When he pushes open the bedroom door and walks in he discovers a room with a single bed, a reading lamp next to a stuffed chair and hassock, a six-foot-wide bookcase with four shelves stuffed with books and a virtual art gallery with pictures hanging on all the walls as well as on the inside of the bedroom door and on the door of a clothes closet.

Each print is bound in a frame crafted from old barn boards. All the prints are copies of paintings by Joan Miro. Ian walks around the narrow spaces between the bed and the walls and studies the baffling pictures. He can see scant connection between the pictures and the titles that are sometimes printed on the frames, sometimes handwritten on the bottom of the print, some of them in Spanish, some in French, some in English: *L'Oro Dell'Azzuro*, *Personnage Et Oiseaux*, *Senza Titulo*. The *Carnival of Harlequin* nearly nudges some vague recollection in his memory, but *Cat Encircled by Flight of a Bird*, *Dog Barking at the Moon* and *Singing Fish* brings back his smile and with a shrug of his shoulders he moves on to the bookcase.

The bookcase, like the frames of the pictures, are crafted from weathered barn boards, some of them with the cut marks of an adze once used to shape tree logs into rafters. The titles are all in French. He opens one at random, *La belle bête*, and realizes at once that his high school French enables him to make some headway. He recognizes most of the words but the meaning of many of the sentences eludes him. He closes the book and looks at the author's name, Marie-Claire Blais. He pulls a few more titles, takes a quick look inside, closes them to look at the authors' names on the back of the books, Saint-Denys Garneau, Gaston Miron, Anne Hébert, Paul Chamberlaine. He puts them back and turns to look in the closet.

He files through the clothes hangers in the closet, finds a garment he can wrap around himself, a black leather kilt with enough overlap so he can pin it over his hips, and a T-shirt large enough for him to squeeze into. He looks in the mirror and laughs, pushes the sheet back over his shoulders like a cape, clenches together the two panels in front with his fingers and tucks them under the belt of the skirt over his belly button. When he lifts his arms up out of the sides of the hanging sheet it is still ample enough to cover most of his body.

Where the clothes were pushed aside he notices on the floor a cardboard box, a little mildewed along the edges of its cover. He pulls it open and finds another collection of books giving off a slightly musty smell. He picks up a few: *Marie Chapdelaine, Bonheure d'Occasion, Le Survenant, Un Homme et son Péché,* all in French. The name of the book *Marie Chapdelaine* seems familiar but the others mean nothing to him. He puts them back.

When he turns from the closet he notices several notebooks on the table beside the chair. The one on top, a half-inch-thick scribbler with a hard, black cover, is half full of notes and poems. He perches on the bed and opens the cover to a title page: *Le Cahier d'Yvette.* Then he opens it at random and reads a short poem:

L'Excès Chercheur

(…)

Gelé

pris dans le bloc de glace
fixé

la même où respirer
c'est vivre avec une lame
dans la chair
à chaque instant mourir
mourir et sourire en flame

The handwritten lines are transcribed in slightly wavy lines with the author's name, Paul Chamberlain, written underneath it. Again he understands most of the words, *Gelé pris dans le bloc de glace, fixé:* something was frozen in a block of ice, *la même:* the same, *où respire:* where to breathe, *c'est vivre avec une lame dans la chair:* it is to live with something in the skin. But he can make out little of the meaning and nothing of the wavy lines or the three dots in parenthesis under the title. He puts the notebook back on the table, thinking to explore more of the house and come back and study the notebooks to look for clues. Where am I? he wonders. Who am I? Who is Yvette?

Across the hall he finds the living room containing a chesterfield, a couple of stuffed chairs, two wooden rocking chairs facing a television in a corner, a wooden box full of split hardwood next to a blackened fireplace, a mantelpiece displaying family pictures between two candles in their holders: two late middle-aged adults, a balding man of medium stature with a smile and a bemused look on his face, a petite, laughing woman with greying black hair tied in a bun at the back of her head, a skinny teenage girl with black hair looking as if she had just asked a question and is waiting for an answer. Outside the picture window the branches of four budding apple trees vibrate in the breeze, the adolescent leaves preparing hopeful mangers for blossoms about to be born. He turns on the television. An auditorium full of standing people, waving banners bearing the name René Lévesque, applaud while a man stands behind a microphone and takes a long drag of smoke into his lungs, watching the end of the cigarette between his first two fingers glow bright red and turn to ashes.

He goes back through the kitchen and out into the porch. Between a freezer and the wall of the porch he finds a pair of rubber knee boots that are much too small for him, but he manages to squeeze his feet into them and hobble out onto the back step. The dog, barking once in welcome, comes running over wagging its tail. He steps to the ground, scratches the dog's ears and pats its head.

"What's your name, pooch—Rex? Prince? Butch maybe? Whose dog are you?"

The dog lies down and rolls over on its back. Ian kneels on one knee, scratches the dog's belly and looks around. No sign of a neighbouring house so he leads the dog across the yard, clutching the sheet around his body, and opens the barn door to the sweet smell of hay and manure. The rooster announces his entrance and the chickens pause for a moment from their pecking and cast their wary eyes on the stranger. The sunlight from the few dusty windows and the manure hatch barely illuminate the two cattle stalls but he can see there are no animals there. He calls out hello and waits in the sweet silent smell. He climbs the short ladder to the hayloft. In the dim light coming through a dusty window he can make out nothing but a pitchfork on top of a mound of hay and two pairs of cats' eyes shining from the dark corner of the loft.

He leaves the barn and crosses the yard back to the house and in the kitchen finds some bran flakes in the cupboard. In the freezer he discovers a grocery bag full of frozen blueberries, mixes a handful into the cereal in a bowl and douses them with milk from a bottle he finds in the fridge. He eats quickly and fills the dish again. He boils some water, makes a pot of tea and fills up on toasted sandwiches made with slices of homemade cheese cut from a wheel he finds wrapped in a towel in the refrigerator. He watches the cat jump up on the table and finish off the milk he left in the bowl.

☆   ☆   ☆

On her way back home after work Yvette goes to a clothing store and buys a pair of pajamas, a denim work-shirt, a pair of coveralls, a couple of pairs of work socks and a pair of rubber knee boots.

On the ferry home, she leans against the railing and watches the sun drop over the western horizon, drenching the St. Lawrence and its banks in crimson. She thinks she is alone and she begins to sing.

I'm going home where I belong
I'm going home, he waits for me

It won't be long before we speak
I'm going home...

She hears a footstep behind her and turns her back to the sun. "Oh. Hello, Dr. Rench."

"Call me Monc, Yvette, I'm not in my office now. I'm just me, a farm boy going home from the city. A farm boy without a farm, just an empty barn and a field of weeds."

"I didn't know your first name before now."

He glances at the men's store shopping bags hanging from her hands. "I was born in Moncton. My mother was a wonderful warm woman but not much imagination. You have a beautiful voice. You could sing for your supper. Might be more fun than nursing. Not much money in it though."

When the ferry bangs into the dock they lurch sideways toward the bow, and he grabs her by the elbow. She smiles. "I'm fine," she says, and places her shopping bags by her feet on the deck. "I'm used to the bump when Jacques is at the wheel. Sometimes I think he does it just for me," she laughs. She points to the wheelhouse and waves. "He always gives me a big smile and a wave. I don't even think about it. I believe my legs remember it for me, because they're always ready when it happens."

"Sorry," he says. "I thought you were going to trip over your shopping bags." He gives the bags another puzzled look.

"I'm fine, Monc. Takes a lot to trip me up. My legs are strong from walking that hill. When I'm on the ferry I always feel like I'm rooted to the deck."

"Here we are disembarking again already. Can I carry the bags off for you? They must be heavy."

She bends to pick up the bags and smiles up at him, lifts them by the handles with two fingers, hefts them a few times to show they are not too heavy then dangles them at her legs.

"No thanks, I'm fine. They're not heavy."

"It's funny, you know," he says as they walk off onto the dock. "Taking the ferry seems to make the trip to the city and back home more important. Embarking, debarking, sailing, it all seems so much more romantic than driving a car across the bridge, don't you think?"

"I don't know. I don't drive. I've never been on the bridge. Is it faster? Is that why people go that way?"

"No. It takes longer, especially in the morning and after-noon, people going and coming from work."

"Maybe they like the view."

"You don't even notice the river from the bridge. You can't take your eyes off the road in front of you or you'll bang into someone or someone will bang into you. The sunrise, the sunset, you might as well be in bed for all you see the sun."

"So why do they do it?"

"I don't know, maybe they like to sit down. Or maybe they like to listen to the weather forecast fifteen times," he laughs. "I never take the bridge unless I need the car over there for doing errands. The boat ride is pleasant in good weather, quicker and less bother, no parking problems. I leave my car here but I'm thinking of moving across the river, getting an apartment. There's never a moment's peace when you own a house, especially a big old farmhouse—the windows, the doors, the roof, don't even talk about the barn, empty as it is, you still have to deal with it, and when the winter comes, the snow, the snow, the snow." He hesitates before he moves off toward the parking lot to his car. "Would you like a drive home? That hill must be quite the drag after a long day."

"No, thanks," she says, walking backwards away from him. She stops, turns and over her shoulder, she says, "I love the walk. I need the exercise. Gives me nice thoughts about my father, and a chance to plan supper." She waves goodbye.

"Okay, Yvette," he calls after her. "But, let me know. Anytime. The weather can be nasty some days. Just let me know. If it's a bad day call my office and I'll wait for you in the lobby of the Frontenac. I take the car over on bad weather days when the ferry ride is too cruel. You cook just for yourself now too. That must be lonesome," he says as she continues to walk away from him, turns and gives him another wave with a lift of her chin.

With a worried smile, Yvette approaches the house. The dog runs to greet her and, sniffing the packages, follows her to the back step. She lifts the metal latch, pushes open the door with her foot, carries her shopping bags into the porch and through the open door into the kitchen. Silence. She looks at the cereal bowl and spoon on the table, looks up the stairs, listening, and seeing nothing, hearing nothing, she lays down her bags quietly by the bottom step and tiptoes up the stairs and down the hall to her father's room. Empty.

Back downstairs, she creeps silently down the hall. The door of her room is ajar. She pushes it open with a finger. He sits there wrapped in the sheet with his back toward her, facing the bookcase, peering at one of her notebooks on his knee, following the script with a finger. She quietly pulls the door closed, knocks, and pushes it open again and smiles at his startled face as he looks over his shoulder.

"*Je m'excuse,*" she says. "*Bonjour.*"

He closes the notebook. His face takes on the surprised, blank look of the discovered intruder. He puts the notebook back on top of the other books on the table. His face crimson, he gets to his feet and turns to face her. The sheet falls back over his shoulders like a cape, revealing a red T-shirt split down the middle by the fleur-de-lis necktie, his thighs wrapped in the leather kilt.

Yvette bursts into laughter. "*Est-ce-que tu es Superman, Super-woman ou Le capitaine du Quebec?*"

She waits for his smile but he frowns. "Ah," she says, "he reads but he does not speak. We'll fix that. Just wait here a minute." She rushes downstairs, plucks the pajamas from one of the bags and comes back upstairs, pulling the plastic, the cardboard and the pins from the pajamas.

"*C'est pour toi,*" she says and places the pajamas on the pillow. She picks up the notebook he was reading when she entered the room, puts two more notebooks with it and places them on the pillow beside the pajamas. She pats the pajamas and then the books and repeats, "*C'est pour toi.*" She smiles, leaves the room, pulling shut the door, then opens it again, and leaning on the handle she laughs, "Stay right here now until I get the supper ready." She takes several pieces of clothing from her closet and leaves the room.

Left alone, smiling, puzzled, Ian removes his bizarre attire, stuffs them in a drawer of the dresser, puts on the pajamas and examines himself in the mirror. A collection of trains, planes, ships and cars decorate the tunic of the pajamas. Each vehicle bears the same tiny inscription. *"Es-tu arrivé?"* That much he can understand and translate and he repeats it to himself several times, "'Have you arrived?' I guess so," he answers with a wry smile, "but where?"

Yvette spends the next hour or so preparing the meal, singing, humming, smiling. With everything ready, she goes to her father's bedroom and brings down to the kitchen the bed-table she borrowed from the hospital when her father became bed-ridden. She goes back upstairs, takes a shower and changes her clothes.

"Always begin with wine," her father told her, so she begins with two chalice-shaped crystal glasses, wedding gifts her mother kept but never used, filled with dusky-tasting red wine that she knows will cling to the taste buds like a piece of cloth. She places the wine glasses on the tray, lifts the tray onto the bed-table and wheels it down the hall to her bedroom.

"Here I am," she says, as she wheels the bed-table into the room, "at long last."

Ian is sitting in a lotus position leaning against the head-board, one of Yvette's notebooks in his hands. He gives her a quizzical look. *"D'accord,"* she says. She takes the notebook, claps it shut, puts it with the others back on the bookshelf, pushes the hospital table across the middle of the bed and sits herself cross-legged on the mattress, her back against the footboard, the table between them, her pleated skirt fanned across her legs. In the dimming light of dusk they sit silent looking at the tray with its two wine glasses.

The tray too, like the crystal wine glasses, was a wedding gift never before used, a square fashioned from two thin planks of maple fitted together by tongue-and-groove. Her father had carved on it the outline of an Atlantic salmon and the word "*toujours*," chiselled across the furrow created where the two pieces join. Her mother used it only as a wall hanging so she would see it every day. One glass of burgundy sits on the tail and one on the head of the fish. Yvette leans forward in her cross-legged position, crushes the dirndl skirt of her dress between her legs, picks up a glass of wine from the tail of the fish, raises it in a toast and beckons him to follow suit.

"*A nous*," she says, "*un petit goût du Châteauneuf-du-Pape.*"

He raises his glass in silence, but she sees a little startle in his eyes. They sip at their glasses and watch each other until the smell of baked salmon wafts in from the kitchen. She takes his empty glass, puts it with her glass on the bookcase and takes the tray to the kitchen.

She returns with the bottle of wine, a newspaper, a notepad, and two plates of food on the tray: the baked salmon, mushrooms picked from the pasture and sautéed in butter, the celery sticks filled with homemade cheese, potatoes from last year's garden, baked, split, covered with sour cream provided by Mimi the cow, frozen peas from the garden thawed and sautéed in the dregs of the butter, lemon juice, olive oil and salmon fat. She pours more wine into the crystal glasses and puts them on the bed-table beside the tray.

They take their plates and eat from their laps. When they finish she offers more and he understands her gesture and nods acceptance. "Ah yes," she says, "a meal first goes to a runner's feet and then we have to feed the belly."

In the kitchen she sings while she loads his plate with more food.

Oh I'm half drunk on wine
And I'm half drunk on food
And I'm all drunk with a silent
Hunk and I think I feel just fine.

While he eats his second helping she tries to start a conversation. "*As-tu eu une bonne journée?*" she says. But he stares blankly as if he didn't know what kind of a day he had, so she decides to just talk and perhaps he will understand. She picks up the newspaper and reads to him.

"'There will be a congruence of events and strangers will stand at a crossroads.' That's my horoscope for today. When is your birthday?" He takes a sip of wine. "I have a feeling it is today. Listen to this. 'The slate is wiped clean. A new beginning is possible. Leap before you look.' Isn't that interesting?"

When he finishes eating she picks up the utensils and names them. "*Fourchette,*" she says and prompts him to repeat the sounds. This time he responds.

"*Fourchette,*" he says and smiles.

"*Couteau.*"

"*Couteau,*" he repeats.

"There you go. You are a good parrot. Now we got the idea."

She takes away the dishes and comes back with glasses full of wine. She puts the tray with the wine glasses on the bed between them and pushes the bed-table to the wall beside the bookcase. They sit watching each other over the wine glasses half full of red wine and a notepad and pencil between them on the Atlantic salmon tray.

"Here's to learning to talk." She raises her glass. He raises his glass and says nothing.

"*Je m'appelle Yvette.*" He looks at her and opens his mouth but says nothing. She writes her name on the notepad and hands it to him.

"Yvette," he repeats.

"Yvette," she says and pokes herself on her breastbone.

"Yvette," he says and points at her.

"*Et toi?*" she says and leans forward and touches his chest. He shakes his head and shrugs his shoulders. "Abraham is what I will call you, Abraham Runner, because they found you fallen from running on the Plains of Abraham." She reaches over and pokes his breastbone.

"Abraham," she says.

"Abraham," he repeats.

"*Formidable,*" she says then she writes down, "*Je m'appelle Yvette.*"

He takes the notepad, looks at it and says. "*Je m'appelle Yvette.*"

"*Je m'appelle Yvette,*" she says and pokes her breastbone. "*Tu t'appelles Abraham,*" she says and writes on the notepad, "*Je m'appelle Abraham*" and pokes his chest.

"*Je m'appelle Abraham,*" he repeats.

"*D'accord,*" she says, "*formidable.*"

"*D'accord,*" he repeats, "*formidable.*"

"*Je suis une femme,*" she says, and cups her breasts with her hands. His eyes light up with understanding.

"*Tu es une femme,*" he says in his high school French.

"*Tu es un homme,*" she says and points between his legs. He smiles and nods understanding.

Now with the footings and foundation in place, Yvette begins to build.

"*Je m'appelle Yvette et tu t'appelles Abraham.*"

"*Je m'appelle Abraham, tu t'appelles Yvette,*" he repeats. He takes a sip of wine.

"*Je suis une femme, tu es un homme,*" she says, and takes a sip of wine.

"*Je suis un homme, tu es une femme.*"

They smile. They laugh. They relax. Yvette carries the tray to the kitchen and comes back with the glasses of wine on the head and tail of the Atlantic salmon and between the glasses, on the body of the fish, a chocolate cake with a candle burning in its centre. She places the tray with cake, candle and wine on the middle of the bed and they sit cross-legged on either side of it, Abraham in his new pajamas with its trains, planes and automobiles, Yvette in her dirndl skirted dress with its blouse printed with bouquets of *fleur-de-lis*.

"*Souffle la bougie,*" she says, and purses her lips and mimes blowing out the candle. "I'm making a wish. You too, make a wish." She puts her fingers to her lips to indicate they should keep the wishes secret.

He leans forward, purses his lips and blows out the candle and they watch a thread of smoke the shape of an exclamation mark rise to the ceiling. Yvette rises to her bare feet as if pulled up by the rising thread of smoke and raises her glass. "Here's to Abraham," she says, but her knees buckle and land in the cake and the glass of wine topples from her hand and lands upside down on Abraham's head and the crystal glass falls into his lap and wine runs down his face and splashes on the legs of his pajamas and over the white sheet covering the bed. "My God, my God, what have I done? My cake is crushed, my legs are wet with frosting, my sheet is stained, my bed is a mess, I should be angry, I should be frustrated, I should be crying, but I'm happy and I can't help laughing."

Abraham is laughing too and sipping wine. "Your *fleur-de-lis* are beautiful," he says in high school French.

"Yes, my flower is beautiful like the flower on your necktie," she says and gives him a measuring look. She sticks out her tongue. "*C'est la langue,*" she says and sticks it out again.

"*C'est belle, la langue.*"

"Yes, and your tongue is speaking very well. Put a little wine on my tongue." She gestures, dipping her finger in his wine glass and letting a drop fall on her tongue. Abraham puts his finger in his wine glass and touches it onto her tongue. She takes his free hand in her two hands and pins it down under their scrambled feet. "There, now see if you can do it without hands."

☆　☆　☆

Once the speaking lessons are well under way, and he is managing in French, she brings him the coveralls, plaid work-shirt, grey work-socks, and rubber knee boots and places them on the kitchen table. "These are your barn clothes," she says, "never take them farther into the house than the porch." She pinches her nose with her thumb and forefinger and scrunches up her face. She leads him to the back porch. "Don't be shy," she says. "Get the good clothes off and put them on those hangers over there. Put them back on when you come in from the barn."

He strips off his shirt and pants, shoes and socks and hangs the clothing on the hooks behind the freezer. The wounds from his accident are fading from his body and the colour is back to normal. His nose has new skin and the scars on his back are barely visible. Yvette strips to her underwear and changes to coveralls and denim shirt. They pull on their rubber knee boots and she leads him to the barn where she teaches him how to milk the cow.

In the barn dust floats in the squares of sunlight flooding through the windows. The sour smell of manure from the floor mixed with the sweet scent of hay from the loft make Abraham gasp and sneeze the minute he gets past the door. "You'll get used to it," Yvette laughs. "It won't take long."

The two barn cats, Minou and Minute, sit facing each other on a window ledge as Abraham and Yvette approach the cow waiting in its stall to be milked.

"Give her a good slap on the rump to show her you mean business," she tells Abraham, "or she'll try to bully you out of the stall." He whacks the cow with a back handed fist and leans on her with his shoulder and upper arm and she sidesteps to the other side of the stall, giving lots of room for the two of them to set up beside her. Yvette sits Abraham down on a three-legged stool and crouches behind him, bending her knees, leaning against his back, looking over his shoulder, her arms stretched under his armpits and out to the cow in front of him. She positions his hand on the cow's near right teat and wraps her fingers around the cow's near left teat. "Hold it like this," she says and squirts a stream of milk against the inside of the bucket, making a sound like heavy rain. "Now you try it." She repositions his hand. "Does that feel comfortable?"

"Yes, that feels good."

"Yes, it's a nice handful. Now squeeze down. No, no, squeeze don't jerk, firm and gentle, like a nice tube of toothpaste upside down." She covers his hand with hers and guides it and a bit of milk drops into the bucket. "Okay now, there's a splat, try it again, like this," she says and squirts a stream of milk from the left teat into the bucket and then turns up the teat and squirts milk all over his face. "Open your mouth, Abraham, it's a warm surprise," and she fires a stream of milk into his mouth making him cough and laugh at the same time.

"Try it again now, do it together, there, that's better, am I hurting your back, no, good, it's no longer sore, do it again." The cow takes a moment from munching to turn around and give them an indifferent look.

With their four hands on the cow's four teats, his head against the cow, her head against the back of his head, her chin on his shoulder, they rain milk into the bucket and every four or five squeezes into each other's faces. After they drain the cow, they carry the milk pail between them and walk in their milk-soaked barn clothes to the house. In the porch they empty the milk pail into the creamer and change to their regular clothes.

"Tomorrow we'll start the garden," she says, "so we can eat good food next year. Isn't it nice to plan a future? Now let's cook supper and later tonight we'll churn some butter."

The next day Abraham and Yvette kneel head to head at the end of a two-foot-wide, twelve-foot-long patch of fresh forked-up soil. A six-inch-deep furrow runs from one end, where she directs him to stick the prongs of the garden fork into the ground, to the other end, where Yvette, on her knees, bends over the furrow holding a small spice bottle half full of seeds. She uncovers the bottle, takes Ian's hand and pours a little mound of seeds into the cup of his palm. He looks at the seeds and laughs.

"Why is the furrow so deep? These tiny little things are gonna get lost down there."

"No, no. Leeks are like children. It takes nine months for them just to get to be babies. We plant them deep in the bottom of the furrow and put a little earth and compost over them and when they show, we'll put more earth and compost around them, then when they get to ground level in the sun and the rain, they'll have deep roots in the soil and grounded in all that support they'll grow tall and strong so the winds can't knock them over."

Yvette picks up a fistful of earth and picks out the lumps and rocks until she reduces it to fine grains, about the same volume as the leek seeds in Ian's cupped hand. "Here, take this earth and mix it with the seeds so you won't sow them too thick or we'll have to waste a lot of time later thinning them." She puts the earth in his hand and mixes the seeds and earth with her finger. "Now just let them file out of your hand from here to the end where the fork is. You put them in and I'll cover them up so they'll be nice and comfortable and ready to grow."

Abraham moves along the furrow on his knees, spilling the mixture of earth and seed along the bottom until he reaches the garden fork. Yvette comes after him folding a bit of earth and compost around the row of seeds until she catches up to Abraham at the end of the row and stands beside him.

"There now," she says, "some of them will die but the good ones will spring up healthy and we'll cultivate them and keep the weeds away and when they are grown up we'll put them in the root cellar and we'll have great soup all next year."

"Really?"

"Of course. We do it every year. We look after them all summer, they look after us all winter."

"That's a comfort."

"It is. Now how about you take the fork over there and dig up the same kind of furrow for corn kernels so at the end of the summer we'll have lots of corn on the cob to eat, and some for the pigs in the fall and lots to freeze for the winter."

"Where? Over where?"

"Start at the far corner of the garden, see, by the three currant bushes and work your way to the other side."

Abraham takes the fork and starts to dig at the corner of the garden but after he turns a few forkfuls he pushes the tines into the ground with his boot, stands with one foot on the shoulder of the tines, both hands on the handle of the fork, turns and stares at the currant bushes, then gazes over them at the horizon, his mouth half open. Yvette looks up from the other end of the garden where she is mixing sifted earth and compost in her homemade wooden wheelbarrow. Her face freezes in alarm. She watches him stare, her eyes wide. She stands up straight and calls to him.

"Abraham."

No response.

NINE

Lack of communication has held Canada
together for one hundred years. Once we
can speak each other's language the
mystery of being what we are is gone.
—*Dave Broadfoot as The Honourable Member from Kicking Horse Pass*

IAN'S WANDERLUST BEGAN EARLY in a garden of bushes and trees surrounded by a square of picket fence. In each corner of the fence a silver maple tree stood like a sentry, each tree pruned on the sides that face the others so on the east, south and west a corridor free of branches and leaves allowed the sun to beam in on a rectangle of currant bushes, a row of black, a row of red and a row of white. It looked like a miniature vineyard in the middle of the front yard of his grandparents' house. It was all bushes and trees except for a row of crocuses on either side of the front step and along the path leading to the currant bushes. When they popped up in the spring his grandmother potted one yellow and one purple and took them inside and placed them on the sunny side of the living room facing the garden.

When he was five, the eldest of five children, Ian went off to school, leaving behind two skinny brothers, two skinny sisters, a bulbous mother, Mamie expecting another baby and an exhausted father, Mick. A coal miner, his father often worked overtime to provide for the endlessly developing appetites of his brood for food and clothes and on occasion to hire a morose teenage girl to assist the beleaguered mother or at times replace her when the doctor ordered the mother to bed or hospital.

By the time he was six, after spending a few weekends and part of a summer with his grandparents, where he enjoyed a taste of freedom and tranquility, he took to going there straight from school to avoid the chaos of chores, frantic, skinny siblings, cranky cat, yapping dog, depleted father home from the mine, the unpredictable cooking of his mother, or worse, a can of beans fried in lard by the morose teenager of the month.

Relatives and neighbours of Morag, Ian's grandmother, addressed her when they could not avoid the encounter simply as Mam. She never gave them any reason to fear her; they simply read her demeanour as a no-nonsense woman, a woman you never knew how to speak to. She welcomed Ian as a rare and willing companion and made few demands on the young fellow's time and energy. She had acquired tape recordings of radio programs from the forties that she played on a tape recorder installed in the body of a defunct floor model radio she'd bought with her first paycheck when she was a nurse. When Ian landed from school at dinnertime they sat in the living room in front of the radio and listened to *The Happy Gang*.

After school they ate a snack, a homemade bread, peanut butter and black currant sandwich, and listened to a soap opera, usually *Ma Perkins* or *Pepper Young's Family*. Then she helped him with his homework. Afterwards if it was raining or snowing or otherwise inclement she would play her fiddle and teach him to play simple tunes or speak to him in Gaelic, which he didn't learn to speak fluently but eventually did learn well enough to understand basic conversation and sing a few Gaelic songs. Or she would tell him stories of their ancestors in Scotland.

In good weather in spring, summer or early fall, once they listened to their programs they postponed the homework, fiddle and story session and he went off to the ball field carved out of the blueberry barrens that stretched from their street to the coal mine. When dark closed down the ball game he came home to his supper and after homework they sat in the dark dining room, illuminated only by the florescent light from the plaster of Paris grotto and statue of the Virgin Mary and they listened to *Boston Blackie, The Green Hornet, Lux Radio Theatre,* or some other radio drama and then went to bed.

In the late fall and winter, after the men and boys fenced in the baseball infield, transforming it into a hockey rink, he played until dark and went home for supper and while she told her stories they sat on wooden kitchen chairs at her quilting frames and she taught him how to select rags, shape them to fit a pattern and sew them onto a sheet. Or in late summer and fall they moved the radio/tape recorder into the kitchen and listened while they made red, white and black currant jelly, which they waxed into recycled bottles of various sizes.

For a while Ian's mother objected to the arrangement. When she called to complain, Ian's grandfather Calum would drive him home in his antique pre-war Ford, have a cup of tea with his son and daughter-in-law and talk about the boy after he went to bed. Ian's mother did not approve of her mother-in-law, whom she considered to be too strict, but the inconvenience of the extra and active child, a climbing, clambering menace to every moveable, breakable, tearable object in the house, the convenience of one less responsibility in the frenzy of breakfast in the morning, supper in the evening and homework at night, gradually wore the rope of her disapproval to a thread and stretched it until it broke.

Consequently he gradually settled in with his grandparents. Holidays evolved to weekends, weekends augmented to weekdays, then weeks in a row until, somewhat estranged from his family, his brothers and sisters became as cousins, his mother and father like aunt and uncle, and his cousins who lived near his grandparents were his playmates. When he went home, usually accompanied by his grandfather, he behaved like a visitor, he took off his cap, left his shoes at the door, he was polite, unassuming, thankful for the tea and biscuits.

As much as she was wary of the grandmother, Ian's mother adored her father-in law. Her own parents died when she was young and she welcomed Cal, as he insisted everyone call him, as part of her family. He often took the kids off her hands giving them rides in his car, taking them to a movie on Saturday afternoons, and to the beach on Sunday in the summer, or for a skate on a pond in the winter, and buying them treats.

Once Ian settled in with the grandparents, Cal insisted on taking him home for a visit every week in the hope that he would not lose the connection with his family. But it didn't work. Having two homes made Ian feel homeless, except when he was playing hockey or baseball. As he grew toward adulthood, graduating from rink hockey and pick-up ball games to organized sports, his real family became the ever-changing teams he played for. And his coaches became his surrogate parents. He got used to waving them goodbye as he moved from one age and skill level to the next.

Only after several years, as Ian approached his teens, did he notice that Morag and Calum never talked to each other, although they both talked to him in each other's presence.

☆　☆　☆

The first flash of memory flicks onto the screen of Ian's imagination when he brushes by the quiescent black currant bushes as he bends over the fork at the corner of Yvette's garden.

His grandfather is driving him back after their weekly Sunday evening visit to his family.

"Grandpa, how come you and Mam never talk to each other?"

His grandfather laughs, and considers the question during a long silence. He eases the car into the driveway and cuts the engine as darkness begins to settle over the yard. The sun is gone over the horizon and the sky is filling with black clouds. He looks across the front seat at Ian who is waiting for his answer. "I talk to her sometimes but she just gives me a level stare or walks into another room. So usually I just talk to myself and hope she'll overhear me so at least she'll know what's on my mind."

"But why? Why won't she talk?"

"Well, she does talk to you. But to me? Well, it's a bit of a mystery, but my guess is that even though I only married her the once, she has never forgiven me."

"What does that mean?"

"It's like a joke. You can't explain it. You get it or you don't. But let me put it another way. I think it's that she's disappointed."

"In you?"

"Not in me personally, no. But when she was a nurse she had money and she took music lessons. And she went around playing the piano and the fiddle at all the dances. Not many women got to do that. Then she got married and with the children she had to stay home because she had neither money, energy nor time enough for music and travelling. And I was away a lot and couldn't help her out."

"Where were you?"

"I was a sea captain. We shipped lumber and coal and other stuff to places like Jamaica and brought back molasses and rum and bananas, pineapples and stuff that we couldn't get here, especially in the winter. And during the war I was in the Merchant Marine. Her mother warned her if she married a sailor she could expect he'd be going to sea, but she wasn't one to listen to her mother."

Ian pulls on the bill of his baseball hat. "So she's disappointed," he says, as if he just invented the insight himself, "in everything."

"No, oh no." Cal looks over the steering wheel and says into the black windshield, "She's happy with her children and grandchildren. But I don't think she's ever figured out that it had to be one or the other. And, oh yeah," he laughs, "she's happy with her bushes of currants, especially those bitter black ones that you and she love so much, which makes me think why don't we go in and make some peanut butter and black currant jelly sandwiches. They can't make up for things you never had but it reminds us of what we've got now."

Calum gets out of the car, shuts the door and leans on it, looking over the roof at Ian, who shuts the door on the passenger side. "She talks to you, Ian," he says across the dark top of the car. "What does she say to you?"

"Not much. We don't talk a whole lot. When I'm home I read a lot. Mostly we listen to the radio, or she tells stories, or fiddles, or we make jelly or quilts. Old-fashioned stuff. Once in a while she gives me some advice."

"Like what?"

"Like, whatever you do, don't let life stand in the way of your dreams."

"Abraham?" Yvette hollers to him against the wind, watching him standing there at the other end of the garden as if wondering what to do. "It's for the corn. Dig a trench, about four inches or a little more so we can fill in around the stalks as they grow, just like the leeks. We don't want the wind to knock them off their roots. I'll be there in a bit to help put in the seeds."

He doesn't answer but waves a salute to show he heard but then he stands still, his two hands resting on the handle of the garden fork, the foot of his bent leg resting on the shoulder of the prongs, his eyes fixed. Yvette, trowel in hand, digs into the compost and watches him stare at the horizon.

☆ ☆ ☆

Ian carries the last box of groceries out the back door of the Co-op grocery store, down the steps and places it in the back of the truck. He shuts the tailgate and closes the two doors of the cab of the half-ton Ford. With his deliveries ready to go he walks back through the double doors of the store into the back shop, pulls a banana from a stalk hanging from the ceiling. He continues down an aisle surrounded by wire racks of seeds, cartons of canned goods, shelves of dry goods, boxes of hardware, plumbing supplies, small farm equipment and tools, some furniture, kitchen and bathroom appliances, animal feed, pet food, boxes of apples, oranges, pears, just about everything light enough for two, three or four men to lift, small enough to fit into the box of a half-ton pickup truck: an old-fashioned store trying hard and hopelessly to compete in an encroaching supermarket world, its customers diminishing almost as fast as churchgoers attending Mass across the street.

He sits on the end of a row of hundred-pound sacks of oats with his feet propped up on a carton of canned corn, looks at his wristwatch, then at the

swinging double doors of the main shop as Marie steps through and he begins to
peel his banana.

They sit in silence on the bench of oats. He puts his arm around her
shoulders and she leans into him. He whispers something through the hair
hanging over her ear and she lets out a little yelp, leaps from his embrace,
knocking him off the sacks onto the floor, and flees across the space and through
the swinging double doors into the front shop.

☆ ☆ ☆

"Abraham," Yvette yells across the garden into the wind. "What
is it?"

He doesn't budge, stands rigid, a statue, eyes fixed. Yvette
straightens up from the wheelbarrow, drops her trowel to the
ground, walks across the garden and puts her hand over his
knuckles on the handle of the fork. "What is it, Abraham?
What? Are you all right? Are you hungry? Are you sick?" He
turns his head and looks at her.

"Yvette?"

"What?"

"Who am I?"

She gives him a long look. She takes him by the wrist with
one hand and peels his fingers off the garden fork with the
other and leads him out of the garden toward the barn. "Come,"
she says. "We'll feed the pigs. No training necessary. You dump
the food in the trough, they eat."

He stops her. "Yvette?"

"Never mind. Come on, enough garden for today. We'll
talk. Feed the pigs first. Then we'll eat. And rest. We're tired."

"And talk?"

"Yes, Abraham, we need to talk. But first, the pigs."

"Okay. Sounds like fun."

The pig pen is a corral, a pole fence on three sides built out from one side of the barn. Inside the corral, against the wall of the barn, are two shelters like two large dog houses, so that each of the pigs could take refuge from the hot sun or otherwise nasty weather. Inside the barn Abraham loads a bag of feed onto a wheelbarrow and pushes it out and over to the rail fence. Yvette cuts open the bag and Abraham lifts it over the top rail and pours each of two troughs full of feed.

"You might think it's fun now. We'll see how you like it when it comes time to kill them."

"You kill them?"

"Somebody has to."

"Yeah?"

"Unless," she laughs, "you want to eat them alive."

"Yeah, I guess."

"Think you could do it?"

"I don't know. How do you do it?"

"You shoot them. And you cut their throats. You hang them up to bleed. Then you butcher them. Pork chops, bacon, roasts, ribs. Lots of fun."

"Is that what the rifles are for? In the closet?"

"Yes. The big one for pigs and deer. The little one for rabbits."

"I don't know. I don't think I've ever done anything like that."

They lean against the top pole of the corral watching the pigs gobble up the feed. "Don't worry, Abraham," she laughs. "I'll train you. First I'll give you a swatter and you can kill some mosquitoes. Then some black flies, then some houseflies. Then we'll dig some worms and you impale them on hooks and use the fishing rod to kill some fish. That's when we start eating." She looks at him with her laughing eyes. "Then you can take the axe and chop the head off a chicken for dinner, then after a few chickens you can take the .22 and kill some rabbits. That's not too hard." She picks a long stick off the ground and laughs. "Look, you just whistle when you find one running through the woods—" she whistles and the dog who is hovering around a circle of clucking chickens looks up and wags its tail "—and they'll stop and look at you with their pitiful little eyes and wait for you to whistle again and you shoot." She whistles, aims the stick at the dog and makes shooting noises. "Just work up from killing small things to bigger things and after a while you'll be able to kill anything."

"Did your father teach you that?

"I learned that from Kuznetzof."

"Who is ...?"

"He's a Russian. He wrote *Babi Yar*, a novel. I didn't read it, it was in English I suppose, translated, too much for me to read, but I read about it."

"You read a lot."

"Yes. But don't worry," she says, picking up the empty feed bag, "I'm just teasing you. We send the pigs to the abattoir. You won't have to kill them. Just feed them. And eat them. In between is somebody else's job. Just don't think about it." She ties the empty feed bag around the top pole of the corral. "We feed them all summer, they feed us all winter. That's the way it works. Just like the vegetables."

Yvette has two pigs, one to sell and one to eat. As she predicts, getting the pigs to eat is not a problem. And after the pigs are satisfied she takes Abraham by the hand and leads him back to the house. They sit at the kitchen table and drink tea and eat muffins and Yvette tells him how she met him, took him home, dressed his wounds and taught him to speak French. She tells all the details she can think of whether or not he already knows them, prolonging the story, trying to gauge his reaction.

He stares at her through the long story looking astonished, half amused, half agitated and at the end, blank, impassive, silent. With a touch of panic in her voice Yvette says, "You couldn't speak, Abraham. I taught you how to speak."

"I could speak. I couldn't speak French."

"I thought you forgot how to speak. The doctor said you had amnesia."

"I do have amnesia. I don't know who I am."

"Did you remember something today, in the garden?"

"You abducted me. You kidnapped me. You stole me from the hospital."

"Abraham, my dear." She puts her hand over his on the table trying to smooth, to lighten. "I took you home to heal your wounds. To teach you. Look at you. You're better. You're almost a farmer." She gives a weak laugh. "You can milk the cow, you can feed the pigs, you can plant leeks, you smile, you laugh."

He takes a moment to consider her words. In the silence the dog comes into the kitchen and sits by his chair. He reaches down and scratches the dog's ears and lets him lick his hands. "I think I used to have a dog," he says.

"Look at the wounds on your back. If you could see your back, they have all healed, and they healed in the form of letters, a sentence written on your back."

"Really." He smiles.

"Yes. A beautiful sentence."

"What does it say?"

She gets up from her place, walks behind his chair, lifts his shirt off his back and writes with her finger across his back.

"Can you read that?" she says.

"Just the first letter, J," he says. "I lost track after that. What does it say?"

"It says, *J'y suis, J'y reste, Je ne m'en souviens pas, mais je suis content,*" she laughs, goes back to her chair and squeezes his hand across the table.

"I'm sure," he says. His smile is gone.

"I read a lot, as you know, but I don't always read exactly what's there, if it's boring sometimes I read what I want to see. It's often a lot more interesting."

He feels his forehead and smiles. "My body is better but my mind is half gone," he says and after a silent moment he blurts out, "You can't just take people prisoner."

Exasperated, Yvette gets up from the table and leans over the teapot, her two hands on the stove. When she calms down a bit she says, "What are you saying, what do you mean? You came with me, you stayed with me."

"You took me. You hid me. You hid my clothes. Where could I go in a bed sheet? What about the hospital? Do they know you took me?"

"Somebody asked after you and I told the truth. I said I took you home. They didn't believe me. It was very busy. They don't remember. Yes, I hid your clothes. You didn't know where you were. I thought you might wander off and get lost when I wasn't here. I had to go to work."

"Where's my wallet?"

Yvette comes back to the table, pours some tea into her mug, puts the teapot back on the stove and turns to him. "When they carried you into emergency you had no wallet. You lost it, maybe, or somebody stole it. Who knows? It was gone. Nobody knew who you were. You didn't talk. Not a word. The doctor said amnesia. I thought you forgot how to talk. In the garden, did you remember something?"

"Yes."

"A woman?"

"Yes."

"Where were you? What were you doing?"

"I was in the grocery store where I worked. In the back."

"What was she doing?"

"She was crying."

"Why?"

"Because I was leaving, I think."

Yvette returns to the table, folds her arms and stares at the plate of muffins. Abraham gets up, goes to the stove for the teapot and fills his mug. He sits again at the table, leans on his elbows with his chin in his hands and stares through the window at the light fading on the horizon. She waits for him to speak. Finally he breaks from his reverie, takes a sip of tea and speaks.

"What are you thinking, Yvette?"

Yvette puts her thumb under her chin, her forefinger between her teeth and bites on it, moving it from side to side and biting, finally speaking out of the side of her mouth.

"I'm trying not to cry."

She laughs then cries. "Abraham," she says and she puts her hand on his shoulder and gives it a little squeeze and looks at his eyes. "The grocery business, you were in the grocery business. My uncle Pierre runs a grocery store in Quebec City. Maybe I can get you a job. I'm pretty sure. I told them there about you and they are very curious to meet you. Especially Pierre. He thinks he's my father now that my father is dead. Working could help you to remember; doing what you used to do. If you work in a grocery store you might remember more about that part of your life, and then you might remember everything. But you keep away from Thérèse. She's my cousin, but I think she's a witch anyway," she laughs.

"What's wrong with her?"

"She always wants whatever somebody else has."

"Is she good looking?"

"She thinks so."

"What do you think?" He smiles.

"I think she's a little overexposed. But look, you're smiling. That's better. You're teasing me. Maybe she'll remind you of the woman in the store. Maybe then you'll know what you want. Maybe when you remember everything you'll leave me and go back to your other life. Maybe I'll cry when you leave, if you leave. But we better find out before we plant any more leeks."

"Does she have a boyfriend?"

"What do you care?" She smiles. "Yes, Georges, he works there too. Very nice fellow."

"Is my name Abraham?"

"I don't know. I called you Abraham because you came to me from the Plains of Abraham. Maybe I should have called you Montcalm or Wolfe," she laughs. "I might think different about you. What was her name?"

"Who?"

"Who? Who do you think?" She mock-punches him on the muscle of his arm. "Don't play with me. The woman who was crying in the grocery store. The woman you were leaving. The woman you are thinking about."

Now Abraham is biting his fingers. He closes his eyes.

She comes through the swinging double doors from the main store with her lunch in a brown bag and sits on the oat sacks next to Ian. He puts his arm around her shoulder, offers her a bite of his banana. She shakes her head. "No," she says, "keep your banana, I've got an apple." She leans into him and speaks. "What do you want?"

"You know what I want."

"Yes. And you're going away. Tomorrow. Great."

"Everybody goes away, Marie, like they say, down the road. I'll come back." He whispers something through the hair hanging over her ear and she lets out a little yelp, leaps from his embrace, knocking him over the sacks and onto the floor, and she flees across the back shop and out through the swinging doors to the front shop.

In the darkening kitchen, lit only by light leaking from the hall-way, Yvette warily watches the movements of his face. She sees him smile and wince as silence and darkness deepens around them. The windows turn black in the moonless, starless night. The grandfather clock in the living room runs out of momentum and the tick-tock stops. When his face settles into a stare she says, "You were leaving. Where were you going? Stop biting your fingers, you're worse than me."

"I was leaving to join the air force."

"Do you remember that?"

"I remember some. It's coming back in bits and pieces."

TEN

You can't go home again.
            —*Thomas Wolfe*

WHAT AMAZED IAN even more than the amazing future he imagined for himself as a fighter pilot is how easily he left his past behind like a forgotten suitcase full of inessential clothing. He got on the train in Sydney and watched the harbour and then the rest of Cape Breton's lakes and wooded hills disappear into oblivion.

In Halifax his knowledge caught up with him and he eased through the tests and interviews for the air force, finding the answers to the questions as if by instinct. He had been an indifferent and distracted student in high school and he soon began to realize that his grandmother's storytelling and his own voracious reading, which had allowed him to escape stormy and rainy days when baseball and hockey were impossible, had helped him pass high school exams for which overnight cramming did not much dissipate the fog between his brain and the curriculum. And now it rendered him more knowledgeable and articulate than most of the young men who preceded him in those military chairs of inquisition. The psychologist and medical doctor could find nothing wrong with his mind or body. He vowed his loyalty to Queen and country and signed his name by the X on the bottom line, committing himself to five years of dedicated service.

He was amused to discover that although he was going to join the air force they provided him with train tickets to transport him to his destination. At the station he bought a paperback copy of Jack Kerouac's *On the Road* and once in his seat buried himself in it, sparing himself the lakes, rivers and wooded hills of Nova Scotia, the flat fields of the Tantramar Marshes and the long wide rivers of New Brunswick. By the time the train reached Quebec he was cocooned in his upper berth and rode through the dark until he emerged somewhere in Ontario as if from a tunnel. At the train station a corporal escorted him up to street level and into a van and whisked him off to a Canadian forces base a dozen or so miles out of town.

The base, an isolated community of isolated communities, contained various messes for the various ranks: the officers' mess, noncommissioned officers' mess, the other ranks' mess, the permanent married quarters (PMQS); aircraft runways, hangars, parade squares; several linguistically isolated NATO communities from Norway, West Germany, Italy, Belgium, Turkey and more. Most of the flat land was pavement, punctuated with carefully shaved rectangular lawns and artificial-looking real trees. The people were mostly men. The few women who appeared in the open seemed only to exaggerate the community's insulation. There were no dogs or cats except those living with families in the PMQS, which were set back, as if an afterthought, behind the base proper and the few animals belonging to the families were either housebound, roped or fenced in the yard. The only visible sign of chaos were the uniforms; the military was still in the process of unification and the new rifle-green outfits were interspersed with the old blues and khakis.

Ian, sequestered in his own unit, a squad of about thirty aspirants, found ways to increase the chance that he would be one of the dozen who would be passed on to flight school after orientation, indoctrination and training.

Having been exposed to Hollywood war movies depicting army soldiers being eaten alive by drill sergeants, he was relieved to discover that basic training was a matter of endurance: run faster, shoot better, climb higher, stand at attention longer, make your bed, shine your boots, clean your rifle, press your uniform, shut your mouth better than everybody else. Ignore the mental and physical abuse, treat it with the inward smile of a connoisseur of B movies. Just do what they ask and do it better.

The officers, the non-commissioned officers and even his fellow aspirant cadets in the barracks, who looked askance at the little library he had collected over the years, little realized that this collection of paper was a subset of a bank that provided him with the currency to quickly absorb the manuals of information and transform them into clear, precise and correct answers to oral and written questions. The details of military history, etiquette, ethics, rituals, of meteorology, navigation, geography, theory of flight, he scanned quickly and they flowed fluently from his mouth or his pen.

The downside of his intellectual armory presented itself only twice in his progress from the ground to the clouds. In Halifax, the interview was inching along smoothly until one of the officers asked him if he had any hobbies.

"I write poetry," Ian said.

The two officers turned quickly toward each other and exchanged a glance.

"What kind of poetry?" the other officer asked.

Alarmed, Ian replied, "Oh, just jingles for the high school newspaper."

"Do you have any other hobbies?"

"Hunting," Ian lied. "And sports, I play baseball and hockey," he said, mixing in the truth. All three faces relaxed and breathed a silent sigh of relief.

At officer training school a second alarm bell rang while the duty officer and sergeant were doing their routine inspection, checking his bed, his rifle, his boots and uniforms. The lieutenant examined his little collection of books stacked on his foot locker: Kerouac's *On the Road*, Steinbeck's *The Grapes of Wrath*, Durant's *The Story of Philosophy* and a few others. "What's this about?" the lieutenant said in a crisp British accent.

"It's just a bunch of essays about philosophers."

"Philosophers. What do they do?"

"They think. They write," Ian said, getting nervous, while the sergeant stood back and looked on amused.

"I hope you're not one of those," the lieutenant said, holding the book between his thumb and first finger and putting it down on the footlocker. He moved on to the next bed.

The sergeant lingered a moment, picked up *The Story of Philosophy*. "Young sir," he said, "if you don't mind, I'll borrow this. I'll bring it back as soon as I finish it, and I'll bring you a book you might like. In the meantime, put your books inside the footlocker."

Ian graduated from officer training and moved on to flight

school. He began training on Chipmunks and moved on to more and more complex aircraft until he was flying F-86 Sabres, Starfighters and Voodoos and was penciled in to fly with the Snowbirds aerobatic demonstration team when the floor fell out of his daydream in the sky.

☆ ☆ ☆

Ian cannot remember his ascending career in the military but when he tells Yvette he remembers leaving to join the air force, she asks him if he remembers anything more.

"Like I said, some of it, bits and pieces."

She waits, watching his face in the shadows, across the kitchen table in the darkening, silent kitchen. She waits. She gets up, goes to the cupboard for a candle, which she puts on a saucer and places on the table between them. She ignites a piece of newspaper on a burner of the electric stove and lights the candle. Then she goes to the grandfather clock, winds it up and starts the tick-tocking of the time. She sits again and watches in the flickering light. "Tell me," she says. "Tell me a bit you remember."

☆ ☆ ☆

Ian flies his saber jet fighter aircraft into the sun across the top of a cloudbank, noses down through the white clouds, heads toward the airfield, drops to 500 feet, tries to drop his wheels and nothing happens. He tries again. Nothing. He calls in his problem and listens for a while.

"I don't think so," he says into the mike. "Come and get me. I'll be in the lake." He skims under the clouds until he comes to the lake, then climbs to 2000

feet, flattens out until he finds a hole in the clouds, aims his aircraft at some empty water in the middle of Lake Ontario and bails out.

☆　☆　☆

"Wow," Yvette says. "What happened then?"

"They gave me the boot. A medical discharge."

"You hurt yourself jumping out?"

"No, I landed in the water and floated. They got me pretty quick. My body was okay. The medical discharge meant I was crazy. Psychologically unfit, I think is the way they put it."

"Wouldn't you need to be crazy to be flying around in one of those things?"

"I wasn't really crazy. That's not what they meant. They needed to get rid of me and that was the easiest way. They were probably right. The shrink explained it to me. 'Look,' he said, 'you were sliding around on the air with two tons of crippled aircraft strapped to your back and they wanted you to land without wheels so they could test their new procedure for crash landings of crippled aircraft. In that situation a sane pilot jumps.' 'That's exactly what I did,' I told him."

"So, what was the problem?" Yvette says. "You did the right thing."

"Well, he explained it to me. 'Jet fighters cost a lot of money and now they'll have to buy a new one because you threw yours into Lake Ontario. That's crazy. So from your point of view you're sane. From the air force point of view you're crazy. But we won't put that on your discharge papers. They will say, Honourable discharge: for the greater efficiency of the service.'"

Yvette gets up and steps around behind the stool he is

172

perched on and leans into his back, snuggles her head next to his, reaches her arms under his and takes his hands and squeezes. "Did you mind getting the boot like that? Do you remember how you felt about that?"

"Yes, I did mind. But I think I changed my mind."

"Why?"

"I'm trying to remember. I remember the padre, Father Ouelette."

"What did he say?"

"I'm trying to remember."

Yvette brews a pot of strong tea and laces it with a bit of new cream from the cow, brings down two of her favourite *fleur-de-lis* cups from her mother's china cabinet and places them on the table with a plate of her biscuits and homemade butter. She takes a handful of hair at the top of Abraham's head, tilts it back and plants a long kiss on his lips. "I'm glad they gave you the boot, because if you were still there you wouldn't be here even if you hadn't gotten killed, but even so you've got to stop running in front of taxis." She crosses the kitchen and brings the tea she'd left steeping on the stove and pours their cups full.

"I don't guess I'll be in a big risk from taxis walking or running between the house, the barn and the garden. There are lots of dangers in a prison but getting hit by a car is not one of them." It is a sore point between them.

"Prison," she laughs uneasily. "You're not in prison. You're not a prisoner. This is your hostel; you're a guest. And you know, sometimes hostels can become homes. You just have to stay in them. You couldn't go to town in my father's clothes, especially to find a job. I could have made them over on the sewing machine but there's no way to make the legs longer, or the arms.

Anyway you've got work clothes now. You can go out any time you want. But I think we'll go and get something more stylish and a better fit. I'll take your measure again. I can't wait to do that, I think about it all the time." She grins. "Especially the pants. Let's do it after supper. No, it's getting late; let's do it now and eat later."

"And you're gonna get me a job?"

"That should be easy. You've been in the grocery business, and you can play baseball. That will clinch it. They're nuts about baseball. Show up in a splashy outfit and the job is yours, I'd bet the barn. And I can't afford to lose the barn. Come on, let's go to the bedroom and measure your legs."

"Could we plant some peas tomorrow? Is it too early for peas?"

"No, peas can go in the cold ground and they grow pretty fast. But carrots and parsnips and beets first. The more you remember the more I want to plant roots. Especially beets— they're full of blood and their roots go deep in the soil. They have only one leg and no foot on the bottom of it, so they can't go anywhere. Comforting but not much fun. I love them, but I love you more. You're more fun but we have to keep control of those legs and feet. Come on, we'll take your measure and we'll make supper and you can tell me what you remember about Father Ouelette."

☆ ☆ ☆

Father Ouelette sat at his office desk in jeans and khaki T-shirt trying to push a dark thread through the eye of a needle, the jacket of his military dress uniform draped over his knee. A

174

calico cat sat on the corner of the desk. She watched for a few minutes before jumping to the floor and walking to the corner of the room to examine the contents of her dishes of milk and food. She moved with a lazy contented rhythm, her feline beauty marred by a cloudy eye and an ear scarred in a recent battle. She sniffed the air over her dishes but without drinking or eating. She walked across the room, jumped to the windowsill, closed her eyes and purred, basking in the spring sunshine, unperturbed by Ian's knock or entrance.

The padre invited Ian to sit in the chair beside the desk. "They promoted me," he chuckled, "so I skipped lunch to change the rank on my uniforms." Ian watched the frustrated priest fumbling with the needle and thread then held out his hand.

"Want me to give it a try?" he suggested.

"Yes, indeed," said the priest, giving the needle and thread to Ian. "It's a job for young eyes. I'll make some tea." He went to the counter where he had a sink and filled an electric kettle full of water. "I suppose I'll get a new posting now. Seems to be an unwritten law, if you get promoted you get moved. I don't know why. We do the same work wherever we go, marriages, baptisms, funerals, confirmations, counselling, confession. So, I guess you're moving too."

"Yeah, but no promotion. I'm checking out. You're my last stop. You sign the sheet and I'm gone."

"You're going to be a civilian. What do you think about that?"

"Aach, I'm not sure. In a way I'm glad. I guess I'm not cut out for military life."

"You left home for it though," the priest said and sat at his desk again to wait for the kettle to boil.

"Yeah, I needed to leave home though. I needed a job for one thing. "

"Mmm, mmm. What about for another thing?"

"Well, I guess I just needed to leave home."

When the kettle boiled Father Ouelette went back to the sink, filled a tea caddy full of loose tea, put it in a Pyrex teapot and poured in the boiling water from the kettle. He turned his back to the counter and faced Ian.

"Are you going back home?"

"Yeah. To start with anyway. It's the only place I can think of right now. I was planning to go to Toronto and find a job there but I went down to visit my brother and I didn't much like it. He likes it. I guess I could get used to it. But I don't know, working in a factory, making pop cans…"

"It won't be there when you get back, you know." He poured tea into two mugs and brought them over to the desk, sat down in his chair, took the threaded needle from Ian and began to attach a crown to the epaulette of the jacket. "Ouch! I'm not very good with this needle, that's three times I've stabbed myself. My mother would have a fit if she saw me with a needle and thread. Sorry, I don't have anything to eat. Just cat food."

"I'm not hungry, Padre. Yes, that's what they say, you can't go home again."

Father Ouelette managed to get a crown positioned on an epaulette of the jacket and a needle and thread through two corners of it to hold it in place. "There now—" he smiled "—looks like I might get these things on yet."

"You think it's true? You can never go home again?"

"I think it depends on why you leave home and how long you stay away." While he talked the priest finished sewing up the sides of the epaulette. "When you leave to join the air force it's like becoming a priest. It happened to me twice, when I went to the seminary and when I joined the air force."

The cat on the windowsill rose to her feet in the sunlight, yawned and arched her back in a long stretch, dropped to the floor and walked lazily across to her dish, ate a few bites, lapped up some milk from the other dish, went back to bask in the sunlight of the window and resumed purring.

Father Ouelette finished sewing on the epaulette and looked up in triumph. "There now, that's one crown sewed up on one coat. That makes me half a major. Now if I can get another crown on the other epaulette, and do a few shirts and a couple more jackets, no matter how I dress a whole new level of underlings will have to salute me."

"What difference does it make?" Ian said. "People go away, they come back. The same people are there when they come back. The same schools, same churches, parents, sisters, brothers, old friends, the ball field, the hockey rink. It's all there."

"Yes, it's all there. The people are the same, but you are not the same, and you are no longer all there. I mean in both the geographical and the cultural sense. Perhaps you have heard this old joke: A man is coming home to his village and his brother is going to meet him at the airport in the city. A friend asks the brother how he will recognize him. The man says, 'He said he'd wear a black hat and carry a brown umbrella.'

'But what if there are other people dressed like that and you miss him?'

'If I miss him he'll recognize me.'

'How will he recognize you?'

'Oh, he'll recognize me easy enough. I haven't been away.'"

The padre continued. "When you go away you leave your history behind you, especially if you leave when you are young. Your village history, your family history, what you knew fades away, and you aren't there to hear the stories they wouldn't tell you when you were a child. You are away when occasions happen. Your grandmother dies and nobody thinks to call you in time for the wake. You make it for the funeral but have to leave the next day. The post-mortem circle goes on without you. Your cousin gets married and you don't know her well and you are on a course and can't get leave so you send a card and money. But you miss the party and the stories. Her husband and the kids will be strangers. An uncle is killed in an accident and you find out two weeks later."

He paused and took a few sips of tea. "After a while it's all like news you read in a newspaper. Even when you are there on a holiday your mind is half somewhere else and they treat you like a guest. Your allegiances change. A priest has his duty to his bishop and to the Pope who lives in another country. An airman swears allegiance to Ottawa and to the Queen who lives in England. When I visit my village in Quebec my cousins talk to me about family affairs but half the time I don't know who they are talking about and I am ashamed to ask. Sometimes I see my father laughing behind his hand at the way I'm speaking French." He laughed and looked up from admiring his work. "Have some more tea, Ian."

"Yes, Major Ouelette," Ian said and gave the priest a quick salute. "I will. You don't get good tea in the mess. Good coffee though."

"That's it. That's what happens. You lose good tea, you gain good coffee."

"Too bad it isn't that simple, eh?"

"Oh, I don't know. Probably just as well it's not simple. You haven't been in the air force for very long, but you'll find you've changed. You lose something, you gain something too when you do such a thing."

"What? Such a thing as what?"

"To join the air force, to become a priest, that sort of thing. I think of it as leaping out of history. Why would anyone leave everything he knows—family, friends, village—and leap to another world where he knows nobody? A sad but exciting thing to do. It's what they talk about when they talk about joining the French Foreign Legion. People call it escapism and I guess it is but it can be escape in a good sense. If it weren't for explorers I'd probably be a peasant farmer in France, half starved, and you'd be the same in Scotland. Adventures have good consequences and bad. You make your choices; you take your chances. Sorry, Ian, you came here for me to sign a paper and I end up giving you a sermon. It's an occupational hazard I guess."

"No, sir. This is very interesting."

Father Ouelette stood up and tried on the jacket. "What do you think, Ian?"

"Looks great. Good job."

"Good. I'll do the next one as a major, maybe I'll do even better. I'm just telling you this because you are going home and soon you will have to decide again. To leap or not to leap. Because that's the type of person you are. Your commitment is vague and general and hard to engage. It doesn't lend itself to gradualism. You made the wrong leap this time, joining the air force. You and the air force don't suit each other, but it changed you. I notice your faith is getting weaker. You miss Mass sometimes. You don't get to confession much anymore. That happens to a lot of people but in you it is significant. Have you ever considered the priesthood?"

"I've thought about it."

"I'm not surprised."

"Do you think I should?"

"Oh, no idea. Probably not. Like the air force it doesn't suit most people. But you are the type. You'll have to think it out. Think hard, but don't join the French Foreign Legion," he laughed, "that wouldn't suit you either."

"Why do you think the air force doesn't suit me?"

He handed Ian the needle and another length of brown thread. "Here, thread this for me again, would you? I'll answer your question but it might sound like another little sermon." He smiled. "Have you got time for that?"

"Oh yeah, my immediate future is empty."

"I've watched you play ball. You're a good athlete. Did you ever notice a lot of good athletes are not good umpires, and umpires are not particularly good athletes? Umpires are good at paying attention to arbitrary rules and making quick decisions. They don't have to think. They don't create, they don't have to and they're not supposed to. They don't care what happens next, they know it will be something they will recognize, so they don't bother to imagine what might happen, they wait until it happens and they record it. It's happening to somebody else."

He sewed while he talked, looking up over the top of his glasses at Ian. He was getting better at it, more rhythmical and now seemed to be enjoying the experience.

"If you had to fly your aircraft from here to Europe you'd have to struggle to keep yourself awake, never mind keeping alert.

You know what they say about military life, ninety-nine percent boredom, one percent terror. You'd be an awful umpire, distracted by the beauty of the plays and missing the consequences of them. A fighter pilot who wants to stay alive needs to be a great athlete and a great umpire at the same time. Do you understand me? It's something you should know about yourself."

"I think so. I'm not sure I like it."

Father Ouelette passed a jacket and a crown to Ian along with a needle and thread. "Here, how about you sew one on. Even though I'm getting better, my fingers are getting numb. Now if you were in the American air force you'd probably be in Vietnam. You'd pay attention because if you didn't you could expect to get killed. Of course you'd have to kill other people and you might not like that."

"Isn't that what the military does—kill people?"

"Not necessarily. Where I come from every farm has a dog. The dog's job is to keep other animals away from the farm, not to go to the next farmer's land and kill the guard dog there. But if any critters come into the dog's farm he chases them away and if they don't run he kills them. That's what an army is for. The dogs in neighbouring farms bark at each other to remind them and other animals that the farms are guarded but they leave each other alone as long as they stay on their side of the fence.

"As a ball player, if you were an outfielder you would probably be a failure. You'd be distracted in the boredom of waiting for something to happen. But as a pitcher every play is a possible crisis and you are forced to pay attention. If you were in Vietnam you'd pay attention all right."

"Perhaps I should go to the United States then, join up there."

"Why would you want to be a dog in somebody else's yard?"

He let Ian think about that for a while and concentrated on his sewing. Ian sipped his cold tea. "You probably saved your life by bailing out of your aircraft," Father Ouelette said after a long silence. "And the air force may have saved your life by packing your bags for you."

"I guess it's a consolation. I can't be a pilot but I'll stay alive."

Ian finished sewing another crown onto an epaulette and sat back and they sipped their cooling tea in silence until Ian asked, "What about you, Padre? Do you like it?"

"Which, the priesthood or the air force?"

"Both."

"Truth is I find it hard to untangle them in my mind. They are very different but the consequences are similar. The priest's work is important—baptizing, hearing confessions, saying Mass, visiting the sick, comforting the dying, trying to teach people and himself there is something beyond all the fiddle-faddle we go through every day. And I guess we need the air force too, and the army and navy, although the daily routine is boring and an awful waste of gas." He laughed.

"Do you keep in touch with your family?"

"A letter now and again. I call my mother once in a while. And you?"

"Not much. If someone writes me a letter I answer it. But they're not much for writing letters either unless it's something important. I got a telegram once and it scared me. I thought my father had been killed in a mine accident but it wasn't that and now I can't even remember what it was. I can't even imagine why they would send me a telegram."

"You see? That's what happens. While I'm speaking to you now I may have a cousin in Trois Pistoles who is in some kind of trouble and I'll never hear about it unless I go home and happen to ask after him and even then they'll probably think, 'Oh, he's on holidays, don't bother him with it, it's over now anyway.' They never write me bad news. Except for my mother and father who will soon die, my relatives and neighbours have become snapshots and postcards. My brothers and sisters who stayed home know each other and our parents in a way I'll never know them because they have lived with them as adults. I lived with them only as a child. That is happening to you. If you go back and stay that would change after a while but I doubt you will. You're not the type."

"I could change."

"Sure you could. Go home, marry the girl next door, get a job in the plant or start up a little store and sell groceries, play ball with the boys, take your kids to hockey, join the Knights of Columbus, build a nice picket fence around your lawn, a little half-court basketball floor in the backyard, but you'll never forget your jump in the lake. Nobody in your world will ever have jumped out of an aircraft and that makes you exotic. You will always be different and you will always feel different and everybody will know that and give you a little more space than they give each other."

Ian finished sewing the crown on the jacket epaulette and started on a shirt. Father Ouelette poured more tea. "I wish I could say I'm happy," he said. "Sometimes I feel happy, when I'm baptizing babies or marrying happy couples, and sometimes I feel useful and even necessary when I counsel sick or dying people, but I have to confess what I feel most is comfortable.

When I go home I feel happy but uncomfortable. Here I am today sewing my new rank on my uniform. It's of no importance but it's nice to be promoted, to feel secure and know you can go on working. To know or at least to have the illusion that others think you are worth the money they pay you."

☆   ☆   ☆

Yvette watches him across the table in the fluttering candlelight. When Bougie the housecat, leaping to the table, knocks over the candle, Yvette thinks she sees a flicker of recognition in Abraham's eyes before the room goes black.

"Are you remembering?" she asks in the dark.

"I remember a cat."

"That's all?"

"No. I think there's more."

Yvette puts the candle back on the saucer and relights it as Ian relates his memory.

☆   ☆   ☆

The cat jumped to the floor from the windowsill, bypassed her dishes and pushed her head and body through the swinging cat door.

"There she goes." Father Ouelette smiled. "She'll walk around the house a few times and pee here and there, I suppose to let the vermin know she's still on the prowl. She won't be long now but tonight she'll be out for God knows how long and God knows where, looking for something to kill."

"A nice life," Ian laughed.

"Yes. For a cat. We have a saying back home. We say so and so is comfy as a kitten in a basket of laundry. That's me, sitting in my den with my needle

184

and thread happy as a kitten in a basket of laundry. Of course kittens grow up and become cats. It's my job to counsel you, and God knows, I may be overdoing it today, but this is my last chance. So take heed, Ian, you are a bit of a cat. Think hard before you choose what to do. You found out already that when you fly off into the wild blue yonder you may not be able to land back where you started. You might have to crash land or bail out and find yourself where you never expected to be."

"I'm a cat?"

"Yes, but a human cat. You think, so you suffer. Choose your suffering wisely. But make sure you choose it, or it will choose you."

"Cats have a nice life. Your cat soaks up the sun, purrs away like a furry little engine."

"They appear happy when we see them. But their real lives happen when we don't see them, in the dark, away from home. Unlike dogs, they don't belong to the house or anybody in it. You never hear of a one-man cat. Cats have no masters but their work in the dark. Their allegiance is to their work. They use our houses for inns and first aid stations. Like soldiers, they don't have homes, they have a home base where they march or fly or sail back to for temporary respite."

"They have families, kittens."

"Yes, the females have families, but the males don't bother with them and anyway the females abandon them as soon as they can find their own food. Or they leave them for others to look after. Their families are not their lives, just unavoidable interruptions. Like sailors, it's what they do in port. But cats are lucky, they don't have to think about it. But me, I do. Look at her when she's on the windowsill. Every once in a while she looks over at us, indulgent and amused, happy to have a place in the sun, rent free, while she rests up for her next adventure in the dark. Like me, she lives in solitude except when she's doing her work. Fortunately, I have a better job."

"What's her name?"

"Brief candle."

"What a weird name for a cat." Ian laughs. "What's wrong with Tabby or Ginger?"

"Never mind. Perhaps now you'll decide to go to university—that would be a good idea for you—and if you do you'll study Shakespeare and you'll come upon my joke and you'll get a good laugh and if you have forgotten me you'll remember me then. There now, I have both crowns on my shoulders but I'm afraid I've counselled you while I was still a captain. Would you like me to do it again as a major?"

"No, Padre. Just sign the paper, then I'll be a civilian and it won't matter."

"Okay, what about confession?"

"No, I'm not ready for that," Ian says.

The candle is nearly burned down to its setting on the saucer, little more than a blob of wax, and Ian and Yvette sit motionless in the shadows and the flickering light at the table, the teapot between them, the tea in their cups cold. Yvette's eyes wide and round as nickels stare at Ian's dream-like face as he ends, almost in a chant, his recollection.

"He called you Ian."

"Yes."

"That's your name, I suppose."

"Yes."

"I never heard that name before."

"It's Gaelic for John."

"Ah yes. My Saint John of the Road. Come with me Saint John, I want to welcome you back and remind you where you are," she says, and takes him by the hand and leads him like a sleepwalker to bed. "This is not a basket of laundry but it's pretty comfy. Take off your clothes and get in under the sheet, pussycat, I want to scratch your ears."

In the morning, in spite of the late hour going to bed, they both wake early and lay back, their hands behind their heads on the pillows.

"Are you comfortable, Abraham?"

"Yes."

"I'll call you Abraham. As long as you're here."

"Do you know the song 'The Cat Came Back'?"

"No, but I don't think I'd like it if I did."

"You don't think it would be encouraging?" Ian laughs.

"No. Cats always come back, so they say. But that means they always go away again. Your padre was wise about cats. Now, human cats, they have to think. And sooner or later they have to choose their suffering."

"I guess that's true."

"So this is your port, your respite, your home base. Your basket of laundry, your windowsill in the sun. Do you sail tomorrow? Do you fly the day after tomorrow? Do you fold your tent and march off next week?"

He does not answer her questions. They stare at the bedroom wall brightening in the golden light of the rising sun.

"Ouch!" he yells. "What was that for?"

"I'm scratching your fur. Cats like that. And they usually stay put while you do it. What are you thinking?"

"I'm thinking I still have some remembering to do."

"Tell me, Abraham, would you like me better if I got my teeth straightened?"

"What kind of a question is that?"

187

"It's an interesting question and practical and easier to answer than some of the other questions I'm asking. I guess I'm looking for a question you can answer."

"It's an interesting question but I don't have an interesting answer. I like your teeth the way they are."

"Well, I guess we're not going to go back to sleep. Today is a big day. You are going to fix the roof on the barn and I am going downtown to buy you some more clothes and tomorrow we'll both go to town and get you a job. You be careful on that roof because I hate to tell you but we are all out of parachutes. So tie yourself with a rope to the top because if you slip it's a crash landing for you and I'd have to take you back to the hospital and we'll see if you like it better there than here in your minimum security prison."

ELEVEN

Only sages know why pairs are lasting
Or why hair and bone make three out of two
—*Peter Van Toorn,* Mountain Tea

IN THE COOL of the next morning Yvette, with Abraham fitted now into a fresh outfit—a lightweight work-shirt under a windbreaker and a pair of jeans and running shoes—walk to the ferry, sail in the yellow sunlight across the St. Lawrence to Quebec City, ride up the funicular, walk up Rue St. Jean to a grocery store and stop while Yvette talks to a tall young man busy carrying boxes of produce from the back of a truck into the store.

"*Bonjour, Georges.*"

"*Bonjour, Yvette. Ça va?*"

"*Ça va bien.* Is Pierre in today?"

"I think. Ask Thérèse. She's on cash today."

They enter the store, a long narrow space with a kiosk forming a countertop and cash register near the door. Two walls of freezer space and three bulging aisles of general groceries divide the area into narrower spaces. Thérèse stands in the

189

centre of the kiosk and beams a smile to greet them. She is wrapped in a green smock partially covered by a white butcher's apron splattered with animal blood. Her hair, bunched in a net on top of her head, sprouts strands in every direction. But unflattering garments and wild hair cannot disguise the beauty of her tall athletic body or the energy flooding from her eyes, as blue as her hair is black, shining with confidence and mischief.

"*Bonjour*, Yvette, what is that?" she exclaims. Then she hangs her mouth open in a silent *O*, as she looks Abraham up and down. Then she turns her eyes on Yvette. "Well, look at you in your good dress and your nice old-fashioned shoes all shined up. Are you on a date?"

Yvette, stone faced, stares at her, making no attempt to hide her annoyance. "Is Pierre in?"

"Oh yes, he's in. Down in the meat market. You want to see him go right down, you can leave this one here. I'll look after him."

Yvette grabs Abraham by the hand and leads him to the other end of the store. Pierre, a stout, round man, wearing a white, spotless butcher's apron, looking like a jolly butcher in a children's story, comes out from behind the meat showcase.

"*Bonjour, Yvette. Comment ça va?*"

"*Ça va bien, merci.* Pierre, this is Abraham—" she puts her hand on his shoulder "—who I mentioned to you yesterday."

Pierre cups his hands around his mouth and yells at Georges, who is now in the store chatting with Thérèse, "Georges, could you come here a minute?"

Georges finishes his chat with Thérèse at the kiosk and ambles down the aisle to shake hands with Abraham.

"This is Abraham," Pierre says. "He wants a job. Yvette tells me he can drive a grocery truck; he's done it before. Can you use some help on the truck? When you're not too busy he could help me in the meat market."

Georges smiles and looks Abraham up and down, feels his upper arm, measuring the bulge of his muscle with his thumb and forefinger. "Seems healthy enough," he says and points to his head, "anything upstairs d'you think? Any lights on?" Georges pretends to check Abraham's eyes. "Thérèse is impressed," he says, "but I don't know if she checked the lights. Did you give him the test yet?"

"Not yet."

"Test?" Yvette says. "Are you kidding? What kind of a test have you got for a grocery jockey?" She opens the sliding window of the meat showcase and pulls out a T-bone steak and dangles it in the air. "Look at this, Abraham. What do you think—cow or shark?"

Abraham takes the T-bone from Yvette and lets it dangle between his thumb and forefinger. "Well it looks kinda fishy to me. I don't know, sardine maybe?" They all laugh.

"We do have a test," Pierre says, "a skill-testing question. And here it is, Abraham. Are you ready?"

"Fire away."

"Do you know the suicide squeeze? Yvette told me you could play ball, so we just want to check that out."

The pitcher catches the ball from the catcher, stares at the batter until he calls time and steps out of the batter's box, looks at the third-base coach for guidance. When the batter steps back in, the pitcher throws immediately with no windup,

the batter sets to bunt, the runner breaks, the batter ducks under the ball, sits on the ground and scrambles out of the way. The catcher catches the ball and stands astraddle the plate while the runner tries to knock him over but the catcher has lots of time to plant himself and is immovable. He tags the runner out.

☆　☆　☆

Pierre, Georges and Yvette stare at Abraham who stands in front of them with the T-bone steak dangling from his fingers. His eyes closed, a slight smile on his face, he seems to be weighing the meat. He opens his eyes and stares trance-like in silence at the T-bone while they wait for him to answer the question. Finally Yvette pokes him on the shoulder and, smiling encouragement, says, "Abraham, would you rather another question? I'm sure there are lots of questions."

Abraham lowers the steak and lets it hang by his thigh. He re-focuses his eyes and looks at Yvette and the others in turn and gives a little laugh. "No, that's fine. Yes, indeed, I know all about the suicide squeeze."

"I don't know what it is," Yvette says. "Tell me."

"It's in baseball," Abraham says. "The batter tries to bunt the runner home from third base. The opposing team has to anticipate the play and try to prevent them from getting away with it."

"Baseball," Yvette asks. "Why are we talking about baseball?"

"You know very well, Yvette," Pierre says. "Everybody who works here plays baseball."

"There you go, Abraham, you're a lucky man, you qualify. Not everybody would, certainly not me. Can you drive the truck, who knows? Can you cut meat, who knows? Can you tell the

192

difference between a sardine and a cash register, who knows? Can you squeeze play? Yes, of course. Well, that is the main thing."

"Will you play, Abraham?" Pierre says.

"I'd love to play."

"What position?"

"Pitcher or somewhere in the infield or whatever you need."

"Are you good?"

"Depends on how good the batters are."

"Would you be willing to coach the girls' team?"

"Sure."

"You got a girls' team?" Yvette asks.

"Yes."

"Everybody in the store plays?"

"Yes. Everybody."

"She plays?" Yvette asks, pointing down the aisle to Thérèse who is standing in her cash kiosk smiling at them, sending them a little finger wave. "She plays baseball?"

"She's the captain of the team."

"Can I play?"

"Well, can you? If you can play, you can play."

"I don't know the squeeze play, or any other play for that matter, but Abraham can teach me. I can learn. But now I have to go, I have some shopping to do." She embraces Abraham, kisses him, gives him a stiff look and walks down the aisle. She attempts to hard face Thérèse and pass her by without comment but Thérèse, standing in the middle of the kiosk, stops her with one word.

"Thanks."

"For what?" Yvette says, stopped now and leaning over the kiosk, palms down, fingers splayed on the countertop.

"For the gift," Thérèse says, laughs and points with her head down the aisle toward Abraham.

"Hands off," Yvette says, trying to look menacing, but her diminutive body and delicate face make Thérèse, by contrast, look like an Amazon, and the more Yvette tries to face her down the more she reminds herself of a chipmunk. But she feels she can't move without saying something or she will lose something she can't quite define. Thérèse moves to the counter and places her palms opposite Yvette's hands so that they are eye to eye, nose to nose.

"You are married already? Hm? Engaged?" She looks at Yvette's bare fingers on the countertop. "I don't see a ring."

"Our rings are in our hearts."

"I guess that's a no," Thérèse says, smiling. "Sounds to me like he's just another fish in the river. I've got some bait, I'll take my chances. I'll throw in my hook, line and sinker, see what I can reel in. Did I hear you say you're gonna play ball, Yvette? You'll be on my team. I'm the captain. I'm also the pitcher. I think I heard he's a pitcher too. We can compare our curves."

Yvette's big eyes narrow to the size of two nickels on edge, her sensuous lips tighten to a line under her nose, her fingers curl on the countertop as if they are looking for a handle.

"I bet he could show me how to hold the balls, how to swing the bat. I bet I could show him a thing or so too. Sometimes the men and women play together. I love to pitch to the men. Sometimes I let them get to first base just to see their moves. Sometimes I let them steal second, sometimes third. Once in while I can't help it and a man might get a home run.

But mostly I strike them out. Or I let them get to first on balls and then I pick them off. Unless I like them."

Thérèse is having a lot of fun but Yvette is not amused. "Yes, they told me you played ball," Yvette says, acknowledging the three men at the meat counter. "I didn't know that, that you played, I didn't know that," Yvette says and realizes she is starting to babble and just stops. She needs to leave and walk off the weird pain in her belly, but she can't move. She feels like jumping over the counter with her claws out but she knows how ridiculous that would look to the three men. She can feel them watching. They can't hear the women talking but they can feel the tension.

"Oh yes," Thérèse taunts, sensing the audience of men watching, "baseball, soccer, basketball, any game with balls in it. Especially baseball. I specialize in the squeeze play." She slowly licks her lips, and Yvette, against the advice of the voice in her head, the voice of caution, straightens up, hauls off and slaps Thérèse in the face.

The two of them freeze, face to face, their three hands still on the countertop, their fingers almost touching, Yvette's right hand still in the air, the two women frozen for an eternal moment like two obsidian sculptures while Pierre and Georges race down the aisle. Georges takes Yvette by the hand and leads her away. Pierre takes Thérèse and brings her to the meat counter. Abraham, startled and immobilized, just watches.

Moments later Pierre hands the meat cleaver to Thérèse with a grin. "Perhaps you feel like hitting something, Thérèse. Here, take this and whack those pork chops, break a few bones. You'll feel better and you won't go to jail. What the hell was that all about?"

"I was just teasing her. I think maybe she lost her sense of humour. I never knew she was like that."

"Now, Thérèse, you were pissing on her gatepost. It's not easy to keep your sense of humour when someone is doing that. It's a lesson we have to learn."

"Are you the baseball coach or the sexball coach?"

"All the games have rules, Thérèse."

"You know what, Pierre?" Thérèse slams the cleaver down on a rack of pork chops, sending half a bone flying across the room, the tip of the meat cleaver stuck an inch deep in the chopping block. "You are the coach of the ball game not the coach of the sex game. Yvette needs to learn a lesson, and if she thinks about it she will. I owe her a whack but I think I'll let it steep for a while. Maybe by the time she learns to play ball she'll be tough enough to take it."

Yvette flees the grocery store, her grim-faced head hanging, her shoulders hunched, her hair falling past her ears over her shoulder and bouncing as she hurries along the sidewalk looking at her shoes jerking in and out from under the hem of her dress. She comes upon three little girls in an alleyway, two of them swinging two skipping ropes, the third between them skipping double-dutch over the swishing ropes and singing.

On a mountain stood a lady
Who she is I do not know
All she wants is gold and silver
All she wants is a fine young man.

The rope tangles in the girl's feet and when they stop and see Yvette watching them they stick out their tongues at her and flee down the alleyway, laughing and dragging the ropes behind them. Yvette laughs too, shrugs her shoulders and walks on.

When she comes upon a McDonalds coffee cup discarded on the sidewalk, she kicks it along, one shoe after the other, banging it in a three-quarter rhythm that begins to make her feel a little better, kick step step, kick step step, until finally the toe of her shoe catches the inside of the cup and she kicks it high into the face of Father Légère who grabs it on the ricochet off his nose and, smiling, offers it back to the startled, embarrassed Yvette.

"*C'est à toi, Yvette?*"

"*Je m'excuse,*" she says, then she recognizes him. "Oh, it's you. I'm so sorry."

Father Légère stands smiling, his tall frame a little bent, the battered cup in his outstretched hand, his other hand gripping his grey beard. He wears a grey flannel sport coat over a white shirt and a blue-and-grey, julienne-striped tie, grey flannel slacks, horn-rimmed sunglasses hiding his eyes and on his head a grey fedora with a wide black band and the brim pulled down over his forehead. Except for the glasses he looks like a bearded, septuagenarian Gregory Peck playing the retired, aging Tom Rath in *The Man in the Grey Flannel Suit*.

"Never mind, Yvette, never mind, it's only a paper cup, no damage. Good shot though, right on the nose." He laughs.

"I didn't know you at first. But now I recognize your voice and the beard and the smile. Other than that all I can see is your nose. I don't think I've ever laid eyes on you outside the church. Come to think of it, I've never seen you out of your soutane."

"I know. Nobody recognizes me now. I'm surprised you did."

"Well, I barely did. Just by a nose," she laughs.

Father Légère laughs too and looks at the crumpled cup in his hand. "Your cup is empty," he says. "Let's go and I'll buy you a cup of coffee."

"You want to go to McDonalds, it's back there."

"No, no, let's go to Le Duche on Rue Étroite." He throws the paper cup into a wire garbage basket attached to a utility pole.

"I've never heard of that place."

"Not many people around here know about it, but I find it's a nice comfortable spot. Not busy. And once in a while I run into an old friend there. It's one of my favourite little retreats. Only the older crowd goes there; you seldom see young people, well, except for the two idiots they hired to work the counter."

Halfway down Rue Étroit they arrive at a small portico, actually a fancy hole in the wall of an archaic firebrick building. It contains a couple of imitation Roman pillars, set back from the sidewalk in a small dark recess and nearly invisible from more than a few feet away. Even in the brightness of the day the available light barely exposes a dull green neon sign on a thick black oak door identifying the place as Le Duche.

Inside, Le Duche is glimmering under the glare of neon lights that hang from the ceiling and reflect off the linoleum floors, formica counter, round table tops, and the plastic seat covers of the wire-legged chairs surrounding the wire-legged tables. The tables form a circle around a hardwood dance floor shining with wax. A handful of similar chairs and tables form an inner circle on the dance floor itself.

A counter runs along most of the left wall. Behind the soda fountain, leaning over the counter, head to head, sipping milkshakes from the same glass through two straws, two teen-agers, trying unsuccessfully to look like Jimmy Dean and Sandra Dee, mug at each other and patently ignore Father Légère and Yvette, the only two customers in the shop. Father Légère leads Yvette to a booth across from the soda fountain.

"Have a seat, Yvette. I'll get your coffee. I don't know if they make good coffee here, I don't drink it myself, it burns my belly."

Father Légère manages to persuade the Sandra Dee look-alike to serve him and brings back to the table a tray of food and drink, a coffee for Yvette and for himself a cherry coke, a banana split and a large paper cup full of french fries. He brings two spoons so Yvette can perhaps share the banana split. He hands her an extra straw so she can try the cherry coke. He places the tray on the table between them with its contents like a puzzle for Yvette to solve, takes a quarter from the change on the tray beside his sunglasses and goes to the end of the room to a huge Wurlitzer jukebox dressed in red-and-yellow neon tubes and silver- and gold-plated strips of metal. Inside the machine, behind a convex window, an accordion of 45 rpm records fans in a semi-circle in front of a turntable.

Behind the jukebox a panoply of pictures of mid-twentieth–century celebrities paper the wall: Marilyn Monroe in a white shawl, print skirt, black umbrella and stiletto heels smiling as if delighted with the cameraman's joke; Yogi Berra, blocking home plate and reaching to tag out Jackie Robinson; Willie Mays, at the top of his leap, his back to the camera, making a spectacular catch in centre field, the ball like a vanilla ice cream cone caught in the web of his glove. Mickey Mantle, Joe DiMaggio, Ted Williams, taking their famous swings, the ubiquitous Elvis

Presley, Pope Pius XII, Bill Haley and the Comets, Alex Guinness marching his squad of sorry-looking POWs across the bridge on the River Kwai; Humphrey Bogart and Ingrid Bergman standing in their hats and trench coats in the foggy airport in Casablanca; Gregory Peck, his arms around Grace Kelly, reassuring her as he is about to face a showdown with four outlaws out of prison and determined to murder the man who put them behind bars; Marlon Brando, Hank Williams, the real Jimmy Dean and Sandra Dee and a host of dimmer luminaries.

Yvette leaves the booth and walks across the dance floor between the tables to watch as Father Légère works the jukebox. A bank of tags identifies the names of all the tunes on the records inside, and beside each tag a button to push to set the machine in motion.

"I know what this is," Yvette says as she looks through the window at the fan of records, "but I've never before seen one. They don't make records like that anymore. They must be old."

"Just like me——" he smiles "——old, and they don't make them anymore. If you want a tune you put in a quarter and press the letter/number button that corresponds with the record. The recordings are all by the Duke Ellington Band and the various singers he hired."

Father Légère casts a cursory look at the list of titles to make sure nothing changed since his last visit, drops a quarter into the coin slot, presses D3 and they walk back and sit in the booth. He smiles and says, "So, what do you think of this place?"

Ella Fitzgerald, accompanied by the Duke Ellington Band and noises from the scratchy record, sings "In My Solitude."

"What is that?"

"That's a banana split. Try a bite. It's just a banana sliced in two down the middle with a filling of ice cream and cherries or whatever else you want to put in there. I like peaches but they don't have any here."

"A banana sandwich."

"Yes, and this is a cherry coke, take a sip with the banana sandwich—they go together, like a horse and carriage, as we used to say. Here's your straw."

Ella sings:

In my solitude, you haunt me
With reveries of days gone by
In my solitude you taunt me
With memories that never die.

"They're nice and tasty, but I don't know if I could eat or drink a lot of these things. To me they're very sweet. I recognize the french fries though. I like to make my own, but I'll give one a try."

"Yes, in those days grease and sugar were the order of the day. It's my little indulgence, my little treat in my little retreat. Try the french fries with a little of this," Father Légère says and takes the salt and vinegar shakers from a tray at the side of the table. "A little salt, a little vinegar and you have a paper cup full of transubstantiated french fries. Please excuse my little ecclesiastical joke."

"What a sad tune. But she seems to be enjoying it."

"Yes. It's funny how people like to be sad. She reminds me of my girlfriend when I was a teenager."

"So you split up?"

"Yeah. She got tired of waiting for me to make up my mind.

It never occurred to me then but now I think maybe she thought I was a homosexual, or gay, as they say these days. She teased me a bit, nearly driving me crazy, but in those days nice girls didn't believe in the test drive. Too risky."

"Are you sorry about that?"

"Who can tell? Who knows the consequences of a path not taken? One thing though, although she is in her seventies now, when she haunts my reverie she is still a beautiful, vibrant young woman with a long mane of black hair down her back. No doubt she has a husband and children, grandchildren, and a host of problems, but I know nothing of that. I imagine she still lives, if she lives at all, in New Brunswick where we lived in those days. We spent a lot of time dancing in front of the jukebox. 'In My Solitude' was one of my favourite tunes and I guess it still is. Perhaps that tells me all I need to know about myself."

They sit in silence, listen to the music and nibble on the french fries. Father Légère takes a spoonful of his banana split, lifts it into the air, holds it a moment and says, "But what about you, Yvette? Why are we talking about me? Anyone would think you are the priest and I was the penitent and this pseudo soda fountain was some sort of psychedelic confessional. Not that I think you are a penitent. You seemed pretty sad yourself today out on the street, and a bit angry, kicking your coffee cup and staring at your shoes."

Yvette smiles and thinks about it for a minute and decides to tell Father Légère about her encounter with Thérèse. She tells him how she met Abraham and how their relationship developed, and how Thérèse made her so cross she slapped her face. And now, instead of being cross at Thérèse, she's down on herself.

"There you go," she says. "I never knew I could be so talky."

"It always helps to talk about it. It's not too serious, Yvette. She was probably just pulling your leg."

"I guess that's right. I guess my sense of humour abandoned me. But now what do I do?"

"Apologize. Find out what she likes and bring her a gift. Nobody can resist that. Is that why you're not going to church, because you're living with your friend?"

"No. I left the church when my father died. I kept going for his sake after my mother died. It meant a lot to them, going to church; I couldn't break their hearts. And my father needed someone to go with him. He needed to go. It was a big part of his life."

"So do you believe in God?"

"I try to." She smiles.

"That's a good answer. That was Saint Peter's answer. He said: 'I believe. Lord, help my unbelief,' or something like that. We all have our doubts, that's normal, but don't you think the church could help you try?"

"No, I don't think so. I've spent a lot of time reading about it, thinking about it."

"Ah yes, Quebec writers have not been kind to the church. And what have you learned from your reading?"

"Mostly they think the church is just a suit of clothes that power puts on to make it look harmless and helpful to people who believe, and dangerous to people who don't."

"Power? Now what power do I have, Yvette? I can't even get people like you to keep going to church."

"You're not part of the power, you're part of the suit. Do you want to know why I think people don't go to church anymore?"

"I do."

"Because they don't need to. They have their own sources of information."

"But when they want to get married they come. And a lot of people come at Christmas, and Easter, even Ash Wednesday they come and get a smudge on their foreheads. And they want their children baptized. And when their loved ones die they want them buried by the church, they want a priest."

"Of course. Those are things they need. It's not just their religion; it's their identity. It's what they belong to, their group, their family, their relatives. But they don't need priests telling them what they can do and what they can't do. They know what's legal and they avoid what's not and other than that they do what they think is right. Sometimes they're wrong, they make mistakes, but sometimes the church is wrong too."

"Do you pray?"

"I pray all the time."

"What do you pray for?"

Yvette nibbles on a french fry, snipping off a few small bites. "I don't pray for anything, I just pray. You know what? I'm not crazy about vinegar on french fries. Funny thing though, the last time I was in church I did pray for something. It was half in fun but the funny thing is my prayer was answered."

"You sound like a regular St. John of the Cross. Maybe we're too serious when we pray. Why do you pray at all? Myself I really like the vinegar. The salt too, though I'm not supposed to eat salt. High blood pressure."

She sticks her hand deep in the paper cup and pulls out an unsalted, un-vinegared french fry and takes a bite. "The french fries by themselves are pretty good though. But not as good as the ones I make for myself. I'm not an atheist. I know a lot of the Quebec writers say they are atheists, which I think is pretty stupid. To me an atheist is like—I don't know if I read this or if I just made it up. An atheist to me is like a speckled sea trout coming in from the Atlantic Ocean and swimming up the St. Lawrence River, and guess what? Looking for water."

"Good lord, Yvette, I should get you to write my sermons. Will you get married to your friend Abraham?"

"I don't know. When he gets all his memories back, will he stay? I don't know. Who knows what voices will call to him? I know he had a girlfriend who cried when he left. If he goes back to his memories I guess I'll be left singing in my solitude."

"All right then, if you decide to get married give me a call. You'll need me for that," he laughs. "And then maybe I'll see you for baptism and confirmation and Christmas and Easter, and maybe Halloween," he laughs again. "If you're not an atheist you must be a theist. Why do you say you try to believe? How do you try?"

She finishes off the french fries and tries the coffee but it is too cold. "I guess what I meant was not quite that. Like if you asked me, do I believe there is a universe? I would say yes. If you asked me if I understand it I would say I try to, but it's too big for me. I try to, I'll keep trying, but I don't guess I'll ever get to understand more than a bit of it, and I don't guess anybody else will either."

"Some people do think they understand it."

"Yes and they probably do, but I suspect they are thinking of a very small universe. Or maybe they think the part of it they understand is the whole thing. Some people probably think they understand God too but I imagine it must be a pretty small

God. But what do I know, I'm just a farm girl with a few books. Didn't even finish school."

☆ ☆ ☆

Abraham immediately makes himself a useful employee, hauling in supplies, stocking shelves, delivering groceries when Georges is not available, relieving Thérèse or Pierre at the kiosk or the meat counter. He seems to know how it all works, especially as a cashier, teasing and flirting with the mostly women customers who keep coming back for fun if not for groceries.

Yvette, apprehensive, watches the grocery business from the sidelines, but she practices hard with the ball team every evening and discovers she likes it and learns a lot faster than she ever thought she would. Her diminutive body is compact and sturdy and what she lacks in power she makes up for in speed on the base paths and quickness on the field. Because of her size she is difficult to pitch to. When she crouches at the plate as Pierre taught her to do, the strike zone between her knees and her armpits almost disappears and to throw a strike a pitcher has to place the ball in a space the size of a small roasting pan. So the choice is easy: walk her on four balls or throw strikes down the middle of the zone and you better have wicked speed or a lot of movement on the ball and hope the ones she does hit are picked up by the infielders.

Abraham, a useful and profitable grocery store employee, soon becomes an all but indispensable member of the ball team. After many practices and a few pre-season exhibition games, Pierre knows he has a winning pitcher on his team. Georges, the catcher and team captain, begins to feel that the team's tactical and strategic problems can be solved and he feels free to worry about the team's personal problems.

In their fourth exhibition game with runners on first and second and one out, Georges calls time and goes to the mound to talk to Abraham.

"What's up, Georges?"

"Just a chat. They might be thinking a double steal. I want to give them time to think we know what they're up to. If we get one of them they'll still have a man in scoring position. If we get neither they'll have two. This guy is not a good hitter but the next guy is a sure clutch hitter. This one might try to bunt them over but he's not good at bunting either. If he tries and I get to it first I'll go to third for the force out. If you get it you might not have time to turn and get the runner at third, so go to first for the sure out."

"Play ball," the umpire yells, but Pierre calls time out from the dugout and runs to the mound.

"If we strike him out," Abraham says to Georges, "we can walk the next guy. I've watched the guy after him, he couldn't hit a barn with a pan shovel full of beans."

"What are you doing?" Pierre says.

"Just chatting, Pierre. Did you ever hear of a pan shovel?"

"Abraham, I know you understand the squeeze play. Did you ever pitch against it?"

"Why?"

"You've been pitching games and practices since we started and nobody has ever got to third base. Does anyone ever get to third base with you?"

"Just Yvette," Georges says.

"Don't get him going, Georges."

"Don't kid yourself," Abraham says. "I'm not that good. These hitters just aren't used to me. They'll soon figure me out."

"How do you know how good you are or who you played against before? Do you remember?"

"Here he comes," Georges says. "The umpire."

"What I do know," Abraham says, "is that you have to have more than a fastball and a change-up. But I do remember a few things. I get flashbacks nearly every day, bits and pieces."

☆ ☆ ☆

Ian stood on the mound, two feet on the rubber, hands hanging by his side, glove in one hand and the ball in the other, staring under the bill of his ball cap at the batter. He holds that position until the catcher feels the umpire is about to lose patience so he calls time and runs out to the mound.

"What's up?" Ian said.

"The usual, just take a minute but, careful, the umpire is getting pissed off. Just remember we got a party tonight; we want to celebrate a win not a loss. We got two strikes on him. Throw him a fastball across the buttons, make him think, push him back a notch, then a change-up on the outside. He'll swing like a windmill."

TWELVE

In the Big Inning, God created heaven and earth.
—*Wilbur Evans*

A DRY, HOT, ALMOST STILL summer evening. The sun sits on the horizon and spreads a maroon glow over the wrinkled skin of the St. Lawrence River. On the ball field in the meadow beside the river, weary from the heat, dirty with dust, their lungs parched, skin wet with sweat, the players yearn for the game to end, but the plays seem to inch along in slow motion. Abraham on the mound, his eyes squinting against the sun, wipes away the sweat falling from his eyebrows with the sleeve of his jersey. He peers in to pick up the sign from Georges crouched behind the plate. His team, the Patriots, scored early and lead by one in the bottom of the ninth. One out, a runner on first.

Pierre calls time out, trots onto the field and beckons Georges to the mound to chat with Abraham. "Got a curve ball at all today?" Pierre says and Georges and Abraham shake their heads.

"No, I don't think, too chancy. I might hit him," Abraham says. "The next guy is a good hitter. We need this guy."

"Play ball," the umpire yells.

"We need the double play," Georges says. "The next two batters are clutch hitters. This is our best chance to finish the game."

The umpire yells again, "Play ball."

"Fastball low inside for a strike," Georges says, speaking quickly. "He won't know it's coming, he'll never catch up with it or he'll foul it off. After that he'll swing at anything. Throw him one high and outside. If he swings he'll probably foul it. Then maybe a change-up for a strike. He'll be hoping for a walk but if he swings he'll flub it on the ground. The guy on first is too slow to steal second. If we get two strikes on him they might try a hit and run, so keep him tight at first. If he strikes out we might get the guy on second if he's running. If we don't get the double play we'll have to deal with the next guy."

"Here comes the umpire," Pierre says. "Let's go. Don't piss him off at this stage of the game. Say something nice to him, Georges, and mean it—no sarcasm. Abraham, you wet the ball with a little sweat, you got a cup of juice backed up over your eyebrows, just let it drop when the ump turns his back, make that fastball jump."

Georges puts his mask on behind the plate, turns to the ump. "Sorry about that, ump. I got something in my eye out there, hard to get it out." He hunkers down behind the batter. Abraham stands on the rubber and stares at him until the batter calls time and steps out. When the batter gets back in position he throws to first base, forcing the runner to scramble back to the bag. After that the play goes as planned and the batter flubs a hit back to Abraham for an easy double play.

In the dugout Pierre congratulates everyone and they pack their gear. "See you all at the pub. I think the women's team is there already, and now it's party time. We beat a good team today."

Abraham, Yvette, Georges and Thérèse, still in their uniforms, dry now and cool in the air-conditioned bar, still in the sweet and sour sweat smell of their afternoon effort on the field, sit and sip beer from their draft glasses half listening to Dianne Dufresne's voice drifting over the room. All four men's and women's teams are there, the winners and the losers, relaxing, teasing each other, reviewing the best and the worst moments, almost everybody in a good mood.

René, Pierre's brother, the manager of the losing team, is not in a good mood. He and Pierre stand together at the bar, beer bottles in hand. Despite Pierre's teasing, René can't drop the scowl from his face.

"Did you run into a bottle of sour beer or what, René? Losing a game is not the end of the world, man. Lighten up for God's sake. Everybody's happy, we won but only by one run, your best game so far. You have to be pleased with that."

"Where did you get that guy, Pierre?" René says, pointing his beer bottle at the table where Abraham, Georges, Thérèse and Yvette sit laughing.

"Who, Georges? You know where I got him. He's our nephew, he lives in the big white bungalow across the street from your house. You must run into him once in a while."

"Very funny. You know fuckin' well who I mean."

"You mean Abraham, Yvette's friend. She brought him to me. He's a gift. You know nearly as much about him as I do. Truth is you know almost as much about him as he does about himself. He has amnesia. She found him hurt in the street; she nursed him back to health. He says he comes from Nova Scotia. He's okay. I like him. He works at the store—good worker too. Customers like him. He's good for business. And he sure can play ball. Don't tell me you're pissed off because we beat you?"

"He can play ball all right, if you can call it play. Pretty vicious."

Pierre smiles, turns to the bartender and orders another beer. Outside the glass door of the pub the wind is pushing scraps of paper along the sidewalk and at the same time the first drops of rain dot the dusty windows. Pierre takes his beer from the bartender and turns back to René.

"Vicious? He's not vicious. He's a little bit ruthless. You know that, to be successful in business, in baseball, in almost everything, you have to be a little bit ruthless."

"Oh yeah, Babe Ruthless."

"Anyway, what are you talking about? He hasn't hit anybody yet."

"He's burning the buttons off our shirts. It's only a matter of time. If we didn't have helmets I wouldn't send anybody up to the plate with him on the mound. It's too dangerous. This is not pro ball, you know. This is for fun. It's no wonder they can't hit anything when they're all the time getting ready to jump back."

"He's just trying to prove himself in a new place. They're not used to him, his style. They'll get to know him once they've seen him a few more times. He'll make them better hitters. Make them think."

"You're beating us with an Anglo."

"Maybe that's the problem, René. Your batters are thinking in French and he's pitching in English."

"Oh yeah, very funny. You're great at making up smartass answers. I'd laugh if you weren't pissing me off. Smartass answers don't change anything."

"I don't understand why it's getting up your nose," Pierre laughs. "He's not an Anglo, he's a Scot from Nova Scotia, *Nouvelle Écosse*, I guess you'd call him a Nouvelle Scot."

"Scot, Anglo, same fucking thing. Wolfe was a Scot, or at least his soldiers were when they climbed up these hills and took our country."

"You know, René, baseball is like music, it's the same in French or English. And it's a game, it's not the battle of the Plains of Abraham."

"Nothing is the same in English."

"Beer," Pierre says, lifting his bottle up to René's nose.

René thinks about that for a moment. In their silence Diane Dufresne sings "Ziggy" and some of the patrons move to the square of hardwood near the bandstand and begin to dance. "Not even beer," René says, "not even beer. Beer is not beer without talk."

"I'll tell you what, René, I'll tell him to back off the fastball, but he'll have to use his curve ball. He's more likely to hit them with that, but at least it will be slower. Maybe if they get hit a few times they'll realize it's not fatal."

While Pierre tries to sweeten René's disposition and re-establish baseball as a friendly duel using non-lethal weapons, Georges, Thérèse, Abraham and Yvette try to negotiate a truce in the game of hearts. Their ball caps sit on the table next to their beers, the glasses half full, the pitchers of beer on the table half empty, the mood jovial in spite of a residue of wary tension left over from the grocery store encounter between Thérèse and

Yvette. Their dust-covered faces bear the look of teams happy with each other after good performances, enjoying a well-earned rest and a glass of cold beer.

Georges smiles and points to Yvette and Thérèse with his thumbs and forefingers of both hands raised in the form of non-lethal handguns. "Now here's the thing, cowgirls," he drawls in a Gary Cooper imitation, "will you be okay with the table between you or should we tie your elbows to the armrests of your chairs?"

"Oh, you are altogether too funny, Georges," Thérèse says. "Don't you worry about us, we had our little misunderstanding. I made a little joke and we all understand that now. You know we're cousins. We've been fighting since we started trying on lipstick. Like sisters."

"Yes, I'm sorry, Thérèse," Yvette says. "I'm sorry I gave you a slap. A stupid thing to do. I hope it didn't hurt too much."

"It takes more than a slap to hurt this cowgirl, girl, but if you do it again I'll send you a message and it won't be through my lawyer."

"Okay then," Georges says, "it's settled. You belong to me, she belongs to him."

Thérèse gives Georges a straight look, a false laugh and a punch on the shoulder. "I don't belong to anybody," she says, "but I think maybe he belongs to her. After all, she stole him from the hospital. He's a bit of a hostage, don't you think?" Thérèse makes a little humming laugh to show she is just trying to keep the fun going.

"Don't start that again, Thérèse," George says.

"Why not, it's just in fun. You want us to talk about the

weather? It's too hot and sweaty so don't remind me, if you don't mind."

"I just took him home," Yvette says, "to heal his wounds."

"Yes," Thérèse says with a fat smile aimed at Abraham, "he had an arrow through his heart. Or is it you, Yvette, with an arrow through your heart? I understand he's got excellent therapy for that. Sometimes it's hard to tell who's the nurse and who's the patient."

"Okay now," Georges says, palms up in a mock plea for peace, "enough of that. Let's talk about baseball. I hear the women played a great game today."

"She grounded out three times." Thérèse points at Yvette and holds up three fingers. "Three times."

"Yes," Yvette says, "but I got a double and batted in a run."

"Yeah, but that's one run. I batted in two runs. And we won by two runs."

"Yeah, but you made an error that cost us a run, so my run made up for that."

Now they are laughing a little easier and getting deeper into the beer. "That's the spirit," Georges says, "if you have to fight, fight over something that doesn't matter, then we can all go home laughing with lots of good stuff to talk about at work tomorrow. Not like René over there growling about politics, Québécois this and Québécois that, the Anglo cultural invasion, the American cultural invasion, blah, blah, blah. Look at the face on him. Poor Pierre is getting a sermon. What do you think, Abraham?"

"Good chance it's me he's yakking about. He doesn't like my close shave fastball. Did you hear him yelling from the bench, calling me the Barber of Seville? And look at the knives he darts from his eyes when he aims them over here."

"It's nothing personal, Abraham. You're just an insignificant soldier in the army of the Anglo cultural invasion and your fast-ball is but a symbol, an extension of the guns of the Plains of Abraham to the Baseball Diamond of Abraham, and once René gulps down a couple more beers he'll be mellow. Let's dance. This party's getting too talky."

Diane Dufresne sings her melancholy songs. The last light of the sun fades from the horizon and clouds roll in under the stars, blackening the windows of the sports bar. Like shadows in the dark the pairs from the men's and women's ball teams dance their weary legs in a fog of beer and fatigue.

Yvette dances with her ear against Abraham's chest, her eyes wide and pensive, searching, one of her hands pushing against his right shoulder, the other clinging to his left, their athletic bodies, barely moving, balance in the rhythm of the music.

"I can hear your heart beating, Abraham."

"You're trembling, Yvette, what's wrong?"

"I'm scared."

"Yvette, don't worry."

"You remember more and more."

"Yes, but don't worry."

"You tell me not to worry. You don't tell me you won't go back."

Abraham stares over her head across the room. An explosion of thunder and a gust of wind blows a shower of raindrops clattering against the panes and bursts of chain lightning light up the black windows like a wall of blinking, weeping eyes. When the room returns to the dusk of dim light all the dancers stand frozen. Their pupils, dilated by the radiance of the lightning, now adapt to the renewed gloom. Wonder fades and everybody knows it's time to go home.

Later, back home, their last-minute chores done, Abraham and Yvette bring their fatigue and their beer-buzzed brains to bed. Usually, after the games, especially after a double victory, they are sexually alert in spite of their fatigue, but this night Abraham lies on his back, his head propped up on pillows, hands behind his head, eyes on the ceiling. Yvette lies under the sheet that covers them, her tiny body curled against his arm, her hand on his belly, her eyes wide, waiting.

"Yes," he says finally.

"What?"

"Halifax, I remember Halifax."

"And the woman is there?"

"Yes."

"The same woman?" she asks, with a worried look. "The one you left behind at the store?"

"Yes."

"Is it sexy? Don't you lie."

"Yes."

"Turn out the light."

"What for?"

"I want to show you something."

"What?"

"You'll see."

"In the dark?"

"Yes, I'll show you how to see in the dark."

He stretches his arm and switches off the bedside table lamp. The room turns coal-black except for the occasional dim flash of lightning blinking in the window and silent except for the faint lament of distant thunder and the gentle patter of raindrops against the pane.

"Now then, Abraham, will you tell me everything?"

"Yes, I think so. What are you doing?"

"I'm not doing anything. What do you mean, you *think* so? I want to know everything. If it's anything embarrassing write it down."

"What are you doing?" he says. "How could I write anything down? It's totally dark, and I haven't got a pencil. What are you doing?"

"Looking for a pencil maybe. But it's not me, it's my hand. It's walking down your body. It's looking for something. What could it be, I wonder? It's walking down the hill, searching through the bushes, searching, searching, nothing this way, just a big old leg, nothing that way either, just another leg. Whoops, how many legs have you got? Is that another one? An extra? Is that it? The hand is searching. What's it looking for? Yes, yes, it's clapping its fingers and laughing, it wants to borrow the extra one. Now whatever you have to say, write it down in the morning, it's too dark in here for writing, and anyway I've got your pencil."

☆　☆　☆

When Yvette wakes up in the morning she is startled when her hand moves to touch Abraham's body and he is gone. She listens. No sound in the house. She gets out of bed, wraps herself in the sheet. She looks out the bedroom window, the kitchen window, the living room window. The sun is rising above the river, brightening and warming, refreshing the fields, their thirst quenched by the rain. Overnight a south wind blew the thunder-clouds north into the mountains. Back in the bedroom Yvette peers through the window, still shining from the night's rain, and watches Abraham as he walks out the barn door. He heads for the house carrying a cardboard box. She stands still as she hears him come into the house through the back porch door, stop for a few moments in the kitchen then leave through the front door, shutting it quietly behind him. She clutches the sheet tightly around her body, runs to the living room and watches him walk down the driveway, across the road and over the field, down the hill toward the ferry. In the kitchen she finds his note on top of the cardboard box.

Yvette, you asked me to write it down. I've been keeping a journal. What I remember is in it. I'm going to town. See you later, Abraham.

Yvette opens the box and finds four notebooks the size of school scribblers. She sits down at the table with one of the notebooks, opens it to the first page and reads:

Today Yvette taught me how to plant leeks. It is hard to imagine such tiny seeds growing into the strong, substantial plants we sell in the grocery store. But it's only been a month since I remembered the one word, Halifax, and already that one word hidden in a furrow of my mind is growing into a blossoming, complex story, and I am left to wonder if perhaps Marie was right.

"Right about what?" Yvette whispers to herself. She flips through the pages, every one filled with Abraham's writing in a very clear hand as if the writer intended or expected someone else would be reading it. Although Yvette speaks English with difficulty, she can read it well enough. She picks up another notebook and opens the cover to the first page. No dates, no titles, no indication if it is the first, second, third or fourth, just a series of entries of various lengths, some just a line or two, some several paragraphs, and as she turns the pages she sees that some entries are several pages long. She stops turning pages somewhere in the middle and reads:

Halifax. I came to be a seminarian but I went to see Marie at the hospital because Father Angus asked me to look her up and said she would take me to the seminary. Show me where it was. But as it turned out, show me where it wasn't. Father Angus knew Marie was a former girl-friend, he knew too that the seminary was gone, the contents sold or given away and the building a shell about to be demolished. He probably knew too that a group of partners had taken the contents of the seminary and transformed them into a restaurant. He could have told me all that but he didn't. I suppose he thought the irony would have more impact if I experienced the transformation myself. Did he guess? Did he hope for what happened between Marie and me? He would certainly know it could happen if Marie and I were thrown together with a bit of wine and song and unfinished business from the past. Did he want us to get back together? He had that quirky sense of humour. He would enjoy thinking of the possibilities. I know he didn't like the idea of me becoming a priest.

Yvette puts the kettle on to boil, put two handfuls of tea into the pot, goes back to the bedroom, throws the bedsheet back on the bed and fortifies herself with underwear, a pair of jeans and a work-shirt. She takes a look at herself in the mirror as she buttons her shirt and says to her image, "Brace yourself, girl, this does not look good." She goes back to the kitchen, pours boiling water into the teapot and while the tea steeps she stands by the table and reads a couple of passages at random from two more notebooks.

Glace Bay. Marie was a clerk, packing the boxes with groceries, and I was the trucker delivering boxes to the customers who had phoned in their orders. We were pretty thick, Marie and I. It started the first day I came to work and we enjoyed our times together, but in the end...

I don't yet remember joining the air force but I remember leaving it, Father Ouelette giving me advice.

She pours a mug of tea and sits at the table and finishes reading all four notebooks. Then she arranges them as best she can in a time sequence and reads them again, making a few notes.

When Abraham comes back she is still sitting at the table sipping the last of yet another pot of tea, her face blank, as if in neutral, while her mind wanders among a maze of questions that all seem to have multiple correct answers. Abraham's face is a mixture of relief, apprehension and curiosity.

"You finished reading the notebooks? Do you have any questions?"

She laughs. "You sound like a teacher."

"You're staring at the notebooks. I thought you might be psyching yourself up to get started."

"I'm staring at the future."

"What do you see?"

"I can't see anything. The past is in the way. I've got amnesia in reverse. Just like you couldn't recall your past when you had a future here, now I can't get by your past, at least with what I know of it, to look into the future. You were born here, Abraham, but now you are Ian. How can that work?"

The sound of the name Ian startles them both into silence. He holds on to the kitchen chair across from her and they stare into each other's eyes. Ian speaks first.

"I wasn't born here; I was hijacked."

Another long silence. Then, in their stillness, Yvette speaks.

"Abraham was born here. Ian was born in Nova Scotia. Who are you? Where are you from? And what are you talking about? Will you get over it? I picked you up off the street like a bird with a broken wing. I nursed you, nourished you, housed you, taught you to farm, to speak French, got you a job, even a baseball team to play on, and all you ever did was teach me how to fuck and you wouldn't even do that until I seduced you and now that you've fucked me I guess you are a bird, a homing pigeon, you delivered your melancholy message, your broken wing is healed and you're ready to fly back home."

After this outburst from Yvette, Ian eases himself into the chair and in silence they stare blanks at each other until she gets up and makes a plate of toast and marmalade, another pot of tea and pours them each a cup.

"You can't just capture people and keep them prisoner."

"Yes, under lock and key," she laughs. "This is quite the jail. And behind what locked door did you pine for release? What armed guard kept a bead on you while you fed the pigs, milked the cow or chopped the heads off chickens? What ball and chain did you drag along as you weeded the garden?"

"You hid my clothes."

"I hid your clothes, your rags. Yes. You were traumatized. In a daze. What was I supposed to do if you wandered off while I was away at work? Yes, I hid your clothes, a tattered and torn T-shirt, a ripped pair of shorts and a pair of worn-out running shoes. Yes. But when I gave you new clothes you soon took them off again and mine too and you are still here with your clothes on and with your clothes off too. And where did you go today and why did you come back?"

"I took a walk. To think. Were you worried?"

"I don't worry about your walk. I worry about your think. The woman in the store, the Co-op, that was Marie?"

"Yes."

"Why was she crying?"

"I told you that. She was crying because I was leaving."

"And you left her again in Halifax."

"Yes."

"And are you leaving me?"

No answer.

"You abandoned her. Like she was a broken boat. You jumped off her like a drunken sailor. And now you say you loved her."

"I didn't say I loved her."

"No, you didn't say you loved her because if you said you loved her you would need to say more than that, and you would need to do something. You never said you loved me either, you just acted as if you did. And now you sit there looking at me as if you're seeing me through holes in the air."

Ian rises from his chair, walks around the table and puts his hands on her shoulders. She leaps from her chair and turns to face him. "Don't touch me!"

He jumps back from her ferocity. "What's wrong?"

"What's wrong! What's wrong! You know what you are? You

223

are a cat. Like your padre said. I bet he knew lots like you. You use our homes for inns, bed and breakfast."

They stand another silent moment, locked apart by tension.

"I talked to Pierre," Ian says.

"Your coach, your boss, and now your counsellor. And what did he say?"

"He said my decision is a hard one, but simple."

"So you're at the decision stage. Well, at least that's a step. And now Pierre is your guidance counsellor. And his advice?"

"He said if I want to know why I am here I should stay and find out. If I want to know why I left Nova Scotia, go back and find out."

"Well, I got my own counsellor. And I got better advice."

"Who?"

"Madame Teacup. You better sit down for this." Yvette sits across from him, takes her teacup off the table. "Here," she says and hands him her cup. "Swish it around and drain it."

He circles the cup in the air a few times and drinks the remaining cold tea and hands the cup to Yvette. She peers into the cup and studies the configuration of the leaves. "That is very interesting." She points a finger inside the cup.

"So what does it say?"

"Be patient. We're looking for the future. It's not easy."

"You're finding the future in a teacup?"

"I am beginning to think there is more truth in tea than in wine. And you can't trust the newspapers these days to tell you about the present, much less about the future. Well, well, well, look at this." She tips the cup so that he can see inside. "What do you see? What does it say?" she asks him, smiling.

"I see tea leaves. They're not talking to me."

"Ah ha, you can't read. Let me read it for you. It's an old Québécois proverb: *Qui prend femme prend pays.*"

He shrugs his shoulders, repeats the proverb in English. "Whoever chooses a woman chooses a country."

"There's more, Abraham. I'll call you Abraham for now. There's more. A little practical advice. Something to do," she says and she smiles a little wry smile and reads the leaves. "There is a congruence of events. Wipe the slate clean. Confront a stranger. Clear a path. Take a train, or a plane, or a bus, or a thumb."

He smiles. "Well, that's not for me. That's your cup, your tea, your leaves."

"No, we both drank from the cup. You drank last. You configured the leaves. The leaves kissed your lips. I can read your cup if you like, you can swish it around and drain it, but the message will be the same." She picks up his cup and offers it to him but he keeps his elbows on the table, his hands on his chin.

"How do you know?"

"Because I'm the one who can read," she laughs.

"You're giving me the boot? Why? Are you still cross? Because of Thérèse?"

"Thérèse. I can handle Thérèse. I've handled her already. She's not as tough as she thinks she is, and she's a real person, not a ghost from the past. I can't fight ghosts."

"So, why then?"

"I stole you, *remember?* Hijacked you, took you *prisoner,*" she says in a voice he has not heard before, louder and punctuated, *remember, prisoner.* She suddenly jumps up from the table, teacup in hand, and stands behind the chair, one hand resting on top of the backrest.

Startled, he says, "Okay, okay, let's say you didn't steal me, it's a matter of interpretation."

Her face goes blank but her eyes shine, her brows knit over them. "If my father were alive he'd tell me to go to confession. And if I went to *confession*, the priest would explain to me that if you *steal* something you have to be *sorry* for committing your sin and you have to make *restitution*. You have to restore what you *stole* or if you can't do that you have to *compensate*."

Her hand goes to her mouth. She appears surprised by her sudden vehemence. She goes to the sink and washes the leaves out of the cup, picks the teapot off the stove and pours another cup. "Well," she says more calmly, "I'm not sorry for what I did and I don't think I can be, and I can't think of anything to compensate with. I don't have anything valuable enough to compensate for such a valuable stolen object." She smiles, a hint of sarcasm tingeing the colour of her voice. "You can't compensate gold with tin. I thought my love would be enough. So I will have to make restitution. I will restore you. I stole you from the hospital, from your life, captured you, kept you a prisoner and now I release you." She leans back against the stove, closes her eyes against the steam of the tea and sips it as if she were counting to ten. When she opens her eyes she speaks deliberately. "Off comes the padlock. I fling open the gate. I got you new prison clothes. I got you a job in the prison grocery store. You had some fun on the prison baseball team. You enjoyed a pleasant relationship with the warden. Now you are free."

He gives up staring at her now and he hangs his head as she talks. "Go home, Ian, and find a suitable parole officer to guide you, get you reintegrated into society. I hope, while you served your sentence here, you became truly rehabilitated and that your new freedom will not overwhelm you, and trick you into re-offending and land you back in someone else's prison."

She falls silent, holding her teacup half an arm-length between them. Then she drops the cup, picks up his, swishes the remaining tea, tips it so he can see inside. "See," she says, "just as I told you it would be, the verdict is the same. Go home, if you have one."

"What if I want to stay?"

"Stay? Stay in jail? That's absurd. If you want to leave your life you have to leave from there. You can't leave from here. You can't get here from here."

"What will you do?"

"I will make strawberry jam to keep me company over the winter until the leeks arrive."

"How is the crop of leeks? I haven't checked lately."

"Nothing showing yet, but I can feel it coming along. Good-bye, Ian."

PART THREE

THIRTEEN

She would have been a good woman
if it had been somebody there to shoot
her every minute of her life.
—*Flannery O'Connor,* A Good Man is Hard to Find

HEADING FOR THE UNIVERSITY, Ian turns Senator's Corner and walks down Commercial Street past what used to be Eatons, past what used to be a drugstore called The Medical Hall, what used to be a restaurant called The Union Café, what used to be the Co-op, past the new enterprises that replaced whatever used to be in the era of coal mines and churches. Most of the plywood windows have disappeared in favour of glass. Patches of greenery and gaily painted park benches testify to a tax-supported effort to clean and brighten. As he walks he smiles and entertains himself by recalling the introduction to his major thesis in history which, after fifteen revisions under the critical eye of Father Angus, had burned itself into the grooves of his brain. He called it: *Ring around the Rosy, Pocketful of Posy, Ashes, Ashes, All Fall Down.*

"Glace Bay, the biggest town in Canada," boasted the publicity in the thirties; "Ole King Coal, the power behind the war," bragged the headlines of the forties. In the fifties the war was over and Big Oil usurped King Coal's throne and other people's oil fuelled Nova Scotia and the rest of the country, providing other people with jobs. And in the following years as plywood began to replace the glass of storefront windows and able-bodied men and women began "goin' down the road" to Toronto, Windsor, Calgary and Vancouver, the once busy main street, in accidental irony called Commercial Street, became the walkabout and park bench avenue for single teenage mothers pushing baby carriages and old-age pensioners, survivors of the coal mines, coughing away their twilight years.

At the bottom of Commercial Street he stops in the middle of the bridge over the harbour and watches the ducks. On either side of a walkway below the bridge two sets of preschool children holding on to a yellow rope, minded by two caretakers, one on each end of the rope, throw crackerjacks into the water. The ducks swim or take low flights chasing the food from one side to the other. Ian remembers his boyhood days, unsupervised diving and swimming in the dirty harbour. Now, at least, he thinks, it is a more affluent, safer, healthier world.

After King Coal was dethroned, several saviours, disguised as promises, scrambled ashore on the beaches of the bleak island: subsidies for the few inefficient coal mines still at work, subsidies for the neglected, inefficient steel plant, grants to build a heavy water plant, loans to support foreign-owned pulp mills, subsidies for the forest industry, subsidies for the fishery, the establishment of permanent, part-time or seasonal jobs subsidized by unemployment insurance benefits and welfare cheques and on and on; false prophets that just enabled politicians to scramble from one election to the next.

The proper authorities created a causeway, joining the island to the mainland of Nova Scotia and the Rest of Canada, to facilitate the flow of goods and services in and exports out in the new prosperity that kept fading like the horizon on a transatlantic voyage. Alas, the "Road to the Isle" became the "Brain Drain from the Isle," became the "Road to the Rest of Canada" for the lucky ones with educational passports in their pockets.

And the only thing left to brag about: beautiful stretches of spectacular coastline along a vast ocean reflecting the deep blue of the sky, and at each stop along the way, hostels dressed in tartan flags, and kilt-clad fiddlers and bagpipers celebrating the loss of a forgotten language. Tourists flowed in and out. Young men and women followed the sunset to join the army, the air force, the navy, and the factories waiting at the end of the road, hungry for trained and willing hands.

Finally, in cooperation with the zeitgeist, the proper authorities created a jewel, a university to educate and train the evacuees so that the rewards at their various destinations would be more lucrative and their jobs more interesting: accountants, teachers, journalists, editors, administrators, feeding into the burgeoning cities down the road, some of them even writing novels, making plays and movies about goin' down the road.

Ian leaves the bridge and keeps straight on up South Street, keeps on by the miners' museum until he turns up University Avenue, his hand slapping the trunks of the maple trees lining the sidewalk. He passes under the archway displaying the sign University of Glace Bay and walks along the cliff overlooking the Atlantic Ocean. In a fit of optimism, what used to be a baseball field and a dozen streets of company houses have been transformed into a baseball field and a university. It is already apparent that the ball field is diminishing foot by foot each year as the cliffs erode under the encroaching Atlantic Ocean. None of the professors in the geology department can or will predict when the earth will begin slipping from under the nearest building, the university chapel, but if asked they will say probably about the same time there are no priests left to say Mass; it seems to be part of God's plan.

Ian walks into the office and classroom building, keeps along the hallway until he finds the theology department and knocks on Father Angus' door. When he hears Father Angus' invitation he opens the door and sticks his head inside.

"Hello."

"Well, good God, look who's here."

"It's me."

"Where have you been? Did you get lost or what?"

They shake hands and embrace. Ian takes a look around. Books still line the walls, but the heaps of baseball paraphernalia he remembered strewn over the floor are replaced by still more newspapers and periodicals. A map of the Middle East hangs down over several rows of bookshelves. A skeletal map of the Middle East in the first century AD, on a piece of transparent plastic, is superimposed on the modern map. A small red circle surrounds a red map tack. A red string tied to the tack leads to a picture of a ruins identified as Sergiopolis.

"You got a new office."

"Yes. New. And exactly the same as the other one. The woman who had this office is now in my old office. I don't ask why anymore. I think it's the new attitude. The Kleenex attitude. Everything and everyone is identical now. You pull a professor out of his box and another one pops up. I did ask her how she liked her new office. 'I hate it just as much as you must hate yours,' she said. 'You can't open the window. You can't shut off the air conditioner that conditions the air by depriving it of oxygen. The florescent lights buzz like tinnitus so I have to sit in the dark on winter afternoons like a bear in hibernation. By three o'clock in the afternoon I get up and fling myself out the door and flop around the parking lot sucking up oxygen like a salmon on a riverbank gasping for water.'"

"There you go," Ian laughs, "you can almost tell she doesn't like her office."

"So, Ian, what are you doing here? I thought we were rid of you for good, especially since you never bothered to keep in touch. Do you ever write a letter, do you ever make a phone call? Have a seat. Tell me, what are you up to this time?"

"Back to school."

"Here?"

"Yep."

"For what?"

"Study theology, history, Gaelic, maybe help coach the ball team."

"You already did all that. You graduated, remember?"

"I got to be somewhere. I might as well be studying. Anyway I think I need a time out. Find out where I came from, where I'm going."

"Ha," Father Angus replies, shaking his head.

"What?"

"Never mind. So where did you come from? I mean just now. What have you been so busy with you couldn't let us know? Sit down and talk."

Father Angus' chair is loaded with small baggage, a kit bag, an overnight bag, a camera case, a set of binoculars in a case, his passport sitting on top of it all. He sits on his desk and Ian sits in a corner chair and tells him of his sojourn in Quebec, his accident, the baseball, Pierre and the grocery store, his relationship with Yvette, and his leaving.

"You just left her?"

"Well. She sent me packing."

"Ha again—" Father Angus smiles "—in fact ha, ha. Well, now we know where you were. So you just have to figure out where you are going. Looks like you might be going nowhere. But I do know where I'm going. You can coach the ball team but not with me. Colour me gone."

"You're fired?"

"Not yet. Let's say the bishop encouraged me to cultivate another garden."

"You're going to a parish?"

"Yes. Yes indeed. The oldest in Christendom, Sergiopolis."

"That's not in Cape Breton—must be on the mainland."

"Yeah, it is," Father Angus laughs, walks over to the map and points to the red circle. "The mainland desert of Syria. See, here it is on the map."

"Wow. That's a bit drastic."

"I'm one of the new breed of theologians. I don't so much read now as dig."

"Is this a good idea?"

"The bishop likes it, gets me out of his hair."

"And you?"

"I don't like the bishop's hair. And I'm getting a little tired of the pseudo-Gaelic crowd. This year somebody else can do the St. Andrews banquet and talk nonsense to a room full of chauvinist, drunken, displaced Scots who wouldn't know *Et tu, Brute*, from *Agus thu, Bonny Prince Tearlach*."

"What are you going to do in the desert?"

"Like I said, I'll dig. And like yourself, I need to do a bit of thinking." He picks up an imaginary guitar, strums and hums a few imaginary chords and improvises a few lines of 'Cotton Eyed Joe' in Gaelic.

Co ás a tha thu?
Càit' a bheil thu' dol?
Co ás a tha thu?
Eòis na sùla chotoin

"You know, Ian, the desert is a fine and private place, and none I think do there embrace. Good spot for a retreat."

"That sounds familiar. Who said that?"

"There now, you didn't pay enough attention in your English classes. While you're here you might as well take a refresher course. Try the seventeenth century. It's full of good stuff."

"When do you leave?"

"Pretty soon. Just have to tie up some loose ends."

"Really?"

"Really. So hello, goodbye, but first let's eat—the bishop is buying."

In the university cafeteria Ian, Father Angus and the bishop form an equilateral triangle around a circular table. The sides, however, are equal only in geometrical terms: the distance between each angle reveals nothing about the unfathomable mysteries separating the three men. Father Angus and the bishop, like two estranged lovers in another kind of triangle, talk to each other through Ian as if he were a wireless machine telegraphing their coded messages.

The bishop is a nice man, a fact Father Angus is willing to acknowledge, but he considers it a niceness unencumbered by a fertile intelligence. The bishop's naïveté and his innocence, the major components of his niceness, grate on Father Angus' nerves, particularly because they do nothing to mitigate his unwholesome ambition to reach administrative levels of power and influence beyond his level of competence. The bishop got to be a priest by dint of a modest intelligence aided by his athletic good looks and his consistent displays of piety. He was not eloquent but he knew what people wanted to hear. They wanted what he himself wanted. They wanted reassurance that what they already knew was sufficient, so he was well liked for his views and a popular priest. He got to be a bishop for all the same reasons and for being dependable and for his modest virtues: he is prompt and neat. His boat sits solid in the sea no matter what waves of controversy come to rock it off course. A slow boat, going nowhere, but unsinkable.

The bishop, of course, has a different view of himself. "You know, Ian," the bishop says, "—pass the pepper, please—it's great Angus is off to the first century. He was never at ease in the twentieth. Baseball, for example, was never his game even though he could play. Gladiating would suit him better. More blood to it. More whacking at things. Yes, he'd make a great gladiator. Too bad he was born in the wrong century."

"You're gonna study gladiating?" Ian asks Father Angus, just for something to say.

"Just a little analogy lad," the bishop says, like an amused professor addressing a student wearing a baseball cap pulled down over his nose, ignorant but brazen enough to ask a question from the back seat of a classroom. "Just a little analogy. I think of gladiating as a primitive form of baseball. And theology, pretty primitive too in the first century. They didn't write much, eh? Just a few hieroglyphs on shards. Very confusing even if you learn to read them. For example Angus told his students—where's that waiter?—to be real Christians they have to quit being Christians, become Jews or Muslims or something and then become converted to Christianity. I bet he thinks, but I can't be sure in spite of my faithful spies—" he laughs—"I bet he thinks a really good baseball player should first become a gladiator, and then become a ball player. Learn the basics first: fear, intimidation, ruthlessness, get that killer instinct. Then you can defeat an enemy even more skilled than yourself. I'm not a scholar of course. I don't know everything theological, Ian, but—"

Father Angus interrupts. "You know, Ian, that would be a good place for the bishop to stop," he says and winks, "now that he's said something incontestably true. As you can see, Ian, it's not my theology getting on his nerves, it's baseball. Oh, I just thought of something: what century did Christ live in? Was that the first century AD? Never mind, we can figure it out. It doesn't matter, obviously the first theologians, the apostles, and after that, the disciples, what were their names, oh yeah, Matthew, Mark, Luke and who was the other one, it'll come to me in a minute, and then Paul and Augustine, they were too close to the source. You have to distance yourself from the source; you can't be intimidated by the spring. If you want to test the purity of the water, go downstream a few miles, try the water after it's been over the rocks; just a little analogy, but never mind, we were talking about baseball. Now when the bishop was a humble, no, scratch that, when the bishop was a mere priest and I was a humble curate, I beat his humble team. I say they were humble because, as they say, they had a lot to be humble about, no, scratch that, let's say we humiliated his proud baseball team."

"No, Ian," the bishop says, "it's not the baseball. You know as well as I do because you've taken courses from him. He's preaching agnosticism. That's heresy. I can't permit that."

"Yes, Ian, you have taken my courses and I hope you learned more than the bishop's spies. I think it goes something like this: in an odd, limited sense a Christian is like an agnostic. The agnostic claims you can't know; the Christian says somewhat the same thing because religion is not based on knowledge, it's based on faith. If you know, you don't have to believe. If you know, say from experience, that beyond the land there is an ocean, you don't need to believe it, you can just go down, not too far from here, take off your shoes and socks and walk right into it. You know it; you don't have to believe it. Just a little analogy, a shade too subtle for some of his spies, but I'm pretty sure baseball is the sore point."

"Yes, he beat me," the bishop says, "by telling his pitcher to throw a baseball at the brains of my best batter."

"Oh yes," Ian says, "I've heard of that play. It works pretty well."

"Oh sure," the bishop laughs, "stick up for him, after all he's your mentor. Loyalty is always important."

"Except when it gets in the way of truth," Father Angus says and spreads jam over another piece of toast. "Tell the bishop, Ian, the standard defense against the suicide squeeze. The batter's brains are surrounded by a helmet, and the catcher warns him what's coming. All the batter has to do is get out of the way."

"I've never seen that play in any book on baseball," the bishop says, and puts some jam on his toast.

"Well," Ian says, "you might get arrested if you wrote that in a book."

"So there. It's okay to do it but a crime to write about it. I rest my case. That was high school ball, Ian," the bishop says, "not the big leagues, not even college ball, not even senior ball. High school."

"What's the difference?" Ian says. "Ball is ball."

"He threw it at his head."

"It's the easiest shot to duck."

"Oh sure, stick up for him even if he's wrong, loyalty standing in the way of truth. You're probably worse than he is. Oh well, he'll be gone this afternoon. Actually, I thought we'd be rid of him before now. Once I assigned him to that women's shelter in Reserve Mines, chaplain to a household of lonesome, vulnerable women, I thought sooner or later we'd catch him in flagrante delicto with one of them. But never mind, this way is better. He's gone right out of the country, no scandal, nobody hurt, nobody we know anyway, no embarrassment to the church, or the university, and you know what, Ian?"

"What?"

"He's glad. He's going and he's glad. And you can coach his ball team. You can probably have his girlfriend too, if he has one. I have my suspicions. I accused him of it once. You know what he said? He said, 'Well, Bishop, would you rather I had a boyfriend?'"

The bishop stands up and pushes his chair into the table

and stands for a moment with two hands leaning on the top of it and looks at Ian, who is showing signs of getting a little uncomfortable.

"Don't mind us, lad, we're just joking, he's one of my favourite priests when he's not embarrassing me. I have to go now. You two enjoy your coffee and dessert, and I hope you have a good year, Ian, and I hope he has a good year too. I hope he finds a shard with a hieroglyph on it and comes back and teaches us how to read it. He'll write a ten-page paper with twenty pages of footnotes and before you know it he'll be a full professor. Over my dead body."

It is a long year. Heraclitus said it first: You can never step back into the same river. The river you stepped into is long gone into the ocean, where it evaporated, ascended to become a part of a cloud in the heavens from where it will descend as rain and become another river in another country, waiting to kiss the next foot to step into it.

Ian coaches the ball team in the fall, and in the winter plays hockey and handball, teaches first-year Gaelic, tutors students in Gaelic and French, takes courses in history, eighteenth-century Gaelic poetry, seventeenth-century English literature and computer science, but he feels as if he's playing at learning, playing at teaching, playing at playing. Every day Father Angus' words haunt his daydreams: "You've already done all that." And worse than that: "You're going nowhere."

He ponders the priest's words throughout the long winter. And as the snow banks grow and the frost deepens through

January and February and the winds howl through March and over the slush of April, more and more he feels like a man dreaming he is trying to look out from a bright room through black windows into the dark, seeing nothing but the reflection of his own shape, an outline, a shadow.

When the snow is gone from the ball field, the infield drying, the outfield grass showing some green, hope begins to grip his heart. Although he hasn't heard from Father Angus he expects him back soon and looks forward to sharing the summer and the ball team, perhaps a dream from which he will wake in the fall, but at least not a nightmare.

Through the small window of his basement apartment a row of crocuses appear with a false promise of an early spring. He gets permission from his landlord and borrows a trowel and, leaning out the basement window, he digs up a yellow and a purple flower with their corms, root systems and a trowel full of earth, takes them into his bedroom, sets them in two coffee mugs and wets them down from a pitcher of water he keeps on his bedside table. He places them side by side on his television on the foot locker at the bottom of his bed and smiles at them while watching an afternoon game as the New York Yankees put a beating on his favourite team, the Boston Red Sox. After a few innings with the game well out of hand he takes the two crocuses and leaves for the university.

He unlocks the training room at the end of the gymnasium and gets into a clean baseball uniform from his locker and, still carrying the two crocuses, walks along the hallway to the cafeteria. He sits the two coffee mugs with the flowers on a table while he gets a cup of coffee. He sits at the sun-drenched table near a window and sips the hot coffee and stares out the window at the empty courtyard. In mid-afternoon the place is nearly empty of students and professors.

Marie surprises him. When he looks up at the sound of the cafeteria door swinging open she walks in and sends him a greeting wave across the rows of tables, gets herself a coffee and a couple of muffins. She stands in front of his table and puts down the coffee and muffins.

"Are you going to a ball game or a flower show?" she laughs, eyeing the crocuses. "Flower pots with handles and a cute joke, what a great idea." Ian had forgotten and no longer noticed that the coffee mugs, left on his classroom desk by some students, were a pair with a set-up of a joke on one and the punch line on the other. The first mug asks, "Why did the chicken cross the four-lane highway?" The second one answers, "To show the porcupine that it could be done."

Marie, still standing, laughs. "I couldn't have said it better myself."

"Oh, I don't know," Ian says. "I bet if challenged you could probably ratchet that up a notch or two."

"I'll give it a try sometime."

"So where did you come from? Where are you going?"

"I didn't come from anywhere," Marie says. "I'm here. I've been here. Studying. Preventive medicine. Halifax got too lonely without Jocelyn. Not to mention you. When I get my degree I'm going to prevent everybody from getting sick. Too late for Jocelyn, unfortunately. Had to bury her. By myself."

"I know. I ran out on ya. I'm sorry."

"And that was the second time."

"Yes, it was. I'm sorry."

"Why be sorry? If you didn't want me, what's the point?"

"I guess I didn't know what I wanted."

"Isn't that the same thing? If you don't know what you want you don't want anything. But you could have stayed to help me bury my buddy."

"Yes, I'm sorry."

"Okay. Don't get mopey. We're mature now. We understand these things now, heart problems, now that we have preventive medicine."

"Did you know I was here all year?"

"Oh yes."

"And you didn't look me up?"

Marie takes a little while to answer. "Would you believe it was preventive medicine?" She smiles at his puzzled face. She pushes a muffin across the table. "Have a bite of muffin. Just kidding, Ian." She smiles and takes a bite and a sip of coffee. "Well, half kidding, I guess. I just thought we'd bump into each other sooner or later. But I'm off campus a lot doing my practicum. I live off campus too, in Reserve Mines. The old convent is a women's shelter now that the nuns are gone. I live there. I come in once in a while for a tune-up with my supervisor. I thought I'd run into you, and, well, I did. Here we are."

"The women's shelter... What are you sheltering from?"

"Oh nothing, they rent out extra rooms. They give me a room free and I do the nursing. And believe you me they need a lot of nursing. Too late for preventive medicine though, and the fractured hearts are hard to mend."

He turns and looks out the window. Now the square is full of students walking to and from classes, some of them turning into the cafeteria and the room, quiet until now, except for the clatter of dishes coming from the kitchen, is filling up with noise.

"How did you know I was here?"

"Angus told me."

"Father Angus?" Ian says, puzzled. "When did he tell you that? He left not long after I arrived."

"Oh," she says, thinking back, "around that time, I guess, I must have been talking to him on the phone about one of my patients. So what about you, still want to be a priest?"

"I spent the year finding out that's one thing I don't want."

"That's a start then, we all do a lot of that."

"What?"

"Finding out what we don't want. Trying to find something useful to do."

"Who? Who all?"

"You, me, everybody, anybody."

"I guess you've got something pretty useful—preventive medicine. Preventing disease seems like a good thing to do. You won't be wasting your time there."

"Jocelyn always said the only things worth doing are a waste of time. That's the gospel according to Jocelyn."

"I had a good year then, wasting time."

"Too bad you couldn't make a living playing ball, wasting time, having fun."

Ian winces, stung by the remark, or the tone of it. He turns to the window again. There are only a few students in the square now, standing around chatting. The sun still shines but the clouds are approaching. He smiles and turns to her.

"I suppose preventive medicine must have its fun days too."

"That's it, make fun of me, but the thing is, preventive medicine is a waste of time too."

"How so?"

"Everybody dies anyway. Maybe we should call it put it off until later medicine. When you get right down to it I guess we don't really prevent, what we do is try to prevent. I got to go. Will you be around for a while?"

"Could be quite a while, 'til Father Angus gets back, anyway. Maybe all summer."

"Next week."

"Next week, what?"

"He comes back. Angus."

"Oh, you're in touch?"

"He called. He's the chaplain where I work so he keeps in touch. I gotta go. I have a doctor's appointment, I'm getting a brain transplant, but don't worry it's an outpatient procedure now, lots of Cape Bretoners are getting them, then they move to Alberta."

"When can we talk?"

"Call me." She pulls a notebook from her purse and writes down her phone number.

☆　☆　☆

Evening practice in the gym. About twenty ball players, some in pairs, throwing sponge ball grounders along the floor to each other. Other pairs throwing fly balls. Ian stands near the door to the training room watching the pitcher throw a non-flight imitation baseball to a batter who swings and pops it up. Ian approaches the batter. "Show me how you hold the bat." The batter grips the bat and holds it out to demonstrate.

"C'mon now, don't show me how you hold the bat when you're showing me how you hold the bat, show me how you hold the bat when you're swinging at the ball."

"That's it."

"No, it's not. You're changing your grip when the pitcher winds up. Listen, we are not a power hitting team. Shorten up on the bat and hold the bat so that the knuckles of both hands are lined up. That way we'll get more line drives and ground ball singles. We are a bunting, hitting, running team; speed and surprise and frustration is the game we play. Try to hit home runs and you'll pop up and fly out. You know it, I know it. You need to do what I tell you to do. That way we can win ball games."

"I'm not used to it."

"If you do it you'll get used to it."

While Ian instructs the batter, Father Angus, in jeans and sweatshirt, pulling a suitcase on wheels, comes through the door at the other end of the gym. He stops inside, taking in the scene, smiles, retracts the pull-handle of the suitcase and sits on it, folds his arms, crosses his legs and admires the spectacle. After a while when the players by ones and twos notice him and give him a wave he pulls out the suitcase handle and winds his way through them to the other end and surprises Ian with a tap on the shoulder.

"Well, good God, look who's here, just in time for spring training. I didn't expect you until after Easter," Ian says. "Welcome back."

"Thanks. I'll just put my bag in the training room."

"I'll give you a hand."

The training room is crowded with paraphernalia and equipment for treating injuries, a whirlpool bath, a refrigerator/freezer full of cold water and ice, a couple of beds a little wider than a stretcher with thin mattresses resting on plywood, two aluminum chairs, cupboard shelves piled with tape, braces and supports for various joints and limbs, and various pieces of first aid equipment. The spartan room displays one decoration—a poster with a face the shape of a bleeding heart and the caption, Life Hurts. Put Ice On It. Put Heat On It. Try It Out. Get Going. Father Angus sets his bag on the floor and sits in one of the aluminum chairs. Ian sits in the other.

"So, how'd you like the desert?"

"Good. The bishop will be happy—I found a shard with a hieroglyph on it."

"Well, I didn't."

"I heard."

"You did? How?"

"Marie told me. She thinks you're depressed."

"No, no, it's not that bad. I just didn't find a shard with a hieroglyph. I could use a bit of a hieroglyph. Nothing serious. When were you talking to Marie?"

"Just now, on the phone."

"I'm meeting her for a coffee in a bit downtown. Want to come?"

"No, I would but I'm off to see the bishop. Now that I'm back I'd better get my game plan on the table before he gets a chance to think or he's liable to trade me to a farm team in Lower Slabovia."

"What would he trade you for?"

"He'd trade me for a one-armed catcher, or any other priest in the universe."

☆ ☆ ☆

Ian sits in a corner of Wong's Cafe, his back against the wall, sipping black coffee and nibbling at bits of a cut-up egg roll, looking glum. Marie sits across the narrow space between them, her hands folded on the table, looking as if she is not expecting good news.

Ian says, "It's just that I was thinking maybe we might pick up where we left off."

"Where was that?"

"We left off somewhere."

"Where?"

"Halifax."

"Oh, geographically you mean? Yes, Halifax. Yes. We hit it off in Halifax, even though it was a bad time for me, Jocelyn dying. But it was a sad good time, a fun sad good time. It was good. But it went poof. But *we* didn't leave off there. You left off there. You fucked me and you took off and left me with a dead woman. You took off on me to go to Quebec, to become a priest of all things. And my only consolation was, well, why would I want to be married to a hypocritical prick anyway? And are you a priest? No. No, you left me for wide-open space, and that was the second time. Before that you left me for the wild blue yonder. You know the old saying, fool me once, shame on you, fool me twice, shame on me, and that's the end of it; whoever made up that formula for fool-proofing a life assumed there would be no third time. Anyway, the thing of it is, it's too late. I'm not in a position to resume a relationship at the moment." She sounds final but then adds, "Sorry to be so long-winded."

They sit in silence for a while. Marie takes a long drink of her coffee, gulps it down, takes a deep breath, exhales and while she waits for his reaction she tags on to her long speech, trying to lighten the moment, "I don't know if that's preventive medicine or not, I guess I'm not very good at it yet. I think they call it tough love these days, and you know, maybe that's what preventive medicine is." She laughs.

Ian drains the last of the coffee. Just a sniff of a smile curls his lips. He goes to the garbage with the cup, buys another and brings it back to the table, and says to Marie, "What do you mean, you can't resume now?"

"Maybe never."

"You're engaged?"

"No."

"Committed?"

"Not entirely."

"Involved?"

"Yes."

"It's tentative?"

"Yes."

"Who?"

"I can't say."

"It's a secret?"

"Yes."

"From everybody or just me?"

"Everybody."

"Is it dangerous?"

"Yes."

"A married man?"

"No."

"That's all a bit tight-lipped. Nothing long-winded about that litany of puzzles."

Marie picks a fortune cookie from Ian's plate and hands it

to him. "Here, open it," she says. "Maybe it will say something wise."

He breaks the cookie and pulls out the little piece of paper, reads it and smiles.

"What does it say?"

"It says 'Why not talk to the river?'"

"Well, that's wise, I guess. We don't have a river handy, but for now, let's walk to the harbour. I hear we're due for a tidal wave. If it catches us while we're walking along the wharf it will save us from all our options and commitments. Death pretty well does away with the opportunity for options."

They follow Commercial Street down to the bridge that spans the harbour and turn left past the stores, up the harbour road between the long white windowless wall of the fish plant to their left and on their right the lobster boats making rubbing noises against the tires used to buffer their stay against the wharf. Rainwater fills the potholes but the shower is over and the moon appears as the west wind blows the black clouds out over the Atlantic and the moon spreads its white light shimmering over the black harbour water. A breath of the breeze carries the sour sweet smell of sea salt and fish offal.

"Look at the water, Ian. It looks so beautiful, calm, peaceful, friendly, harmless, but you know that under the skin it's full of raw sewage."

"And when you think we used to swim in it."

In silence then they walk the wooden planks of the wharf's extension into the Atlantic Ocean as far as they can go, the only sounds the slapping of the waves and the clopping of their shoes on the wood. At the end of the planks they look down at the black water, obscured by the end rampart of the wharf.

Beyond the obscurity, the light from the moonglow flowing over them imprints the shadows of their heads dancing on the wavelets of bright water.

Marie takes Ian's hand and holds it between hers. "This is the end," she says. "Don't get dizzy. If we wanted to go beyond here we'd have to swim to Newfoundland or drown. And now it's my turn to ask a litany of questions; your turn to answer. You went to Quebec: Did you find a seminary? Did you speak French? Did you meet somebody? Did you get engaged? Committed? Involved? Was she married? Take your time, we have the whole night and the tidal wave might be late. I want to know everything. It's the least you can do after leaving me in the lurch." She lets go of his hand and raises two fingers of her right hand in the air. "Twice."

They turn their backs on the Atlantic Ocean and walk and talk all the three miles back to Marie's home at the former convent in Reserve Mines. "Isn't it odd," she says, as she stands on the step in the dim glow of the yellow porch light. "I left the convent to become a nurse, and here I am, a nurse in a nunless convent. It's like it's all my fault, like I started a trend," she laughs.

The step she stands on raises her up to Ian's height. She takes hold of his shirt with her two hands, takes a long look into his eyes, pulls his head to hers and kisses his forehead goodbye. She turns him around, gives him a gentle push, and as he walks away on the cement path he hears the convent door click behind him. As he lifts the latch of the gate he glances back at the empty space. Once outside he stands a moment and stares at the closed door, then shuts the gate of the iron fence surrounding the former convent, now a home for the homeless. He lets the latch clank into place and walks away.

Ian retreats to his spartan, one-room basement apartment, with his books and language tapes at his study table and on his narrow bed. He shares the bathroom down the hall with the tenant of the other apartment whom he seldom sees and with whom he has never had a conversation, just a nod of recognition in passing now and again. Until now the lack of a telephone has not been a hardship since he has no one to call. His father is dead, his brothers and sisters scattered across the continent. He visits his mother once in a while in a nursing home but she no longer recognizes him. If need be he can use a phone at the university, or the landlord's phone upstairs. But now, after seeing Marie, and with the hill outside his meager basement window budding crocuses, he feels a vague constraint.

Father Angus didn't show up for ball practice, so for the time being he coaches the ball team by himself, busies himself with practice, reading and listening to his tapes, trying to improve his French and Gaelic. He continues using the machines in the training room to do his own laundry. While he waits for the washer and dryer to do their work he cleans and repairs baseball equipment. He can feel his interest in the game draining from his mind.

On the following Friday night he takes a bag of dirty laundry from his apartment to the university gym, picks up another bag full of his dirty uniforms from his locker and carries them to the training room. He unlocks the door and flips the light switch to illuminate the pitch-black windowless room.

When the door clicks open he hears a gasp of breath from around the corner of the short hallway into the room. When he turns the corner he finds Father Angus and Marie on the training bed. Father Angus sits up in the bed, his naked upper body next to Marie who is clutching a blanket to her bosom. The blanket displays the university crest and an inscription in large letters, Provincial Champions.

For a silent moment the three of them absorb the shock and wonder what future this is the first moment of. Ian, perhaps because he is fully dressed, finds the words to speak first.

"I guess," he says, "this is a shard with a hieroglyph on it. A clue in the infinite unfolding of the never-ending saga of roots and wings. Where *do* ya come from, Cotton-eyed Joe?" He suddenly realizes he is babbling and falls silent. He is the only one in a position to retreat, to escape, but he stands rooted to the floor.

Father Angus shakes his head and mutters, "Ian."

Ian says, for lack of something appropriate like *excuse me while I disappear*, "Quite the kettle of fish." He stands immobile, frozen at the opening of the hallway to the door, holding the two bags of laundry like a pair of strangled geese. He doesn't know where to look so he tries, his eyes wide, not to believe what he is seeing.

Father Angus sits holding his knees. "I'm sorry, Ian."

Marie says, "Will you stop that, Angus? *You're sorry.* He's an arsehole, he walked in on us, and *we* should apologize to *him*?"

Ian says, "I guess I came at the wrong time."

"The wrong time," Marie says. "Did you ever come at the right time? Did you ever leave at the right time? Do you ever come at the right time? Do you ever leave at the right time? You just come. You don't care about time. You don't care about place. Why are you here?"

"I came to wash my uniforms and do my laundry," Ian says, lifting the bags by their necks and dropping them to the floor. "I didn't expect…"

"You didn't expect. What did you expect? A kettle of fish? This is not a kettle of fish," she says, and in her fury drops the blanket to her lap, exposing her breasts. "Do you have any idea what this is? I doubt you do, so let me tell you. This is a grown-up man and a grown-up woman, two adults trying to learn to love one another. What *do* you expect? Do you expect everybody to do what you expect them to do?"

"He's a priest."

"What's that to you? He's not your priest, he's not even your coach anymore. Are you gonna need, every minute of your life, a coach and a priest to tell you what to do? I got to admit, you do need that, but God knows it's about time you didn't."

Father Angus says, "Marie, it's just a mistake."

"Mistake, yes, but whose mistake? I know what he's thinking. We shouldn't be here, but what about him? He's never where he should be. He came to Halifax to enter the seminary and instead he entered me and in the morning he walked off like he was leaving the baseball diamond after pitching a no-hitter and I'm the other team. 'That's enough sex for me, Marie, you go bury Jocelyn.' So he went off to Quebec and again he walked right past the seminary and into another woman and stayed there until he thought, oh, that was a mistake. He came back here to see who else's life he can interrupt. You used to be a pilot, Ian. Why don't you see if you can navigate your way *the hell out of here.*"

Ian lets her tirade roar through him and picks up the bags of laundry. "I'll wash the dirty laundry later."

Father Angus says, "We should have got together the three of us and talked as soon as I got back."

"I don't know," Ian says. "We might have been talking for a

month. This way it's all over in one embarrassing minute. Like everybody's mother says, 'Actions speak louder than words.'"

Marie says, "Look, Ian…"

Ian holds out the palm of his hand. "Marie, please, no need to talk. I ran out on you, and like you said, I did it twice. You owe me nothing. I think we got a substantial shard with a clear-cut, legible, translatable hieroglyph. A classic anthropological discovery. I'm gone."

☆ ☆ ☆

The next day Ian goes back to the training room and washes and dries the uniforms, repairs some equipment and makes a list of items in short supply. He leaves a note for Father Angus asking him to find another coach for the team if he doesn't want to do it himself. He goes back to his apartment and packs. His meager accumulation of possessions fit easily into his travel bag: a baseball glove, a winter jacket, a sport coat, a pair of dress pants, a pair of jeans, a few shirts, underwear and socks, a toothbrush, a razor. Everything fits easily into the flight bag, the one thing he still owns from his days in the air force. It is actually two bags attached and folded side by side, designed to carry everything one man would need to travel from A to B if he is not coming back. It would accommodate two uniforms, two suits, sport coat and pants, a pair of military boots and shoes, a pair of civilian shoes, a small pocket for a shoe brush and polish, another pocket for a small travel iron and lesser bags attached to the sides of the main bags to hold two or three more shirts. Lots of empty corners can be filled with extra socks and underwear. He no longer has the need for so much stuff. The carrying handle on top rests on a small silver plaque and on the plaque the RCAF motto, *Per Ardua Ad Astra*. "Through adversity to the stars," Ian mumbles and laughs. It reminds him of Father Ouelette. "You are a pilgrim, Ian. When you get to where you think is home, you will find it is an oasis. Nobody ever stays long at an oasis."

A knock interrupts his reverie. He opens the door to his landlord.

"Ian, you have a phone call upstairs in the kitchen." He notices the suitcase. "Are you going somewhere?"

"Yes. Sorry—a sudden decision. I'm leaving town. Do I owe you?"

"No. You're paid up and I actually have someone waiting for the apartment. I owe you the damage deposit. Is everything all right?"

"Oh yeah, I'm okay. I'm just moving on."

Upstairs, he picks up the phone.

"Hello," he says into the speaker.

"Ian, it's Marie, can we talk?

"I have to catch a plane."

"When?"

"Couple hours."

"Can you leave now? I'll pick you up in half an hour. We can talk at the airport."

At the airport they find a coffee shop, buy a newspaper and coffees and sit at a window with a view of the tarmac. She puts her purse and a gift-wrapped package on the table between them and for a moment they look in silence out the window. Two Dash-8s, an Air Nova and an Air Quebec move around the huge Boeings, trying to find a space. "That one's mine," Ian says pointing to the Dash-8. "I love those planes. When you're in the air in one you can almost feel the pilot flying the thing. On take-offs and landings you can feel the rubber on the runway. You can feel the pilot smile when he gets it up and tilts it toward his destination and levels off, flicks on the auto and sits back and looks at his watch."

"You're going back to Quebec?"

"Yeah."

"To a seminary?" She smiles.

"No. I guess seminaries are a thing of the past."

"You think it'll be the same?"

"I've been asked that question before. Who knows?"

"How do you feel? Or would you rather not say?"

"No. I'm okay with it now. What I came for is not here, which should not be a surprise I suppose, but it surprised me anyway. As they say, you can never dip your foot into the same river again, even though we often think we can. Anyway, it feels good to have a day full of the future, full of going somewhere, full of the possible, full of illusion maybe, who knows? Full of mystery, maybe, is the way to look at it."

"So, what's your plan?"

"You know what they say, if you want to make God laugh, tell him your plans."

She laughs. "So your river was me? Or did you have another river to dip your toes into when you came home?"

"Home?" he says, shrugging his shoulders.

"Well, here, anyway."

Ian picks up an imaginary guitar, smiles and begins to strum and sing:

Came for to see ya, came for to sing,
Came for to buy you a diamond ring?

Marie smiles. "So is there a river in Quebec?"

"There's the St. Lawrence River."

"And does it have a tributary that you'd like to dip your toe into?"

"Maybe."

"Rivers change, Ian, but they all run to the sea. Maybe we'll all meet there one day." She takes his hands into hers and meets his eye. "Ian, last night was not the way to end. I feel kinda bad about that."

"No need, Marie, it was bad timing on my part, but at least it was clear cut. It was final."

"I was too much, I don't know what to call it, but way too much, I don't know, I was too much something."

"With good reason though."

"Yes. But after all, it was your training room, at least more yours than anybody else's, certainly more than mine. You had a key. I should have told you about Angus and me, but I didn't feel I had the right to talk about it yet. Were you shocked?"

Ian laughs. "That's my mirthless laugh," he says. "I guess I was shocked. But when I think about it, I could have, should have known. I didn't pick up hard enough on the clues. Don't take this the wrong way, but why the training room?"

"Not much of a love nest is it. But where? His place? My place at the convent where everyone knows him? Well, it was an impulse. I guess we need a plan."

"I guess you must have wondered why I was so stupid. It did

occur to me, you and him, but I dismissed it. I guess I didn't want it to be true."

"After you left, he proposed."

"Marriage?"

"No," she laughs. "He proposed an ice cream cone. What d'ya think? What else does a man propose to a woman?"

"Sorry, I'm just surprised. Is that what you want?

"I turned him down."

"Why? What do you want?"

"I want to marry him. I turned him down because he doesn't want to get married. Yes, he wants to marry me, he does, I know it, but he wants to be a priest more. If he marries me that's the end of being a priest."

"He'd still be everything else, a scholar, a teacher, a coach," Ian says.

"I've watched him with sick people and dying people. You could see how much it meant for them that he was there, and how much it meant to him. That's where his heart is."

"He'd still be a priest, you know. I don't suppose he could find a bishop to hire him, but he could be an Anglican."

"I doubt he could do that. He wouldn't feel real. I think it's a question of allegiance. Love is never enough. My mother said that. She said it's a question of loyalty. She said: Love by itself is an empty wineskin. You have to fill it, and you have to keep it full or the leather will dry up and crack."

"So what will you do?"

"I love him. If he leaves the priesthood I'll marry him. But I won't see him quit to marry me because he thinks he owes me. Would you marry somebody if you knew she felt she owed it to you, like you might owe somebody ten dollars? I hope not."

"What if he doesn't quit?"

"Oh well, I'll just fuck him once in a while, I guess.... What? What are you wincing for? Are you shocked?"

"That's awful flippant, Marie, even for a flip artist like you."

"You know me, Ian, flip is just a scab to cover pain. Preventive medicine, it's my profession now. So I guess neither one of us knows where we're gonna get to from here. Looks like we need another fortune cookie to tell us what to do."

Ian opens the newspaper. "Both our birthdays are in the same month; let's have a look." He reads the horoscope entry for Pisces. "Go fishing, there are always fish in the river."

"Well," Marie says, "at least it's encouraging." She stands up and shoulders her purse. "It's time for you to go now. Remember, Ian, in Halifax at the restaurant pretending we were Ingrid Bergman and Humphrey Bogart? That was kind of prophetic, don't you think? Although we've got it backwards. You go get on the plane, I'll sit here and watch, like Ilsa, until you're up in the air." She hands him the gift-wrapped package. "Something to remember me by."

He stands up and puts his hand on her shoulder and kisses her forehead. "*Per Ardua Ad Astra*," he says, and leaves her with her face in her hands. He carries his bag and the gift across the tarmac, feeling her eyes on his back. He places the bag on the rack beside the storage door of the Dash-8, climbs aboard and finds a seat ahead of the propellers to minimize the noise of the engines. While he waits for takeoff Ian opens the envelope scotch taped to Marie's package. "Good luck, Ian," he reads, "and wish me good luck in your prayers. Looks like we'll both need it. Here is a little gift. Don't take it the wrong way, I mean it to be helpful. And one more thing. I wanted to ask you but I didn't, so now I will. Didn't you catch on why Angus sent you to me in Halifax? And did you not realize why he went to Sergiopolis? Do you remember him saying to you, 'The desert's a fine and private place but none, I think, do there embrace'?"

The plane scoots down the runway, lifts off, gains altitude quickly and banks to the right giving Ian a last look at the woods and lakes of Nova Scotia. Once airborne the pilot informs them they will be flying at 5000 feet to avoid turbulence. "The weather ahead is uncertain. It is cloudy at the moment in Quebec but the meteorologists say a clearing trend is possible."

Ian peels the wrapper off the package and in the box finds two coffee mugs full of potting soil, the top of a flower bulb making a little mound on top of each. He takes one cup out of the box and reads the line of print going round it: "Why did the porcupine get married?" He picks up the other cup and reads: "To show the chicken that it could be done." So far it is a cloudless day and he watches the blue Atlantic as the plane flies toward the coast of Maine.

The steward offers Ian a choice of *Maclean's*, *Saturday Night*, *L'actualité*, and several newspapers. He takes *L'actualité* and reads an article entitled *"Visions d'autres mondes"* until he falls asleep. He dreams he is face down on a two-by-eight plank half the length of his body trying to paddle with his hands and kick with his feet up the St. Lawrence River. Like a marine Sisyphus he succeeds, inch by inch, against the gentle incline where the river remains at its widest; he manages to struggle past the Matane, the Métis, the Rimouski rivers on his left, the Godbout, the Manicouagan, the Betsiamites and the Sault-aux-Cochons and even the Saguenay tributaries on his right, as the banks of the river encroach on the water; but when the river narrows severely as he approaches Quebec City and the waters pouring from the Jacques Cartier River flood the narrow channel, his small craft becomes static in the stream and as the power of his arm and leg muscles diminish the flood propels him back toward the Atlantic Ocean.

fOURtEEN

She neither turned away nor yet begun
To speak harsh words, nor did she bar the door,
But looked at him who was her love before,
As if he were an ordinary man.

—*Amaru, translated from Sanscrit by John Brough*

WHEN HE WAKES UP the plane is already on the tarmac in Quebec and all the other passengers are gone. He feels a hand on his shoulder giving it a gentle shake. "Yvette," he says, taking the hand in his.

"*Non, c'est Silvie,*" the flight attendant says, laughing. "You are landed in Quebec. You must get off the plane. I hated to wake you, you looked so peaceful, sound asleep."

It is still early enough for breakfast in the nearly empty airport cafeteria. The last of the debarked passengers are already filing out with their coffees. Ian takes a seat at the counter. With a flirtatious smile, the tall, short order cook greets him.

"*Voulez-vous quelque chose?*" she asks.

"*Café, s'il vous plaît.*"

"Sure, sir, what more?"

"Toast, *deux* toasts."

"Yes, but don't you wish for an egg?"

"*D'accord, ça serait bon.*"

"I desire to talk English for the practice. Do you mind, you?"

"No, I don't mind…me."

"You mock me, sir?"

"Just a tiny bit." He smiles and with his elbow on the counter he raises his hand and creates a tiny space between his thumb and forefinger to indicate the minute amount of mocking. "Just that much."

"You make me laugh."

"Why do you want to learn English?"

"Your coffee, sir."

"Thank you."

"You are welcome. I want to do the secretary. You have to talk English to have the best jobs. Do you want your egg sunny side down?"

Ian laughs. "Okay. Is there a bus to the city?"

"You must take the *navette*. It goes back and forth."

"The shuttle."

"Yes, the shuttle. I learn a new word. Take the shuttle. What are you called, can I ask?"

"Ian."

"You want two eggs, Ian?"

"Just one. How do you call yourself, you?"

"You mock me again, Ian. But just a tiny," she says and, imitating Ian, raises her hand and creates a little space between her thumb and forefinger to indicate just how tiny. "My name is Aurore. I get up early." She cracks two eggs and spreads them onto the cooking surface of the stove. "Where are you from?"

"Nova Scotia." Ian continues talking, making gestures,

imitating, just like Yvette when she was giving him language lessons. "My name is Ian. Your name is Aurore. You are a woman. I am a man. You are from Quebec. I am from Nova Scotia. You are cooking two eggs. I asked for one egg."

She laughs. "You are funny. I wish my English teacher would be funny, or at least not cross. Do you want fry potatoes, no, I thought so," she says and dumps a spatula full of home fries on his plate with the two eggs. "Have some more coffee. Do you learn French now or do you speak it?"

"I speak it but not as well as English. I'm still learning. You are learning English very well. I'm learning Gaelic now too."

"Gaelic? What is that?"

"They speak it in Scotland. And some people in Nova Scotia speak it too. Old people mostly."

"Is it useful for getting a job? I don't think so, no. Why do you learn it?"

"I guess because my father forgot it. *Il ne s'en souvient pas.*"

"He forgot his language. Is it possible? Was he sick?"

"It was not useful for getting jobs, even bad jobs."

Ian finishes eating his food as the conversation winds down.

"There, you ate it all, two eggs and lots of potatoes. I know two things men like. One thing is, they like you to feed them. It's the same in English and French and maybe Gaelic also. Have some more coffee."

"And the other thing?"

"Other thing?"

"That men like."

"Oh," she giggles, "I don't know you well enough for that yet, to tell you that. But you can guess, it's also the same in all the language."

267

"Aurore, are there lockers here somewhere in the airport where I can store my bag?"

"Yes, they have the lockers but they are too little for your bag. Will you be long?"

"No, I don't think so."

"You can leave it here behind. I'll keep it safe for you and then you come back to get it."

When he finishes his coffee Aurore closes and locks the glass door of the empty restaurant and leads him through a long corridor past airport offices, restrooms and souvenir shops not yet open for business. "I show you Calvin, he waits in the shuttle. The shuttle, that's a nice word."

As they walk along toward the door of the parking lot they chat. "You speak English really well, Aurore, do you get to practice much at the restaurant?"

"No. Only sometimes a person speaks in English. They just say, coffee, toast, please, thank you. If I ask them a question they just say yes, no, don't know. Not like you. You say funny things. Even me can tell it's funny." She laughs. "In class we talk. But not much. The teacher is too stern. Sometimes a tourist talks to me. Or Calvin. He's funny. He speaks everything, French, English, I heard him speaking Spanish. He says the best thing is get a friend that speaks English and won't speak any French."

"Is Calvin your friend?"

"Yes, he is——" she hesitates "——but he'd rather be your friend." She laughs and rolls her eyes.

Calvin, the shuttle driver, waits, seated on the hood of his vehicle, the heels of his cowboy boots hooked into the front bumper, his kilt pushed down between his legs, his thick woolen jacket unbuttoned, his bowler hat tipped forward against the sun. Ian reads the legend on the door, Calvin Le Pape, and under his name, *A. à B. et B. à A.* His thick sweatshirt reads, *J'oublie.*

Aurore introduces them. "This is Ian, Cal. He wants to go to the city."

"Jump in," Calvin says, pointing his thumb. "Get in the front so we can talk."

"If he makes you read his book, Ian, don't make him a tip," she laughs.

"Oh," Ian says, "I forgot to pay for breakfast."

"Never mind, when you come for your bag you can buy me lunch and give me another lesson talking. *Au revoir, mes amis.*"

Ian sits in the front seat of the van. Calvin gets behind the wheel and immediately plunks a book on Ian's lap. "Just take a peek," he says, and while they roll out of the airport toward the highway Ian looks it over. *Culture and Anarchy,* by Calvin Le Pape.

"You wrote this book?"

"Yeah."

"It's a library book."

"Yeah."

Ian opens the book at random and reads aloud, "'Culture is the final refuge of the dispossessed, hunkered down in their master's tumble-down shacks, mumbling enigmatic wisdoms in forgotten dialects.'" He looks again at the library marking on the spine of the book.

"Why would you borrow your own book?"

"To see if anybody read it, maybe underlined something, good for the ego. Do you like it so far?"

"How about this?" Ian reads: "'Culture is the ballast thrown from the ship of state so it can ride high on the wind of change. But when the storm comes, its mast will serve for a keel.'"

"Cute, isn't it?" Calvin says.

"It seems to contradict the first thing I read."

"Of course. Every truth is the opposite of itself. Like everything is important, nothing is important. If one is not true, its opposite can't be true. Where do you want off?"

"The funicular."

"Is she your type?" Calvin says.

"What?"

"Aurore, is she your type?"

"Why not?"

"Good, she seems to like you."

Ian shrugs and resumes reading.

Calvin lets Ian out in front of the Château Frontenac and from there he walks to the funicular. Once aboard he looks down through the glass wall at the menacing descent. He turns his back to the wall, his face pallid, strained, and sees a woman in a plain dress, watching him, smiling. "Are you afraid of the descent?"

"No. Do I look scared?"

"Yes, you do."

At the bottom of the cliff he leaves the funicular, walks across Place St. Charles and onto the ferry. The woman follows. Clouds coast in from the west, greying the day, and the wind begins to blow, creating waves across the St. Lawrence. He leans against the rail near the bow. When he turns to avoid the wind on his face he sees her again, a quizzical look on her face, watching him from the rail on the opposite side. She waves.

When the ferry docks he debarks and walks through the parking lot, across the highway, up the familiar hill and across the field to Yvette's house. He knocks on the door and waits and knocks again. When no one answers he decides to try the barn but when he turns around he finds himself facing the smiling woman.

"Hello. I'm Vergile, did you come to visit me?"

"I'm looking for Yvette."

"Yvette doesn't live here anymore."

"Where did she go?"

"Moved to town. Come in, I'll give you her address."

Vergile makes a pot of tea and they sit at the familiar kitchen table and she serves the familiar biscuits with the tea in a cup with the familiar legend, *Je me souviens.* Ian smiles.

"You like the cup, or is it the tea, or the biscuits? Yvette taught me how to make the biscuits."

"I like the tea and biscuits. The cup makes me smile. It's a long story."

"Yvette moved last week," Vergile explains. "Sold the farm and everything in it. We don't have to buy a thing, not so much as a soup spoon. She spent a couple of weeks teaching me how everything works, how to milk the cow, and all that, packed her underwear and shoes in two grocery bags and fled down the hill. She left her phone number and address in case I needed to find something or to know how to do something."

"Are you a farmer?"

"I'm going to try. I sing in a nightclub in Ville de Quebec. I came from New Brunswick or as they say here *Nouveau-Brunswick,* with a banjo and various other string things on my knee and my vocal chords. My mother says *ma fille est descendue aux enfers.* You speak French, no?"

"Yes. What do you sing?"

"Acadian, Quebec, Cape Breton, Newfoundland folk songs, the music of the dispossessed. Funny, eh, ironic, the dispossessed survive and thrive in their songs. But mostly I make up my own songs. And now I too have possessions."

"You must do well; you bought the farm."

"She sold it for a song. Not literally. She wanted a quick sale. The bank gave me the money because it was so cheap they could sell it in a wink if I don't pay the bills. My parents backed the mortgage anyway so nobody can lose but them. They didn't want me condemned to hell forever. Here's where she lives." She scribbles the address on the back of an envelope. "If your dream doesn't come true, come back, or come see me at L'Enfer Sous Terre, Rue St. Jean. I'll be there from today until the end of the month at least, perhaps all spring and summer if they like me and the customers come back."

Ian walks back to the ferry, sails across the St. Lawrence once again under a thickening sky. The wind changes and the waves now move in the same direction as the boat, urging it on. He boards the funicular at Place St. Charles and rises to the square and the bustle of the beginning of tourist season. The sidewalk artists sit behind their easels, sketching whatever comes into view to pass the time. The horses, harnessed into tour wagons, line up along the edge of the square, the drivers sitting, waiting for sightseeing tourists. A bride and groom stand under the head of one of the horses while several people aim their cameras.

He walks beyond the square until he comes to rue Napoleon and continues until he finds the large apartment complex, Édifice Waterloo, takes the elevator to the eighteenth floor and walks along the hall until he comes to 1815, takes a deep breath and knocks. Yvette opens the door and stares at Ian, her eyes wide, her mouth open, her hand gripping the doorknob. Finally she says, "You."

"It's me. *C'est moi.*"

"You came back?"

"The cat came back, *le chat est revenu*," he says. But Yvette does not laugh.

"Yes, I see," she says in a flat voice. She makes no sign to invite him in. She stands with her arms like bars across the doorway, one hand on the open door the other gripping the doorjamb, her eyes blank.

Ian tries again. "*Je suis ici.*"

"*Oui*, I warned you about cats. They always come back. That means they always go away again."

"How have you been, Yvette?"

"Okay. And you?"

"Okay."

"I thought maybe you lost your memory again?"

"No."

"Where did you go?"

"I went home."

She smiles. "I thought you were home here."

"I think perhaps I was."

"But you went?"

"Yes."

"You must know by now, home is where you come from, not where you go. Home is a port for leaving."

"Yes."

"Home is where children live."

"You sound like you've given it some thought."

273

"You are arrived. I have to say something. I had lots of occasion to think about it. The day I found you on the pavement, I wondered why that happened to me. I don't know why. You came to me by accident. I was happy with that. But you could not live with that. You went home. But maybe home was gone. And now. Why are you here?"

Ian stands with his arms folded on his chest for a silent moment. He shrugs. Yvette opens wide the door and drops her arms. "Would you like to come in? For a minute."

She lets him into a small room furnished like a waiting room with a glass table in the centre holding magazines and two bench-like chairs against the walls on either side of the table. They sit across from each other. Above Yvette's head a painting hangs on the wall. The name of the painting is printed along the bottom board of the frame. *Lusitania und Unterseeboot.* There is no sign of a craft in the picture. The entire space is devoted to an enormous expanse of uninteresting ocean, disturbed only by the slightest breeze and above the water an equally enormous sky troubled only by a small cloud that almost eclipses the sun; a small mouth at the bottom of the cloud lets through a golden beam of sunlight. Ian stares at the painting.

"You like it?"

"I don't know. You?"

"Yes, I do. I like it very much. I often come here and sit where you are and look at it."

"What do you see in it?"

She stares at Ian's face while he stares at the picture as she talks. "You have to follow the sun—it comes through the cloud that looks like a mouth. Follow the beam to the ocean where it lights up a little bit of foam in the corner of the picture. If you look carefully behind the foam you will see a bit of the nose of the torpedo. So why did you come here?"

He takes his eyes from the painting and looks at Yvette. "I came to see you."

"Is that what you do, go around and see people?"

"I came to see if you would come with me."

Yvette presses her lips together, her eyebrows come down, her eyes change and outrage begins to grow behind them. "Why do you ask me such a question?"

"Because I love you." He laughs a laugh that is almost a sigh and adds, inexplicably, "And you speak better English now. Just kidding."

Yvette emits a dry laugh. "Yes, I know you're kidding. You always had good jokes. I wish I could laugh better now. But I must answer your question, and the answer is no. You cannot stay. I cannot go."

"Why?"

"Because I have my duties here."

"Your job?"

"No. There is a hospital everywhere. I have my duties here. I do not live alone anymore."

"Are you married?"

"No, but as good as, same thing."

"Are you happy?"

"Oh yes," she says in a pensive, flat voice.

"You could not leave?"

"No."

"Why?"

She looks at him, waits a minute, smiling, then a fake smile to show her teeth. "My teeth."

"Your teeth?"

"Yes, my teeth. He made straight my teeth. You must remember my overbite, you were rather fond of it, you said."

Ian stares at her. He thinks, is she joking? He speaks to her in a let's get this straight tone. "Okay, you went to an orthodontist, he straightened your teeth so you moved in with him. You can't leave him because..." he pauses, "you owe him. Is that it? Couldn't we just pay the bill?"

"It's not nothing. You did not make straight my teeth. I have a place to be in. I am not by myself, I have someone who will not go off in the wind like a feather." She smiles, showing her teeth. "And I have nice teeth."

"Who is this? What's his name?"

"Monc."

"You married a monk."

"Very funny. That's his name."

"Do you love me?"

"Since I cannot go with you I cannot answer that question."

"*Est-ce que tu m'aimes, Yvette?*"

"It is a worse question in French. I cannot even think to answer that. *C'est impossible.*"

"Why not?"

"Tell me, what is your name?"

"Ian."

"I do not love Ian. I loved Abraham. People do not stop loving people they love. But love is not everything."

"Do you love Monc?"

"When we were together we did not talk of love, we just loved. It's not something you talk about, it's something you do. It's too late for questions like that. Ask me how I like my teeth.

Such questions are more useful."

"Why did you cut your hair? You had such beautiful long hair."

"Some things a woman can't change, some things she can. A woman can always change her hair and her shoes, even her teeth. Other things she must accept. And hair will always grow back and there are one hundred and twenty shoe stores in Place Champlain." She laughs. "I can be funny too. What do they say in English, might as well laugh as cry?" She looks at him a moment in their silence. "Come with me, I want to show you something."

She leads him down the hallway to another room and he follows her into the darkness. She opens the venetian blind and lightens the blue room to reveal a crib, a change table below a set of shelves storing a stack of diapers, powders, oils and salves, tiny socks and shoes, bibs and a variety of button-up overalls. Yvette reaches down and removes the blue blanket, lifts a sleeping infant, cradles him on his back in the crook of her arm. The baby yawns, eyes fluttering in the light.

"So you have a baby."

"Yes, we have a baby. Come." She leads him back to the sitting room, carrying the baby, sits him down opposite the painting and sits beside him. "Here, hold him like this." She puts the baby in the crook of Ian's arm. "His eyes are shaped like mine, like almonds, but the colour is yours, green, with flecks of brown from me."

Ian's mouth falls open. He stares at Yvette. He stares at the baby and back to Yvette. She smiles. "Don't you recognize him? They always look like the father when they are born. It's so the father knows for sure it is his baby too. When Monc asked me who the baby looked like I said he looked like Jesus because it was an immaculate conception."

"You're joking."

"Yes, I was joking. I learned that from you. When things get tough, you laugh. It helps."

"My God, Yvette. I didn't know."

"How could you know, you were gone."

"I'm sorry."

"I thought to go out in the yard and yell to you. I even did that one night. I hollered and hollered in the dark, across the garden. But you did not hear me. My voice is not big. I couldn't make it go to Nova Scotia."

Ian turns and sits back and stares at the empty sea and sky hanging on the wall, thinking.

"But you must have known before I left. Why didn't you tell me?"

"Because I was angry. I wanted you to stay with me because you wanted to stay with me. I captured you once. I didn't think I should have to do it again. I didn't want a prisoner for a partner. But then I changed my mind. I wrote a letter. I put on it Ian MacDonald, Nova Scotia. That's all I knew. It came back without you." She laughs.

"I don't know what to say."

"I called information for every town in Nova Scotia. I made a list of all the Ian MacDonalds. I called them all. None of them was you."

"I didn't have a phone in my own name."

"Then I thought, he'll come back. Sooner or later. But you did not come back sooner."

"I'm back now."

"Yes, but now it is too much later. Too late. Why did you not come back?"

"I don't know."

"Monc says it's because you are a prick. I'm not sure what that means but I guess you do."

"Yes. I know what that means."

"Not nice, I don't suppose. So I am with Monc. A very nice man. He scratches my back. I like his kids and he likes our kid. He was married too, to a bird that flew, like you."

"I don't know what to say. If I had got your letter..."

"Well, you can read it now. I couldn't throw it away. You talk to the baby. His name is Abraham. I'll go get it." She leaves the room. He does not talk. He lays the baby on its back on his legs and holds its two hands in his and feels the little fists close and cling to his fingers. He cannot bring himself to say the name Abraham. He feels if he tries to say words they would come out sobs.

When Yvette comes back and looks at his face she says, "Yes, it's hard not to cry. I sometimes feel like crying but then I think if something bad happens and then something good happens then it's not too bad. I was not happy with you gone but I had my little companion in my belly for a consolation. Here, read it, it's not long."

Dear Ian, I used to think life is full of chances offered by God and you take them and you do your best. Now I think life is full of accidents and you must use them to find a way. If your father gets sick you look after him. If you find a wounded man on the road you pick him up and heal him. If he loves you and has no other special thing to do he stays. You have children. When you are about to die your children go to airports with their children and fly to your funeral. If you are lucky they get there before you die. It's a decision. Yes or no.

"Even if I got the letter," he says, staring at the page, half full of blurred words, resting on the baby's belly, "even if I did get it, you didn't tell me you were pregnant."

"I did not want you to come back because I was pregnant. There's a hint in the letter. And I gave you a hint before you left but you didn't twig to it, or you ignored it. It must have occurred to you, the possibility, more than that, the probability."

"Well, I'm back now. I did not come back because you were pregnant. I did not come back because of the baby."

She smiles. "You know, Ian, the thing of it is, you can't accept a man's comfort and shelter and love, and let him straighten your teeth and tell him you will live with him and his lovely children, and he is pleased and happy to live with you and your child, and then tell him you are not going to live with him anymore because the prick from Nova Scotia is back. And even if I did…who's to say when your wings will be ready to fly again?"

"You can't marry someone just because he's a man."

"Women don't marry men, Ian, girls marry men. Women marry the future."

"That's it then?"

"*C'est ça, Ian. C'est ça.*"

Yvette takes the baby from Ian's lap and opens the door to the corridor. Ian follows and walks out into the hall. She follows him to the elevator. "Give us a hug, Ian," she says. He wraps his arms around mother and child and they cry. When the elevator doors open she pushes him gently and he backs through the opening.

Still cradling Abraham, she pulls Ian back by the shirtfront, kisses his lips and pushes him back again as the doors close between them like the curtains on the last act of a play.

EPILOGUE

A good book has no ending
—*R.D. Cumming*

DAWN. MORNING SUNSHINE floods in through the street-level windows of L'Enfer Sous Terre. The neon lights are out, the sound system off, the harp on the stage silent. Vergile in her street clothes, jeans, shirt and jacket sits across from Ian at a small corner table, a spent beaker of beer and two empty glasses on the table between them. A few men and women move around doing cleaning and maintenance. Ian finishes telling his story, his sad and woeful tale.

"And that's all of it, Glace Bay, Halifax, Quebec. And that's the end. I stepped back into the elevator. Yesterday Yvette stood in the hallway holding the baby, staring at me with her wide eyes, the doors closed. The elevator descended to the lobby. That is the end of my sad and woeful tale."

"Indeed it is a sad and woeful tale."

"You're the counsellor. What do I do now?"

"First of all, you have to realize that your grandmother had it backwards."

"My grandmother?"

"Yes. You told me she advised you, 'Don't let your life get in the way of your dreams.'"

"What's wrong with that?"

"It's backwards. It should be, 'Don't let your dreams get in the way of your life.' But right now you need to look on the bright side."

"The bright side?"

"Isn't it obvious?"

"No."

"Your son Abraham lives. It's not every mistake in life that results in the creation of a beautiful new life. And you, you are dispossessed. You have nothing. You have nothing to lose. That's a good place to start from."

"It's pretty hard to start if you don't have a place to go."

"There are always places to go. You once thought you had a vocation to the priesthood. You could start by coming with me to the farm."

"I could be a nun?"

"Very funny. You could be a brother, like Bernie, but it's too early for that. You can come and work. We could use the help. You could use a retreat while you make up your mind. Bernie can help, he's pretty good, lots of common sense."

"Who's Bernie?"

"He's the brother."

"How many are you?"

"Just me and Bernie, so far."

"You live together?"

"We live in the same house. We're celibate. So far anyway. We haven't made up our minds about that. I give him a hug once in a while, but there's no fucking, and kissing only on the cheek. When he gets horny I send him out to feed the pigs."

"Well, I'll be damned."

"Let's hope not. Tell you what. I'm gonna sing you a little song. When I finish why don't you take a long walk. If you are interested keep walking and come see us, we'll be there all day. Come see us anyway; you know the place. You can answer some of the questions we've been saving up for Yvette, and you need a shower and we'll wash your clothes for you. This song is in Medieval French, if you find it hard to follow it goes like this, *Life is not a sea you walk into inch by inch, the toes, the knees, the belly, but a sea you fall into. There is no rock, no tree, nothing but a circle of horizon and a sky full of stars. You pick a star and you swim."*

"What does it mean?"

"To me it means it's the star, not each other, that keeps us together."

Vergile climbs the stage and begins to play her harp and sing the song. Ian sits and listens until she finishes and with her smile at his back he leaves L'Enfer Sous Terre and walks the streets of Old Quebec as the artists and tour guides begin to organize their days.

☆   ☆   ☆

Again Ian sails across the St. Lawrence River, climbs the hill to the farm. This time he notices the makeshift sign pinned to the gatepost advertising the new enterprise.

The Retreat Farm
Work
Rest
Recuperate
Think
Plan
Play
Live

He knocks on the door that used to be his door to go in and out of as he wished. Vergile steps out and leads him around the house to the garden where Bernie stands in his jeans and T-shirt leaning on a garden fork staring at the ground.

"Bernie, Ian. Ian, Bernie. Bernie is our gardener today. He actually knows a bit about that."

Bernie lets go of the fork, takes off his glove and shakes hands. "Welcome to our farm, Ian. Glad to meet you."

"Isn't it a bit early for the garden?" Ian asks.

"Yes. But I'm just taking stock now that most of the snow is gone. Not much stock to take though. Just these."

"Onions?" Vergile asks.

"No. The tops look like onions. Leeks. Somebody must have planted them last year."

"You, Ian," Vergile says. "You planted them with Yvette. I remember that from your sad and woeful tale. They take nine months. Just like a baby. I told Bernie your sad and woeful tale and he has a few suggestions."

"Possibilities," Bernie says, smiling, looking at Ian. "Something to think about. Options."

"Ah, yes, options." Ian smiles his wry smile.

"You could talk to Monc and suggest that since you are the father, the mother, child and you should live together."

"You suggest that?"

"No. I wouldn't put much hope in that. But if you dismiss all other options, you might as well give it a shot.

"You could kidnap the child and hope the mother would follow the child. She kidnapped you after all. I wouldn't recommend that though. It's illegal, a crime. Going to jail won't solve your problem.

"You could go to the airport and pick up your luggage from that cook. If I heard the story right she might be your new start, she's looking for a chum who speaks English. That would improve your French, but it wouldn't bring you closer to the baby.

"You could rent an apartment in the Waterloo and hope they would be friendly but I'm not enthusiastic about that either. Could be interpreted as harassment.

"You could stay with us until you decide what to do. At the moment that's your best bet. Stay with us until you decide which star to follow. There are lots of stars but you are never going to get to one if you keep on getting distracted by light from the others. In the meantime if you stay here you can work. Have you got any skills?"

"I can play baseball. I can teach Gaelic and English."

"Good. If we get any language students you could come in handy and if we get some more like you we'll apply for a national league franchise. In the meantime since you learned to be a farmer, stay here. You're a teacher too, don't forget. You can teach us to farm. I'm just a gardener but we got the cows and pigs and chickens to deal with. It's all meditative work and therapeutic. Stay until you feel better, then stay until you know what you want and make the right decision."

"And how will I know if I'm making the right decision? I don't seem to be very good at that."

"That's the easy part. Take your time. When you're ready you make your decision. Then you make it right. That's the hard part."

Acknowledgements

Thanks to Robert and Kelly Deveau for putting us up in their home in Saint-Joseph-du-Moine, helping us participate in the events of *mi-carême* and introducing us to the cultural leaders of Chéticamp and other Acadian communities.

Thanks to Anselme Chiasson for his book *Chéticamp: History and Acadian Traditions* (Breton Books), to Gertrude Sanderson for help with Quebec French, to Catriona Parsons for help with Gaelic, to R.B. MacDonald for help with Latin and liturgical traditions, to Dave and Florence Walsh who showed us around Quebec City while we lived there. Thanks to Pat Walsh, George Sanderson, Jim and Effie Taylor, Reynold Stone, Bill Tierney, Ron Caplan, and Phil Milner for their support over the years. To Hugh MacLennan for *Barometer Rising* and *Two Solitudes*. Thanks to Aaron and Marianna Podolsky for the music and lyrics of the song "The Dispossession Blues."

Thanks to Jane Warren, my diligent editor at Key Porter.

And thanks again to my wife, Dawn, the constant editor of my work and my life.

Some passages in this novel appeared previously in other publications in altered form: in my novel *The Company Store* (Oberon), in two short stories, "Dies Irae" and "On Parle Par Coeur," in my collection *The Story So Far* (Breton Books) and also in a previous collection entitled *The Glace Bay Miners' Museum and other stories* (Deluge).